VC IMAGINATION FACTORY PRESENTS:

BIO-SAPIEN

Book 1 - Destination Optic-warp

Rebirth series: 1 of 30 books. Sponsored by Action Burger restaurant.
Written by: Vlane Carter. Illustrations by: John Buurman & Matt Garofalo
BIO-Sapien series based off the comic book in stores now.

BIO-SAPIEN SERIES SPONSORED BY:

2

Take a 360 video tour of Action Burger:

Action Burger's latest music video on youtube:

VC IMAGINATION FACTORY PRESENTS:

THE REBIRTH SERIES

BIO-SAPIEN BOOK 1
"DESTINATION OPTIC-WARP"

A Sci-fi, Space, Action, Adventure & Romance novel series.
Formally known as the BIAlien series.

NEW PROLOGUE
(continued from back cover)

A young man by the name of Jaden is abducted by benevolent
aliens, bio-engineered to superhuman levels and sent back to
Earth years later to stop an alien invasion.

150,000 years ago Darclonians began on an experimental dark
energy/dark matter weapon that works only with carbon based life
forms. The organic subject would eventually die.

100,000 years ago Darclonian probes sought out thousands of
planets with life on them that could develop into intelligent life
forms. The probes fired Quadrillions of Nanomoles into Earth's
atmosphere seeking intelligent life.
The Nanomoles hid inside of the modern Homosapien brain and
studied humans for thousands of years. The Nanomoles recorded
our feelings, memories, emotions, experiences and DNA from
generation to generation.

Today the Nanomoles await a signal from a Darclonian
mothership to begin it's 84 hour three stage countdown.

Jaden's bio-engineered body is the key to perfecting the
Darclonian's weapon of mass destruction. The rebirth of science
fiction begins.

ORIGINAL PROLOGUE

An average teenager Jaden Marino discovers a UFO landing one evening in upstate NY. The government is also looking for the mysterious UFO in the area. The government eventually follows him to it while trying to kill him. He hides inside of the advanced nanotechnology UFO while the government tries to take it away to Area 51 on a trailer. His mind goes into a comatose state and he has an out-of-the-body experience. The spaceship translates his English language from his mind into its language, enabling him to control the UFO with his mind. As he tries to fly away, the government sends all of their best and top-secret aircraft to intercept this very advanced spacecraft. Jaden quickly learns what this spaceship is capable of and goes against the best pilots in an intense chase over NY. Eventually he leaves Earth and travels 2.1 million light-years into the Andromeda Galaxy. He learns of an advanced alien species called Andromedians, who are 70,000 years ahead of humans. The Andromedians are peaceful explorers and their thinking is very far ahead of our own.

In book 3 Jaden comes back to Earth eighteen years later and is aware of an alien conspiracy that is about to take place on Earth. He tries to warn people, but everyone thinks he is crazy. They lock him up in a mental ward. Society, relationships, values and technology has changed on Earth. He has a microscopic artificial intelligence alien companion in his mind helping him along the way, called AI. His body begins developing its advanced alien nanotechnology weapons system to work on Earth. After the government and citizens do not listen, he tries to help the people he cares about while the government places him on a terrorist list and uses their full military forces to kill him. He goes against the government's future weapons, Motherdrone (a super computer that controls all UAV drone crafts), super exoskeleton soldiers, SWATbots, thermobaric weapons and himself. At the same time, a bad alien race, called Darclonians, are implementing their silent planned strike on humans. An energy knight is the Darclonians new powerful weapon that can manipulate dark energy. Unbelievable movie style action sequences throughout the book and an ending you won't stop talking about. Jaden Marino's adventure of a lifetime begins.

THE REBIRTH UNIVERSE SERIES:

BIO-SAPIEN VOLUME I   BOOKS 1-6

BIO-SAPIEN VOLUME II   BOOKS 7-12

BIO-SAPIEN VOLUME III BOOKS 13-18

BIO-SAPIEN COMIC BOOKS ISSUES 1-30

BIO-SAPIEN VIDEO GAME SERIES

BIO-SAPIEN SPINOFF REBIRTH SERIES

BELLONA SERIES BOOKS 1-3

ANDROMEDIAN CHRONICAL SERIES BOOK 1-3
ANDROMEDIAN CHRONICAL COMIC BOOKS 1-5
ANDROMEDIAN CHRONICAL VIDEO GAME
ANDROMEDIAN CHRONICAL CARTOON

BOMANI SERIES   BOOK 1-2

MARCO SERIES   BOOK 1-2

ROBOGODS & DARCLONIANS BOOK 1-2

TORAGON BOOKS 1-2

QUEEN VALASCA & THE ARACHNOSAPIENS BOOK 1-3

BIO-SAPIEN VOLUME I PROFESSIONAL BOOK REVIEWS.

NOTE: BIO-SAPIEN IS THE SAME STORY AND CONTENT OF THE ORIGINAL "BIALIEN TRILOGY" SERIES. THE FOLLOWING BOOK REVIEWS ARE FOR ALL 6 BOOKS TO THE BIO-SAPIEN VOLUME I SERIES.

"Science fiction fans unite! If the title doesn't say it all, I don't know what will! To preface this review, all of you naysayers out there who shake their heads at sci-fi should remember that, back in the 70's, the names R2-D2, C3PO, Chewie...you get my point, here...were unknowns. Now they are as much a facet of popular literary culture as is Mr. Darcy. Jane Austen, Henry James, Dickens, etc., were beautiful storytellers, but sci-fi has amazingly imaginative beauty surrounding it as well. And this author, Vlane Carter, knows that for a fact....

...there are A LOT of scenes that the reader gets to experience. From the military battle with the UFO, to the alien shark attack on another planet (which is really cool, by the way), this author offers a never-ending parade of amazing creatures and locations that will, perhaps, one day be logged into popular literary culture right beside old C3PO and his little beeping buddy......There are two factions out there in America - Star Wars vs. Star Trek - and I am definitely on the side of George Lucas having the more creative concept. So hats off to this writer, Vlane Carter, who may someday join those Lucas ranks if readers and sci-fi fans everywhere band together and realize that the force really MAY be with this one." – **FEATHERED QUILL REVIEWS.**

"....the bialien trilogy is not your typical sci-fi novel. Think of a comic book that uses words instead of illustrations and you might come close. One thing that the writer certainly has is imagination. It is written very visually....

.....you may tell by his style that Vlane is very passionate about his writing. It takes time and effort to envision and write a novel of this length without losing the energy throughout it. Bialien is his first novel, and, from his marketing material and website, certainly not his last. It is always interesting to see the first story written and how writing styles evolve from book to book. Let's see where Volume Two takes us." –**TOP BOOK REVIEWERS.**

"A Sci-Fi series set on exploring concepts of the deep future, "The Bialien Trilogy" is for the Science fiction fan who likes to be amazed at what the future holds...." - **MIDWEST BOOK REVIEWS**

"Vlane Carter first novel is a huge "tome" of a book. There is lots of action and adventure as our main character, Jaden, meets a host of aliens from across the universe, engages in a host of battles as well as doing some "fun" stuff. There is a lot of "things" in this book to cause the reader to pause and ponder. For the adventurous reader who likes long novels make sure you put this close to the top of your Must Read list.—**STEVEN FIVECATS, EDITOR. YELLOW30 SCI-FI REVIEW.**

"...the first thing readers will notice about this book is the author's manner of storytelling. It's different and can take some getting use to. That said, if you adjust your thinking to the author's way of telling the story, you'll find that it works! He achieves his goal of making the story read as if you're seeing it on the big screen, as an action packed movie. Also worth mentioning, is that to complete the entire scope of the story, Vlane has placed visual images throughout, as well as a book sound track, creating an entirely new dimension to the meaning of author/story/reader interaction....

....Outside of the book itself, this author takes great care to interact with his readers and has a website that includes free chapter plus loads of information about the series. Inside the book, he takes just as much care, and it's clear he has put his entire being into each and every word. Real knowledge can make or break a book, and this author definitely knows his technology. ....

....Give this book a chance and you won't be disappointed by the in your face, non-stop action that leaves you on a roller coaster ride that

thrusts you up and down, side to side, both thrills and chills, and then rockets you out of this world..."
-New Reads Underground. Rachel M. D'aigle, NRU Head and Author of YA Fantasy Series The Journals of The Jacoby Odyssey

----

....This book crosses many topics, from government conspiracies, alien technology, nanotechnology, world domination, love, female empowerment and religion... All which take the reader into new realms of thought and possibility, allowing for outside the box thinking and discussion amongst readers.....

....Sci-fi and fiction enthusiasts will have a hard time putting this book down. Vlane Carter succeeds in his unconventional storytelling style, drawing readers into his vast creation, while the plot twists keep you riveted and guessing until the books final page. Or, make that the final word...." **-M. Penny Harmon, Review SIP "ReviewSIP" (Salt Lake City, Utah)**

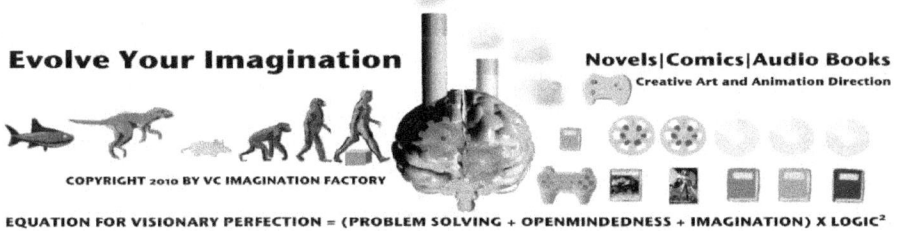

VLANE CARTER'S IMAGINATION FACTORY

Evolve Your Imagination

Novels|Comics|Audio Books
Creative Art and Animation Direction

COPYRIGHT 2010 BY VC IMAGINATION FACTORY

EQUATION FOR VISIONARY PERFECTION = (PROBLEM SOLVING + OPENMINDEDNESS + IMAGINATION) X $LOGIC^2$

Acknowledgements:

I want to thank Jack Cooper for being the first person to finish the novel and filling out a questionnaire in September 2009. Thanks for your constructive criticisms, suggestions and opinions. Good job finishing the vol I series in less than 45 days.

Special thanks to Jack Cooper for listening and analyzing my bits and pieces of the book over the years. I saved your text message when you finished the book: "Your mind is WARPED and I love it...Really good story!" I told you the novel would be hard to put down. Thanks for helping me edit the website content and being supportive over the years.

I want to thank my fiancé Erica Marcelo for being the first girlfriend to finish all my books.

Special thanks to my late mother (Carrie Carter), who was an excellent writer and had perfect English/vocabulary. Thank you for raising me so well and keeping me on track over the years. Your words of inspiration kept me focused over the years, "work hard and don't be lazy." I'm sure you would be proud that I stuck to this 4 1/2 year book project and didn't give up. This novel series, video game design and story, seventy pages of business marketing book notes, hundreds of screenplay scenes, dozens of illustrations and animation designs was the hardest challenge I ever faced. I've used parts of my brain I didn't even know were there. Thanks for being there on the side of me while I typed 16-18 hours a day.

I want to thank my old Facebook friends for responding to my wall and helping me with research on relationships and religion. I know many of you didn't like my outside the box views, but thanks for hanging in there.

I want to thanks my first graphic artist Matthew Garafalo for going through dozens of hours and 40-50 drafts of the Gravhawk, and DEKs book cover. Thanks for having a passion for drawing and proving it's not always about the money. Thanks for a job well done on my first animation book intro. It took a few months, but it was worth the wait. You did magic on the EIS generation 2 in the illustration and in animation. Remember these repetition art directing words in regards to the EIS: "More space between the wings and tail." I felt like a drill sergeant. You definitely gave me my first experience with creative art directing.

I want to thank my other graphic artist Kwan Wilson and John Moriarty for putting up with my very detailed art directing. Good job fellas, thanks for not giving up on me.

I want to thank my main graphic artist John Buurman. John, I've never seen such imaginative sci-fi artwork. Your artwork designs still boggle my mind. When I first saw your artwork, I thought an alien from another galaxy took over your mind and made you draw your illustrations. Good job on the EIS (Exoskeleton Intergalactic Spaceship) generation 4, I knew we could do it. With our vision and your skills we can illustration almost anything (Vol II illustrations will definetly become more challenging; I'm sure you are up   for   it).

I want to thank my editor Kevin Holland for doing such a swell job on editing the book. I know it was challenging editing my unique writing style and content. You finished it and did an amazing job with categorizing all the   characters   and   pointing   out   my   common   mistakes.

I want to finally thank instrumental soundtrack artist: Martin O'Donnell, Hans Zimmerman, Steve Jablonsky, Yann Tiersen, John Williams and many other artists, for making music that stimulated my imagination for tens of thousands of hours. Where do you people come up with these amazing   sounds?

TO ALL READERS AND BOOK CRITICS PLEASE NOTE:

BIO-Sapien series was written in present tense for the following reasons:

1. So the reader can read and experience the novel as if they were watching a movie.
2. Nanotime.
3. Detailed action sequences.
4. Movie soundtracks inserted into different parts of the story.
5. Telepathic communication and talking to another personality.
6. Mind reading and answering questions inside of a conversation.
7. Have the reader experience the story as if they are right with Jaden at all times.

"....Author, Vlane Carter, has created a story told in a unique and unconventional writing style, keeping the action in the present tense, so as to keep the reader feeling as though they are experiencing the action as its happening. It can be akin to reading a script, or make you feel as though you're watching a movie. It is a writing style that can, at first, be jarring and difficult to understand. But if you give it a few chapters it will not only grow on you, but draw you in. And then you suddenly cannot imagine the story written any other way. And, quite possibly, it could be the first book that includes its own music recommendations (to listen to while reading)....." - **M. Penny Harmon, Review SIP "ReviewSIP"**

Single quotes ' ' are used in the book when:

Main character is thinking and talking to himself.
To show main character communicating with another personality in his mind.
High-speed telepathic communications

Even though third person narrative is mainly used throughout the book, the author needed to slowly get the reader used to single quotes by having main character thinking to himself from outside his body in Chapter one and two.

PLEASE NOTE: THE GLOSSARY TO THE MAJOR TERMS AND DEFINITIONS IN THE BOOK ARE ON THE LAST FEW PAGES.
Add author to your facebook page:
http://www.facebook.com/Biosapien
Thank you for purchasing my novel and enjoy!

BIO-Sapien is the first series to use QR music soundtracks in a paperback books & eBooks. Download "Barcode Scanner" in your Google Android or Iphone app store. Scan with your phone and the music score for that page will play on your phone through youtube.

BIO-Sapien's latest artwork & animation music video:

BIO-SAPIEN book 1 – Destination Optic-warp.

Chapter 1: The exoskeleton spaceship

Jaden has been hearing voices in his sleep for the past few weeks, but can't remember specifics when he wakes up. Some of the memories are stored in his subconscious.

"....this isn't his time. I sense his destiny has not been fulfilled and he has a long journey before him," a robotic female voice says.

"...this unknown soul is needed like the rest and isn't anything special," an older man's voice speaks.

"....I sense two anomalies in his twelve dimensions of matter strings configuration," a soft male voice says.

"This universe continues to be unbalanced and there is a shift in the gravitational structure from that sector," the echoing robotic female voice says.

"For the past 100,000 years, we have only been receiving twenty-five percent of organic intelligent souls from that sector...." the old man says.

"The anomaly in his string matter contains the makings of a legendary good force," the robotic female says.

"Or the making of an evil unstoppable force...I sense he will succeed and fail...."

"...your journey has just begun and you must create and choose your own destiny. Goodbye young carbon mortal...."

THE VARIOUS PITCHED VOICES FROM HIS FUTURE CONTINUE IN HIS DREAM.

"...-warp, dark energy, dark matter, plasma fusion...darclo..."

"I love you...."

"..Join us!..."

"Killing the weak and conquering is what your species is good at. You can be the new messiah of the Aquarius age for your people..."

"When a soul dies, the energy, called spirit quarks, on a subatomic level is released into the universe and travels undisturbed...."

"The first female president of the United States..."

"Choose your path, kill those weaker than you. Destroy those who wish to betray you..."

"A Virtualatrix..."

"Die for your species..."

"...you humans are destroying yourselves along with the rare animal species on your planet..."

"...humans are followers you need to be a leader..."

"China thinks they own us now..."

"...terrorist..."

"...you were chosen for a reason..."

"I need you to die...Say hello to your God for me...."

Jaden, a 19-year-old male, runs through a tall, dry cornfield as he tries to evade the military and men in white jumpsuits. As he zigzags through the dead cornstalks in an attempt to lose his pursuers, he notices that he has begun to lose feeling in his hands. Acknowledging the biting effects of the cold, Jaden breathes hot white breath onto his fingers while rubbing his almost numb hands together to combat the cold on this February night. Still running, he peers back and sees no one. Did he lose them, he wondered, but only for a second. He pauses for a moment thinking he lost them and then listens to the distant voices behind him before continuing to dash through the field. The sound of a helicopter closing in on him unnerves him, yet pushes him to move faster. He knows he has to find this thing. The frigid air cools his lungs and causes his chest to burn, but he can't let it stop him. He has to find it before the soldiers catch up with him, or worse, find it first. He scans the area and then decides to dart east and travel that direction for a few hundred feet and then like a mouse in a maze changes direction and pursues a northerly path.

Jaden, standing at 5'9" and weighing 160 lbs, is the child of bi-racial parents, which shows in his fair skin tone as well as in his blue eyes and black, slightly curly hair. He is wearing a black and blue NY Giants jacket, black winter hat that comes down to his eyebrows, blue jeans and a blue jersey, which he thought would be enough to keep him warm, he was wrong. He can feel the chill from his head to his Michael Jordan sneakers. All he can do is ignore it because he doesn't have the luxury of trying to find shelter and warming himself up. He has a mission to accomplish, one that is extremely important to him and obviously to those quickly gaining ground on him.

One mile south of where Jaden found himself, a military helicopter carrying Major K. Robinson cuts through the sky. Robinson yells into the two-way radio that he is holding close to his mouth. On the other end is Sergeant Peters, who has to pull his radio away due to the volume.

"I don't care what you have to do Sergeant. I want this kid apprehended or wounded, and I want the UFO08 found in one piece. This is the most important find we have had in years, not to mention the strongest energy source ever detected in an alien aircraft. We know it is somewhere in the area."

"Okay sir, I understand," Sgt. Peters replies in a raspy voice.

"We know this kid is going towards it now and he will lead us to it," Robinson says as he begins to regain his calm.

"The Ufl-retrac team is with my men, we are less than 100 feet behind the subject. We will shoot to wound him if necessary. We will apprehend him once we locate UFO08," Sgt. Peters says.

"I have confidence in you Sergeant," Corporal Major Robinson lowers the communication device from his face and continues to look out of the helicopter at the massive field.

Jaden picks up his pace as he continues to take deep breaths and exhale the cold winter air. The white breath flows past his chest and disappears. The sounds of his footsteps and cornstalks are heard swooshing around him in stereo sound. The sky is slowly getting darker like a movie camera fade as the leftover sunlight slowly retires over the cornfield's horizon to the west. He is pushing huge five-foot high cornstalks out of his path. Jaden finds a path over some grassy patches and increases his momentum. The nerves in his upper right arm send a pinching, burning sensation to his brain and a split second later his ears report a gunshot.

He hears the sound of a bullet echoing in all directions away from him. The force and sudden pain of the bullet causes Jaden to lose his balance and he tumbles towards the grassy ground. He lands on his stomach, which knocks the air out of him, he slides a few feet. As he struggles to catch his breath, the smell of corn and earth infiltrates his nose and pieces of dirty hay bond with this clothes. The high-speed bullet hit him in the upper right arm, just missing the bone. He is lucky it is just a flesh wound as he looks at the injury to his arm stunned.

Adrenaline releases from the adrenal glands above his kidneys and quickly enters his bloodstream. He can't believe he is shot and begins to panic. The fear of being shot again and dying quickly crosses his mind sending him into a panic. The torn muscle tissue and skin continue transmitting pain to his brain. His heart is beating a mile a minute and he reaches for his wounded shoulder.

His adrenaline diverts some of the pain and energizes him. He takes a deep breath and, while pressing on his wound with his left hand, he quickly stands back up while crouching and looks behind him. He hears voices from a distance, but doesn't see anyone. He slowly jogs off the path and back into the bushy cornfield holding his wounded shoulder. Fear continues bubbling up and he feels a hole in his stomach, but he doesn't have time to be scared.

"We hit him Major, but he got back up and is still running. It was a difficult shot to take," Sgt. Peters says.

"We don't want him dead yet. I'm not far from your location. Make sure your men are using their night vision and heat sensor scopes."

"Yes, sir."

Jaden approaches a small farm on the left, on his right is an elevated flat mound. The winter wind is blowing through his hair and across his face. He jogs into the open area and then back into another cornfield, while crouching down. Three military men in black camouflage clothes are less than 300 feet behind him with their assault rifles drawn. They have night vision goggles protruding from over their eyes. They signal to each other with their fingers as they quickly walk ten feet apart. Two of them can see the cornstalks moving from a distance.

Jaden is breathing in through his nose and out through his mouth. He thanks his training on the track team for allowing him to jog for such a long distance. The blood drips down his arm and soaks his blue jacket. He increases the pressure on his wound, while the wind blows by his face.

Jaden's eyes are scanning in all directions. He knows it's around here somewhere. He remembers it being a little further on the right. This is where he remembers seeing it last. He hopes it didn't move or leave.

A military helicopter with a bright spotlight quickly approaches from behind him. Jaden rolls to the ground and holds cornstalks with both hands to keep them from moving. He lays there motionless and breathes deeply. He listens as the helicopter quickly flies by and over him. He takes his left hand and puts pressure on his injury. He yells to himself with his mouth closed, emiting a loud moaning sound. Panic and fear kicks in as his mind begins to race.

He looks up and the helicopter is somewhere in front of him. He continues to scan the sky and sees the stars glowing. Jaden remembers when he was younger, when he would look through his telescope late at night and look at the billions of stars. That was an innocent time in his life, when he wanted to become an astronaut when he grew up. His mind quickly comes back to reality and struggles to push himself up with his left hand. He wishes he did more one-hand push-ups in gym instead of doing them just to impress women.

He stands up slowly and looks around noticing stalks in the cornfield moving on three sides. He continues forward while crouching coming up to where the cornfield ends and patches of grass cover the ground. He smells the odor of animals and he hears cows mooing in front of him in harmony as if they are singing a song. He hears different frequencies of sounds coming from behind the cows and it doesn't make any sense to him. He walks around the first cow. He pets the second one and it wags its tail faster. The curious cow stops eating grass and turns towards him. Jaden remembers cow tipping when he was younger and hopes these aren't the same cows. A bloodstain is left on the cow's side.

"Moooooo, Mooooo," the cows communicate. The twenty or so cows appear to be standing around something.

The grass makes a slight crunching sound as he walks by. This is where Jaden was a few days ago when he first witnessed the silver-bodied UFO landing on the ground. He remembers how the ship felt as if it was reading his mind when he walked close to it. He approaches the same area, but only sees a large hole in the ground. The hole in the ground is about forty feet long, seven feet deep and thirteen feet wide. Jaden tries to climb down into the hole, but senses something is there. Suddenly his mind feels as if it is being read again and the sensation is making him dizzy and queasy. He doesn't know if it's from losing blood or the feeling in his mind. He thinks that the ship has to be invisible.

Jaden feels as if something is watching him. He quickly turns around and sees a blurry blue shadow of something abnormal about fifty feet in the air. His eyes focus, but he doesn't see anything. He turns back around to the open area and something flashes in front of his eyes. The UFO turns visible and then invisible. This repeats every half second for a few seconds and then it stays visible. Jaden stands in disbelief as the UFO appears, but in a different shape than the way it did a few days ago. The silver metallic UFO now looks boxy and rectangular, but the color is still the same. There is not anything aerodynamic about it. Light particles can be seen moving around inside of the craft. The ship is about eleven feet tall, which is taller than the first time he saw it. A few cows slowly walk away. The volume of their mooing increases as they communicate with each other in a nervous tone.

The soldiers hold position and aim their rifles. Jaden's body heat blends in with the huge cows in the night scopes.

Jaden can't believe how nice the reflective liquid in the body looks up close. He walks around the side of the ship looking for the peculiar opening he noticed the last time he was here. His breath leaves condensation on the body of the ship.

"My men have the UFO08 in sight. We also see a bunch of cows surrounding the subject and the UFO08. We are waiting for your orders," Peters says in a confident voice into the radio.

"Why didn't the HCT55 (top-secret helicopter) spot the UFO08 sooner?" Major Robinson questions.

"It wasn't there before, sir. I'm sure it wasn't there. We didn't even spot it with radar, heat sensors or our night vision cameras."

His voice increases in volume over the small radio, "Listen Sergeant, we need this contained as soon as possible. I want you to take the subject into custody. We'll need to interrogate him later. We never encountered a ship like this and we don't know what to expect. I don't want any chances taken on this, just wound the subject. I want the area quarantined and sealed off, no one within two miles of this site."

"Yes sir, but there is a slight problem, we can't get a clear shot on the subject from here. My closest shooter is twenty-two yards away and the cows are in the line of fire."

"I don't care! Shoot all the standing hamburger if you have to," Major Robinson yells, "I want this subject taken down. Use your silencers; he has nowhere to go. Keep your men away from the UFO08; we don't know what kind of radiation or toxins are being emitted from it. The UF1-retrac team will handle any containment."

"Yes sir."

Jaden is still nervous with butterflies in his stomach. He found the ship, but he isn't sure what his next step will be. He's cold and the pain from his wound keeps entering his mind. Jaden walks completely around the ship, while continuing to press on his injury. He admires its shiny, liquid metal body and boxy shape. Curiosity slowly takes over his fear of the situation.

'I wonder if there are any aliens inside,' he asks himself.

Jaden sees a compartment glowing on the side of the ship in an area he already passed by before. He looks closer and sees a hand-shaped indentation on a flat surface glowing. Curious, Jaden puts his left hand over the blue light. The blue light becomes brighter and then something pierces his hand in several locations. The nerves in his hand send the signal to his brain at 300 feet per second. He tries to pull his hand back, but can't move it. He feels a tingling sensation all over his body. Blood is being drained from his hand. He has a surprised look on his face as he continues to jerk his body back to retrieve his hand, but the ship won't let go.

Jaden's hand feels as if bees are stinging it. He stops trying to move his hand and he suddenly hears two loud thumps behind him. The thumps can be felt from the ground and two cows drop from gunshot wounds. Another cow drops to the ground and they are groaning and mooing. He knows he is probably next. A helicopter approaches and hovers over the area shining a bright light down on Jaden. He looks up and squints from the bright light.

He knows they have him surrounded and not being able to move is continuing to make his heart beat faster. He continues trying to remove his stuck hand. He sees the end of the cornrows moving and hears the helicopter blades cutting the air over him. The wind from the helicopter is blowing in his face and moving the grass around him. Another cow falls to the ground and is laying there silent. Each thump is adding a few hundred goose bumps to his legs. The cows' bodies are shaking and moaning. The wind and noise from the helicopter makes the remaining cows move towards the barn. Jaden's body is still turned around half way, while his hand is still stuck on the side of the ship. The ship has stopped draining blood from his hand, but he still can't move. He turns his body back towards the blue light and struggles to move his hand. The surviving cows are gone. Five are dead on the ground and two are still moaning trying to move their legs. Jaden realizes that he is next and he could die at any second.

"Come on, let my hand go, you have your blood sample! I'm a sitting duck here!" Jaden yells to the ship while continuing to struggle. Suddenly it goes dead quiet around him and he doesn't hear the cows moaning or the helicopter blades chopping the wind over him. The grass on the ground stops moving and the wind stops blowing down on him. He feels as if he is in a closet or has gone completely deaf.

'What the hell is going on?' he asks himself in an uncertain voice.

It is so quiet around him that he can hear his heart beating while he continues to take panicky deep breaths. In and out, his heavy breathing echoes around him. His exhaled breath flows down his jacket and onto the metallic body of the ship creating a slight fog on the UFO. Suddenly there is a very low thumping sound as if a bird hit an outside window from behind him causing Jaden to jump.

He turns back around to see what's going on behind him. It is very quiet and he hears nothing around him. He looks in the distance and his vision is a little blurry. He suddenly notices a dim wall of light. Jaden's pupils contract as he focuses right on a red dot in front of himself. Small goose bumps go up and down his arms and legs. His heart races as he tries to figure out what he is looking at. It captivates all his attention at the moment. He temporarily ignores all of his pain and stretches his left arm from the glowing blue area.

As he gets within a few inches, he notices the red dot has a little sparkle of fire behind it, floating in midair. He moves his head forward to try and discern what this thing is, but his head stops on a solid, invisible force. He looks closer at the sparkling fire in midair and notices it's a long tracer bullet. Jaden stares with his wide-open eyes and mouth in disbelief as his head rests against the solid force. The red dot suddenly moves towards the center of his head. A low thumping vibration is felt throughout Jaden's body in milliseconds. He jumps back towards the ship while bending his left arm and freaks out. His bladder slightly releases itself from the sudden shock of what he sees in front of his eyes, his breathing increases and his hands begin to shake.

Jaden crouches and bends his knees towards the ground. Jaden sees the red dot following him and it stops eighteen inches in front of his chest. He moves to the left and right, but the dot follows him. Another low thumping sound is felt in his body. The wall in front of Jaden lights up. He begins to hyperventilate from breathing so fast. His jaw shudders as his eyes stay focused on the red dot that keeps moving towards him.

He looks in disbelief as the skin around his body is overtaken by goose bumps. His mouth and eyes are wide open. The slightly lit wall turns invisible again and three bullets remain floating. The logic in his brain tells him the ship formed some kind of shield in front of him to protect him.

A drop of blood falls from the right shoulder of his jacket to the grass. He can actually hear the drops of blood splashing onto the grass. The red dot disappears and his left hand is released. He quickly turns his hand around to analyze it. He doesn't see any bleeding or damage.

The red dot reappears lower, twelve inches from his chest in front of him. Again, he hears a low thumping bass sound and he reacts by jumping backwards against the UFO hitting his head. There is sparkling fire like a bottle rocket burning behind the red dot. His eyes focus on the red and orange sparks of fire. He slowly walks to the side with his back rubbing against the ship. His jacket against the ship is making a loud rubbing sound. His eyes are wide open and the slightly lit wall becomes invisible again as the red dot continues to follow him. The low thumping sound hits again and his heart jumps. He stares at the red dot like a deer caught in headlights.

5:42 PM

"That is a negative, sir; I repeat that is a negative! Subject is still standing. It looks like something formed around the UFO08 and the subject protecting him. The bullet from my rifle seems to be sitting in midair near the subject," Private Tandy yells over the two-way radio.

Peters takes a deep breath and responds on the radio, "We need this subject taken down Private; Again, shoot to kill!"

"Yes, sir. I've never seen anything like this. It's like something right out of *Star Trek*!"

"HCT55, do you have the UFO08 and subject in sight?" Peters asks.

Peter's radio comes on with helicopter noise in the background, "We have the subject in sight and the UFO08. We are about 150 feet above the subjects and switched to silent mode. Awaiting further orders," HCT55 says.

"I need to know what your sensors are detecting, HCT55."

"We have little to no radiation being emitted. Heat sensors aren't picking up anything, except the cows near the subjects. X-ray detectors aren't picking up anything. Radar also isn't picking up anything. It's like the subject isn't there, but I can see him with my own eyes," HCT55 unit responds.

"I need you to take down the subject, try not to hit the UFO08. Shoot to kill!"

"Yes, sir."

Sergeant Peters updates Major Robinson on the current situation.

"We need this situation contained as soon as possible Sergeant Peters. I have landed and am walking towards your position now."

Jaden slowly walks sideways along the ship to get away from the bullets. The red dots are gone, but the bullets remain in midair. He starts to feel weak from the loss of blood, which has soaked his jacket, but he knows he has to keep moving. A few minutes go by and he builds up some courage. His fingers extend out like a little kid touching something he never saw before. He tries to touch the fiery bullet and is stopped short by something that feels like a steel wall, but is invisible. The wall has very small light particles moving around on it as he investigates closer and lights up when he touches it. He knocks on it with his knuckles and the force field sounds and feels solid.

After a few minutes go by of Jaden staring at the bullets that could have killed him, he begins to feel dizzy and woozy. He feels as if he is in a nightmare. He wonders how he is going to get out of this. Why did this ship take his blood? Who's inside of here? What do they want with him?

He begins to walk sideways again. Numerous red dots appear as Jaden begins moving sideways again and are following Jaden's body as he walks. He feels trapped with nowhere to go. He hears another low thumping sound and he flinches with his back against the ship. He falls on the ground as several laser dots follow him. He closes his eyes and prays the bullets don't penetrate the shield in front of him. He flinches with each impact. Jaden curls his legs up against his chest while he continues to put pressure on his arm. His hands and legs begin to shake from being scared out of his mind. He opens his eyes and sees dozens of sparkling bullets. With each thump, his eyes jump towards the direction of the sound. He also hears the low thumping sound coming from over his head. The military officer in the helicopter over Jaden fires a few rounds at him. Jaden's bladder releases a few ounces into his underwear as his nerves and adrenaline rush around his body. He feels colder and colder and shivers as his teeth chatter. He feels like a rat caught in a trap. He realizes that each bullet was meant for him.

He feels like crying, but suddenly he hears different frequencies of sounds coming from the ship. One sounds like a dial-up modem. He feels a burning sensation in his chest from breathing so hard. The cold smoke from his breath fogs in front of him causing the vision in front of him becomes very misty like steamy glass in a hot shower. The red dots look like little red stoplights against the foggy energy wall. He calms himself down as he realizes the bullets can't hurt him and the ship is protecting him.

He psyches himself up that the bullets cannot hurt him. A minute passes by and the thumping sounds cease. Abruptly there is a flash of colorful light pulsing where the blue light panel area is and hissing and buzzing can be heard as if pressure is releasing. Jaden turns his attention to his left and he hears simultaneous thumping sounds directly in front of him and over him. He quickly stands up and walks over to where the sounds came from, he is amazed at what he sees. There is a rainbow prism in front of him. A strange, musty smell comes from the opening.

He is amazed at how it just appeared in the body of the UFO. He quickly realizes it is an entrance. He tries to see inside of the ship through the opening, but just sees bright colors. It looks similar to the way a rainbow looks after it rains. The colorful illusion and entrance quickly change to a mirror. He looks at himself in the mirror holding his wounded shoulder.

Jaden is so intrigued by the colorful and exotic entrance to the ship he forgets he was shot and was just fearing for his life. He begins to question if he should enter the alien ship.

He thinks to himself, 'I'm nervous to go inside. What if these aliens abduct me and do experiments with me? Who's inside here? What if I die? What is this ship here for? I heard about what these military people do to people who know too many secrets and how they end up disappearing. On the other hand, this could be the chance of a lifetime for me. There is a fifty percent chance these could be friendly aliens.'

Jaden thinks about the bad aliens in the television show *V*, the Borg on *Star Trek*, Sith in *Star Wars* and the *Alien* movies. He

27

believes he has better odds going in the ship than surrendering to the military. They already proved they wanted to put a bullet in his head, but the aliens could experiment on every piece of his body and never be heard of again. On the other hand, this could be his chance to learn of a different species or see how aliens think and what they know. He could learn technologies and science that no one else knows. He thinks he could come back a hero or with special powers like a superhero. This could be his only chance to see the stars up close. The negative side is that he would be leaving his family and girlfriend. He wishes she was here with him so they could do experiments on how fast her mouth moves.

He stands there thinking while staring into the rainbow and a tear falls from his left eye. The thumping sounds continue all around him. He loves his family and friends a lot, but realizes entering the ship wouldn't be any different from the military making him disappear. He knows way too much. Jaden realizes that this is his destiny.

He looks in the liquid mirror-reflecting doorway to the ship. He sees at least nine bullets floating in midair behind him in the reflection, along with red dots. He looks up and he sees a bright light shining from the helicopter hovering above, but the light doesn't shine on him through the shield. The shield around the ship is reflecting the light.

He feels so weak as if he is about to pass out. He looks forward at himself in the mirror and gains some nerve.

'This is it, I hope these aliens have a good medic and I hope that isn't someone's musty breath I smell.'

Jaden extends his left hand through the liquid mirror doorway and it feels warm inside. He takes a few deep breaths, places his hand over his wounded upper arm and walks through the entrance. The bullets suspended in midair drop to the ground and sound like dozens of beans falling onto a carpet. The shield around the ship disappears along with the entrance.

6:03 PM

Major Robinson walks up to Sergeant Peters, who is huddled around four soldiers looking at a map of the area. Major Robinson is in his early fifties, stands about 5'11" and weighs about 210 lbs. He is wearing a standard light green military uniform adorned with many medals from over 30 years on his still muscular chest. He has served in the military since joining at eighteen. Major Robinson plays ball when it comes to serving his country, he follows orders and doesn't care what they are; he follows them to the fullest. Such devotion has taken its toll on him. His once full head of thick hair has now become salt and peppered and is starting to thin in the middle. Robinson's face shows the road map of his hard life. His brown eyes are set deep into the sockets. His pasty white skin is wrought with wrinkles and a trench-like scar is prominent on the side of his neck; a memento left from a would-be assassin in the Gulf War. Robinson was never much of a family man, instead focusing all of his attention on the army. This left him divorced and estranged from his wife and teenage son.

The soldiers stand up straight and salute Major Robinson.

"At ease soldiers. What's the situation Peters?"

"The subject was being protected by some sort of energy shield from the UFO08. We fired several rounds from sharpshooters and the HTC55 unit, but impact was a negative. The subject was holding his wounded shoulder, while moving along the side of the ship. He eventually walked into the ship and disappeared. The bullets then fell to the ground."

"Oh my God," Robinson pauses and then looks up into the sky, scratches his head and then continues to talk, "We need this contained as soon as possible before the media gets here and people start to see this. How did that little bastard get away? I want to strangle that little son of a bitch!" His loud voice echoes in all directions.

"Sir," Peters interrupts, "He's not going to live long, remember he's been wounded. He has lost a lot of blood by now."

Major Robinson looks into the binoculars and sees the UFO08 with his own eyes.

"My God that is a beautiful ship. There is something different about this ship from the others I have seen at Area 51. The material of this ship's body looks so smooth and defined. This one has to be from another galaxy. I want the Ufl-retrac team to move in now. I want the ship tied down and an electromagnetic cover over it. I do not want this ship to get away. We also need all the oxygen removed and any gases so this ship does not try to take off. I want someone to find an entrance to the ship or an opening. We have a new experimental device called a LRSB to help keep track of it."

"LRSB? What's that sir?"

"I'll tell you about it when it gets here. That is all for now. I wanted this done yesterday Peters."

"Yes sir," Peters says while walking away and quickly gets on the radio. The Ufl-retrac team walks towards the UFO08 in white protective suits with radiation detectors in their hands. Then they bring out computerized devices and start probing the ship. There are loud clanging sounds as some of the men set up spotlights. Robinson walks over to the farm to talk to the owner.

The opening behind Jaden disappears and his goose bumps continue to appear. It is very warm inside the ship and completely dark and misty as if he is behind a waterfall. His curiosity fades away and nervousness returns. The unknown is making his body tremble again. He slowly walks on the sticky, wet floor. He takes off his jacket because of the temperature and holds it between his left arm and torso. Jaden feels as if something is watching him. He puts his hands in front of him so that he does not walk into anything. He continues to take small steps forward.

"Hello! Anyone here?" he asks.

He sees something small and glowing, floating in the air like a lightning bug coming towards him. He takes some steps back to try and avoid it, but it quickly moves at him and goes into his wounded shoulder. It goes pitch dark again. He falls back onto the solid, wet floor and uses his left hand to break his fall.

"What the hell?" he asks while he rubs his wrist.

His voice echoes around him in the silence. Jaden reaches over to touch his wound and it feels numb. Suddenly his shoulder feels a slight burning sensation as if something is eating at the germs, the way peroxide does when put on a cut. He realizes it was some sort of alien Band-Aid to help him. There is a clear seal over his wound. He continues to breath heavy and he coughs a few times. It feels as if something is in his lungs causing him to cough repeatedly.

Jaden hears watery sounds coming from all directions. It sounds like a bathtub filling up. He quickly turns around looking in all directions while he pushes himself with his legs and arms across the wet floor. He hears a small humming sound that quickly dissipates. Jaden feels warm liquid touching his sneakers, making his legs and socks wet. The warm water hits his body and sends warm sensations around his body. He quickly pushes himself up and stands up straight trying to escape this flood. Suddenly his body is frozen and he cannot move. There is an unknown force around him keeping him from moving, the same kind that was around his hand in the blue area. He cannot move his arms, legs or head. His feet are firm against the floor and he quickly moves his eyes around in the darkness. The unknown warm liquid continues to rush up his body. He thinks he is about to drown and he is helpless to do anything. His body feels as if it is stuck in sand as the warm 98.7°F liquid goes up to his stomach and then past his heart. Jaden does not smell any scent from the liquid consuming him.

He starts to panic as he continues to cough and struggles to move. He briefly thinks this is some sort of test, but the irrational part of his brain takes over and he thinks the aliens on the ship are trying to kill him. The liquid reaches the bottom of his mouth and begins to pour in. He pushes out some of the liquid in his mouth. The liquid is tasteless and odorless.

"Help! Someone help me!" Jaden takes a deep breath before being submerged in the mysterious alien liquid completely covering his body.

6:19 PM

Major Robinson slowly walks from the farmhouse where he just finished talking to the owner of the property. He has two soldiers walking near him with guns hanging from their shoulders. He walks to where Peters is standing in a small command post area with television screens of the UFO08 at different angles. The small command post area is elevated on a huge mound of dirt.

"Attention!" a soldier yells.

Everyone stands up straight.

"At ease men."

"Give me an update Sergeant."

"We can't detect through the UFO's hull yet, sir. We are bringing in a stronger instrument, the TC-100, that might be able to scan and penetrate the metallic body. So far, there aren't any dangerous levels of radiation or harmful bacteria. The body is an unknown material, but appears to be some sort of bioship. It has biological components and a

31

strong synthetic liquid type metal. Nothing we've seen before. It's very strong!" Peters announces excitedly.

Robinson continues to look at him with a serious look, "How about the titanium chains? The UFO08 fully secured yet?"

"We almost have it fully secured, sir. The chains are being put around the object."

"Good, Peters, very good. Let me talk to you over here for a second Peters."

They walk to the side together.

Sergeant Peters is a career military man like Robinson, but is smaller and leaner in stature with not as many medals on his uniform. He considers himself in peak condition, standing 5'7" and weighing 143 lbs. He has short black hair and a full moustache with flecks of gray coming through. His tanned skin reflects years of working with his troops. Although he has a gruff exterior, his soft hazel eyes reflect a kinder soul. Peters is married to a Japanese woman and recently celebrated the birth of a baby that he adores.

He has been under Robinson for the past ten years, the past four of which they have developed a friendship. They don't always agree, but Peters is good with following orders and knows the chain of command. His keen sense of right and wrong has cost him several promotions in the past.

Robinson places his right hand on Peters' shoulder and looks him directly in the eyes.

"Listen Sergeant, if we can get this securely back to the base without any problems this would look very good on our resumes. Promotions for everyone by the end of the month. This ship will take years for us to fully dissect and learn its technology. We also need to detect if it is sending out any kind of signal into outer space. We wouldn't want a thousand of these ships down here attacking us next week. I also want a report of how many life forms are on the UFO08 and what happened to that bastard kid. He's probably in there getting probes shoved up his ass right now as we speak," Major Robinson chuckles.

Peters starts to laugh.

"He's having an E.T. probe encounter of the third kind with them," Peters says laughing. Robinson starts to laugh aloud.

"You're going to give me a heart attack Peters; my fiftieth birthday is next month. Oh boy," he coughs and clears his throat.

"This kid is mixed with something right. He's half black and half white right?" Robinson asks.

"Yes sir, his mother is black and his father is white."

"What a mixed up kid, that is surely going to confuse the aliens. When they finish with him, they're going to call him Junglealienfever," Robinson says.

They both chuckle.

"No, he's going to have Jungleborgfever. When they finish assimilating him with their alien probes, he will be a quarter black, a quarter white and half borg," Peters says.

"I knew that kid was going to be a problem from when I first met him a few days ago. I just wish we were able to detect the ship's location without having to follow him to it," Robinson stops joking.

"What did the farmer say to you, sir?"

"He didn't know much. He said his cows were looking and standing around something for the last few days, but he never saw anything out there. I told him an experimental jet landed in his field. He believed me. If he didn't, it wouldn't have been hard to make that old fart disappear. He cared more about if his cows were okay. I told him the jet landed on a few of them and that we would reimburse him for the dead cows."

"Sir, what happens to all those witnesses who saw UFOs in the past?" Peters asks.

Robinson looks around and doesn't see anyone nearby them.

"There is a team called M1. They work out of Area 51 with us, but in different sectors. They specialize in covering up these types of situations. Every state has a secret base where they take these people. We destroy any evidence and we get all the information out of them. Then they are debriefed and/or drugged. We confuse them and get them to believe it was only a dream. Some come back with memory problems, some don't come back at all. standard military protocol."

"Some of these people have families and kids, isn't there another way?"

"It's not up to me Sergeant; there are other people above me, including the Department of Defense and the Secretary of Defense. They all decide who lives and who dies to protect the interest of this country. If we can harness technology from these alien ships, we could upgrade our defense systems and have more advanced spaceships. We could also have more advanced technologies over our enemies. The Russians are doing the same thing when they find a UFO. They are much worse than us to people; they make anyone who has seen or say they saw a UFO completely disappear. At least we return people back to their families on drugs and confused most of the time, in roughly the same shape as before the incident. From our intelligence, they only have one or two little UFO crafts, similar to what we found in the past. According to Project Blue Book, we found five since the beginning of this century that landed in USA. We also uncovered two others buried near the Pyramids in Egypt. We did a successful job keeping it from the media and citizens. This UFO08 surpasses our previous finds from what I can see. We need to keep people away and the media far away. We don't need any pictures or video being sent to television channels across the world. We also need to find out where this craft came from."

They walk back to the area where the television screens are. Robinson lights a cigar and stares intently at the video images of the UFO. The Ufl-retrac team has ladders on the side of the UFO; they are all over the UFO, checking everything. Ten men are on top of the ship, using little scanners and probing devices with metal poles.

The mysterious alien liquids fully submerge Jaden's body in the darkness and he still cannot move. He is holding his breath and he can hear his heart beating all around him through the liquid, echoing like a lost beacon signal. He has been holding his breath for the past minute and he feels a burning sensation in his chest. He feels confused, alone and paranoid as if he is about to die. Unexpectedly, something sharp pierces his belly button causing him to blow out his last breath of air. His nervous system sends shockwaves of chemical messages. The final bubbles are exhausted from his mouth and disappear into the darkness, but he still hasn't breathed in the liquid. Small needles begin to attack and pierce his body in different areas. Jaden has no choice, cannot hold out, and inhales the liquid around him. He coughs the slightly thicker than water liquid back out. Something goes into his vein on his left arm and injects something. Jaden starts to convulse and his blood pressure rises. He gags for air and his heart beats faster and faster. He struggles to move and to break out of this paralyzed imprisonment in his own body. His heart slows down to a very slow tempo and then it completely stops beating. His body lets off a few uncontrollable nervous twitches as his eyes roll into his head. Jaden goes into cardiac arrest.

Major Robinson is sitting in a chair, gazing straight into the screen with the UFO08 on it.

'I'm going to get you alien ship. The military is going to have a field day taking you apart. You think you can just protect people and get away with it. We are going to find out how you created that powerful force field. I guarantee you we will have that technology in the next few years. I would love to interrogate one of you little alien bastards, squeeze your big green heads and put you in the Area 51 circus with the rest of your freak families,' he says to himself.

He continues, 'It is too bad your other E.T brothers died when they landed in their older ships. I do not think you can survive on our planet. I hear our bacteria are very infectious. That is why you are hiding out in your ship. However, you will come out eventually, or I will personally pull you out of there. We have ways of getting you out of there. Come on out and suck up our tasty infected atmosphere.'

Peters approaches Robinson with a smile on his face and says, "Sir, the TC-100 device has arrived. The Ufl-retrac team has already started deep scans to penetrate the body."

"I would like an up to the second update of any findings Peters."

"Yes, sir."

Robinson sits back into his chair. A few minutes go by. Two Ufl-retrac men approach the Major, carrying a shiny metal box with CAUTION written on the outside of it. They stand straight and salute the Major.

"At ease men."

"Your LRSB is here sir!" one of the men yells.

"Can you please sign for this sir?" the other one asks.

Robinson stands up and signs for the LRSB. The men place the box on the table and walk away. Robinson looks at the box with a huge grin on his face. Peters walks over and sees Robinson smiling, looking at the box.

"Sir, is this the LRSB you were talking about earlier?"

"Yes it is; a prototype."

He punches in a code and opens the metal box.

A cool wind blows by them and warm steam comes from the box.

"What is it, sir? What does it do?"

Robinson reaches into the box and pulls out a red glowing device that flashes every few seconds. There are no buttons on the cigar-shaped device. Soldiers nearby turn to look at the glowing device. Robinson holds it in his hand and it glows.

"This is the best in top secret tracking technology Sergeant. LRSB stands for Long Range Space Beacon. This device can be tracked and located 100,000's of light-years away from Earth. We have been working on one of these for years, just in case a UFO gets away from us. It uses subatomic frequency waves, very advanced technology. The signal travels faster than light. It sends out millions of signals a second and they can travel through almost anything. As long as one of the signals reaches our galaxy, we will know the LRSB's location with our long-range satellites. The U.S. government has a special radio telescope in West Virginia that will locate these signals anywhere in our galaxy."

They both continue to stare at the glowing device.

"Sir, where are you going to put it on the UFO08? Has this been tested yet?"

"Peters, we are going to find a spot on the UFO08 or an opening on the ship. This device will stick to anything once it is activated. Tested? I have no idea how this LRSB was tested or if it will actually work. Here! Catch!" He tosses the LRSB at Peters.

Peters quickly extends his hands out and catches the device close to between his legs.

"You don't want to keep that too close to your groin, Sergeant. I guarantee it wasn't tested there," Robinson says while laughing.

Peters looks at the three-inch long, narrow device with a serious face.

"It's cold," he says while extending his arms to give it back to Robinson.

"The box has kept it warm. The device is activated in cold temperatures like space."

"I would hate to drop it and break it. My grandkids will probably be still paying for it," Peters says while carefully giving it back to Robinson.

"Peters, I don't think anything on this planet can destroy this thing. I was told it was made out of a new material the government has been experimenting with called nanotubing metal."

Robinson puts it back into the box and closes it. Robinson's cell phone starts to ring in his jacket.

"I need you to give me an update on the progress Peters."

The phone continues to ring.

"Yes sir."

Peters walks down towards the UFO. Robinson walks away and answers the phone.

A deep voice begins to speak through the phone, "We need an update and a status report." Robinson starts to talk into the phone.

10:30 PM

The floodlights brighten the area as if it is daytime. The full moon shines over the cornfields and a calm wind blows from the west. Sergeant Peters runs over to Robinson.

"Sir, I have an update for you."

Robinson grabs a warm coffee on the table and looks up at Peters while sitting down.

"Tell me what you got, I saw you down there checking on everything and supervising over the Ufl-retrac team very closely. I'm sure you have something good to tell me and when we can start transporting this UFO08; hopefully soon."

Robinson drinks his black coffee and stares into Peters' eyes. Peters has his scrawled notes in his hand. He looks back and forth at the Major.

"We scanned the object for the past three hours. The body is unlike any material we have ever seen before. We are scanning all angles of the UFO08. We have found the following:

Traces of an advanced form of matter and anti-matter.

Unknown microscopic energies moving throughout the ship.

Neutrons, protons, anti-protons, unknowns, radioactive energy, and atoms are being manipulated throughout the ship.

The body is a liquid type of organic metal. There seems to be some sort of nervous system throughout the ship.

Some sort of an anti-gravity drive propulsion engine near the rear.

Numerous unknown materials.

Some things that look like atoms, but are different colors and much smaller."

Peters swallows and clears his throat. He continues while Robinson puts down his coffee and rubs his black beard thinking about what he just heard.

"The matter and anti-matter look stable. The Ufl-retrac team has never seen anything like this before. The head scientist would like to talk to you in a few minutes," Peters says while looking up at Robinson's astonished face.

Robinson stands up and says, "We need this ship back to Area 51 ASAP...."

Someone interrupts the Major and says, "Excuse me, sir."

"I'm John, the head scientist, Major Robinson. I'm in charge of my team down there," John says while shaking Robinson's hand. John is a white male in his late fifties with a hint of Asian descent in his eyes. He is wearing prescription glasses and is wearing a white radiation suit. He carries his helmet in his left hand.

"We need more time to finish scanning the UFO before we move it. I have seen many unknown properties on this ship. We also do not know where the young man is in the ship, if he is still alive and if there are any other life forms aboard. The UFO08 is fully secured and is tied down, but we need to know more about it. This is definitely the best find I have seen in my thirty years of doing this. We need to know what we are fully dealing with here. We could start moving it now and it could blow up half the planet," John says.

"Listen John, I understand your concerns. I have my bosses at the NSA and the Pentagon wanting to know when this object will be secured on a truck and on its way to 51. The media is outside the secured area asking questions and starting their own investigations. Therefore, I have enough bugs up my ass. You have another six hours to finish your scans and have this thing on a truck and on its way," Robinson says with a straight face.

"Yes, sir." John walks away, putting his white helmet back on.

"Those guys are good at what they do, Major," Peter says.

"Yes they are, but they don't have to worry about the politics," Robinson responds.

"Have you ever heard of most of those things they found in this UFO?"

"No, but may God help us that those things don't destroy us."

Robinson sits back down and sips some more of his cold coffee. Peters puts his papers full of notes on the table.

"I've read somewhere that matter and anti-matter have to be separated or they might cause a powerful explosion. Also, that some of those elements are what a nuclear bomb is made of," Peters explains.

"Son, do not tell me anymore. I don't need anything extra to think about. It is bad enough that kid is in there and is an experimental monkey for those aliens. I guess it is only fair for all the times we experimented with their species. I've also seen enough alien movies when I was younger, and I know what a lot of aliens have in mind for us."

"I'm going to do my rounds and check on the UFO08, sir."

"You read my mind, Peters," Robinson says smiling.

Peters walks away. Robinson sees a soldier standing about fifteen feet away, he yells to him, "Hey Private! I need some hot coffee on the double!"

The soldier yells back, "Right away, sir!"

FEBRUARY 16TH 12:10 AM

The moonlight is shining bright over the UFO adding to the artificial lights from the bright movie studio-type lights. A strong gust of wind is blowing harder from the east, making the cornstalks wave back and forth. Inside the UFO, there is a faint heartbeat. The sound is bouncing all around the mysterious alien liquid filling the inside of the ship like an underwater dark cave. Jaden wakes up and gags for air, but something feels different to him. He feels as if he is dreaming and doesn't feel like his normal self. Jaden can't feel anything and is very confused.

'Am I dead and in heaven?' he asks himself.

There is darkness all around him, but suddenly something gets bright directly in front of him. From a distance, there is what appears to be a bright blurry screen with many things on it. He tries to get a closer look at this huge screen; he floats closer to it. The bright light shining on him enables him to look around and he notices he does not have a body. He is having an out-of-the-body experience. As he takes a closer look at this screen, with many different unknown characters, he tries to make sense out of it.

'It looks like alien symbols and alien language.' All the colors and strange characters on this big screen amaze him.

'I hope I'm not dead. I wish someone would tell me what is going on. I felt so much pain earlier and I can remember everything. I think I could be dead. I wonder what time it is, or how long I have been here. I know I'm still on the alien ship.'

He looks around behind him and just sees darkness. However, he notices little clear round things, floating together in a pair. They look like small semi-invisible balls. Jaden looks around more, and notices them all over the place. He tries to concentrate on one of them, and

39

then he notices it disappears and shows up at a different location near him.

'The pair moved so fast.'

He turns and looks back at the screen and he notices he is towards the middle on the screen.

'Interesting.'

His curiosity slowly returns as he looks at similar balls up towards his left and concentrates on them. They also disappear; he turns back and sees another pair where he was just at. He figures out he is looking through a pair of the clear balls at any given time and he is moving from one to another. Suddenly, an alien symbol appears over all the clear balls. Over each of them the word NANOEYE appears.

'Okay, I get it, these are called nanoeyes. Got it!' He looks at this large screen again with strange characters on it. 'This really does feel like a dream. What the hell does all this mean?' he asks while investigating.

He sees unknown characters with strange symbols in the middle of the screen. He also sees small and big unknown symbols on the bottom and top. He abruptly sees something he recognizes on this huge white screen, with black unknown characters on it.

'Jaden! It says my name on the screen, cool!' He notices an alien character on top of his name. He then sees BRAIN SCAN 1% next to his name on the screen towards the middle right.

Then he sees English words scrolling across the bottom of the screen moving to the left. On top of the English words, he sees unknown symbols and alien characters scrolling very fast to the right. He concentrates on the nanoeyes below him and he is up close to the bottom.

"A B C D E F G H I J...U V W X Y Z 1 2 3 4 5 6 7 8 9 0," This line scrolls by faster, then matches up with alien characters and symbols scrolling above it. It continues: THE..., AND.., IT.., DO..., THAT.., OR.., DONE.., FOR...,MY...,SHE,...,HE.., BY. Words are followed by brief definitions, then matched up with alien characters then disappear off the screen.

"VERB, NOUN, TENSE, ASPECT, VOICE, MOOD, ACTION...NOUN, PERSON, PLACE THING, ACTION, PRONOUN, SUBSTITUTES FOR NOUN...ADJECTIVE, ...PART OF SPEECH....." It continues to scroll in opposite directions and Jaden continues watching the screen in amazement.

'The ship is learning my English language. This is cool.'

Jaden moves back, so he can see the complete screen. He looks at the middle right corner and sees JADEN'S BODY. He also notices an alien symbol on top of that. Jaden concentrates on JADEN'S BODY on the screen. The body image glows momentarily then the main screen disappears, and Jaden's naked body in the fetus position reappears over the entire screen.

He sees his body is floating in a clear liquid resembling water, with thousands of micro-tentacles going into his body. On the screen, his body is showing up with light around it.

'Where are my clothes? I'm naked!' There are several nanoeyes floating around his body.

'Wow, that's my body there. I look so pale. This is so weird,' he says.

Jaden also notices a smaller screen to the right, with little alien symbols flashing. He turns around in the artificial eyes and looks back at his actual floating suspended body in the dark. He moves closer for a better look.

'Oh my God, those tentacles are going into my pores on my skin, mouth, stomach, and hair.'

He notices there are some nanoeyes behind his body and focuses on them. He is now behind his body observing.

'Oh my God, there is a big tentacle going in my butt. This is too much, that was not necessary. I am sure that must have hurt. Perverted aliens! There are other ways to get my temperature!'

He focuses and moves back in front of his body and looks at the screen again.

'I look like a freak show; I hope no one I know sees this.'

Jaden looks closer at the screen by his body; he starts to see words he recognizes: BODY TEMPERATURE 99.1 OXYGEN SATURATION LEVEL 98% BLOOD PRESSURE NORMAL. All words have alien symbols on top of them. He looks towards the top right he sees: 500,000 NANOBOTS INSERTED.

'Nanobots inserted? What the hell are those? Oh no, I'm going to change into an alien,' he says.

He concentrates on the NANOBOTS INSERTED on the screen. It lights up and a virtual image of his body shows up in the middle of the screen. He sees tiny dots all over his body, slowly moving around with a high concentration of the dots in his brain. The words and symbols on the screen change also. Jaden looks towards the left of the screen he sees BRAIN, NEURON CODE – DECODED / BRAIN WAVES FREQUENCY

COMPLETE, ELECTRIC/CHEMICAL NERVE SIGNALS FIRING AT 400 FEET PER SECOND, MOTOR CORTEX SCAN COMPLETE, WHITE/RED BLOOD CELLS MODIFIED, ENGLISH LANGUAGE TRANSLATION FROM LEFT SIDE OF BRAIN 75%, …TRANSLATION FROM RIGHT SIDE OF BRAIN 25%, NANOBOTS REMOTE TO BRAIN SIGNAL 100%, ARTIFICIAL ANESTHESIA TO BODY 99%.

'At least I'm still alive. I remember most of those words from science magazines and from school. They are taking all my memory from things I know and translating them. I wonder if I can learn their language. For some reason, I do not think there are any aliens on this spaceship.'

Jaden looks around the screen again. He sees something in red: UNKNOWN NANO REMOVED. He thinks to himself, 'Unknown nano removed? If it is unknown to them, what does that mean? What was it doing there? Maybe it was cancer?'

Jaden concentrates on the red words, just those words that change, and UNKNOWN NANO PARTICLE REMOVED FROM REAR BRAIN–SAFELY STORED. He concentrates on those words, but they stay the same. Jaden remembers the alien symbol on top of the words.

'I don't know if that's good or bad.' He looks at the virtual body of himself on the screen and sees a red dot where the unknown nano was removed.

'That would suck if that thing they removed was something I might need, if I ever wake up. Let me see what else is around here.'

Jaden concentrates on the part of the screen that says JADEN MAIN. He sees the original screen with all the alien symbols and words being translated. Jaden moves towards the bottom of the screen, he sees small images related with the English words. $A2 + B2 = C2$, $PI=3.14$, he reads, and it continues, 65% BRAIN SCAN COMPLETE.

Words, numbers, and sentences continue to scroll by and match up with alien symbols scrolling towards the right. 'These are the things I was learning in college and in high school,' Jaden says, 'Oh my, I hated learning that algebra, calculus and statistics.'

Jaden continues to look at the screen, 'Cool, some of the biology and pre-med courses I took in college.'

JADEN BODY STAGE 1 60% COMPLETE

'60% complete? What is that about?' He concentrates on it, but it does not flash or do anything.

5 AM

"Sir," Peters runs over to Robinson who is dozing off in the chair.

"Huh?" Robinson asks with a confused look on his face.

"This contact lens is hurting my eyes. Hold on a second Peters."

"Yes sir."

Robinson pulls out eye drops, looks straight up, blinks his eyes and uses a few drops.

"Oh that feels so much better." He blinks his eyes a few times, and then takes a sip of his cold coffee.

"Did that happen from staring at the UFO08 on the screen too long, sir?"

"Possibly, when you look at it long enough, it looks like a smaller rectangular version of the Borg cube from *Star Trek: Voyager*," Robinson says.

"You are right, sir. It does resemble it somewhat," he says while looking at the screen with Robinson.

Robinson continues to drink his now cold again coffee. The coffee tingles his tongue and mouth. A cold chill moves through his body.

"When are they going to make something that keeps coffee hot for hours and days Peters?"

"Sir, I would definitely buy something like that."

"What do you have for me, Sergeant?"

"I have an update. The UFO08 has been fully scanned and penetrated to the best of our ability. We have found the following: We located a human life form, who we assume could be Jaden. The body is in a fetal position. It looks as if it could be hibernating or frozen. There is movement as if it is breathing."

Robinson interrupts, "How is the body breathing? How is it alive?"

"We don't know sir, but there seems to be some sort of artificial arms or tentacles connecting him to the ship. Somehow, it's keeping him alive. There are very faint sounds resembling a heartbeat. He's not moving and seems to be floating in something."

"Something?" the Major asks in a puzzled voice.

Peters continues, "Some sort of liquid, we can't make out what it is." Robinson looks at the television screen of the UFO and starts to think.

"What are these aliens up to? Are they turning this kid into a space fish? He's probably going to come out of the spaceship and be able to breathe underwater. Then he will be able to talk to fish. I can see it now, Aquaman with tentacles, communicating with all the fish in the ocean," the Major laughs.

Then he continues, "Have you found a location on the ship for the LRSB to be placed?"

"Yes we have, we found a little compartment opening, with a blue light inside. It should fit your LRSB device," Peters says.

"Let's go and insert this bad boy."

The Major grabs the box and walks down to the UFO with Peters. The Major looks at all bright lights and walks slowly with his eyes wide open looking at the UFO in person. He steps over dead cows.

"I just stepped in cow blood!" Robinson yells, "Someone clean up this mess over here."

The soldiers are standing up straight around the UFO saluting the Major as he walks by. Robinson pulls out sunglasses with his left hand and puts them on.

"The bright lights make it seem like it's daytime here."

"Yes sir, it's very bright here."

John walks up to Robinson and says, "We have the spot for your device right over here, sir."

"Thank you John, I see you are getting a lot done."

John, Peters and Robinson walk over to the area where the small compartment door is on the UFO. Robinson stares at the blue light inside.

"Has anyone stuck their hand in there, since it looks like it could be a handprint for opening the ship?"

John responds, "We tried that already, sir, it didn't do anything."

Major Robinson bends down and puts in the combination for the box. He opens it up and hands the LRSB device to John. John places the device inside the compartment door. The device sticks over the blue panel area.

"Does it need to be turned on sir?" Peters asks.

"It will turn on when it senses movement."

Major Robinson stands back and looks at the ship's body.

"John, do you think these ropes and cables can safely lift this ship onto the tractor-trailer?"

"Yes, it should sir; the tractor-trailer should be here any minute. The small crane is in place and we are ready to transport her."

Robinson takes a deep breath, while touching the UFO with his left hand.

"John, where do you think this alien ship is from?"

John turns back to Robinson and says, "I don't know sir, there is only one human life form on this ship that we believe to be Jaden. We have detected some kind of life forms or live energy all over the ship, but they are too small to detect what they really are from outside. Maybe when we get this ship open back at headquarters we can determine everything inside. I think this is the best find I have ever seen, sir. However, I'm puzzled as to why a UFO like this would land here in the first place, and where are the aliens inside? Did they leave on foot and could be coming back soon? What are they doing with the teenager inside?" John wonders aloud. He then continues, "Maybe the kid could be infected with something that could kill everyone. This kid is going to have to be quarantined for a long time, if we ever reach him."

"Good questions John, but I don't have the answers. I guess in time we'll discover all the answers," Robinson says.

John closes up the opening on the side of the ship while talking to the Major, "I'm looking forward to working with you again, sir."

The tractor-trailer blows its loud horn while it pulls up a narrow dirt road. The tractor knocks over cornstalks from the sides. Soldiers move out of the way, while Sgt. Peters walks up to the tractor-trailer and directs it.

"How much longer, before we can transport this UFO08, John?"

"Less than forty-five minutes, a little after 07:00 hours, sir."

"That's good John, thank you," Robinson says while he walks away and starts to dial numbers on his cell phone.

"Yes, sir. Yes, sir. Forty-five minutes," Robinson says on the phone.

Jaden is staring at his unconscious, floating lifeless body. He notices small light particles lighting up in another area of his brain. He drifts off thinking of being on the *Ripley's Believe It or Not!* television show with superhuman powers.

"Well Jack, there weren't any probes stuck up my ass or anything like that. Those rumors are untrue. They were friendly aliens and just wanted to share their technology on faster than light space travel with me. They were shorter than I am, so I was like a god to them. Then they asked me what type of superhero I wanted to be and I chose to be a cross of Superman, Wolverine and a Jedi. As you can see, I have lightsaber claws as hands and I can see through your wife's clothes backstage Jack from where I'm sitting."

45

"Freak!" someone in the audience yells.

"Well you look like a freak to me. What do you think audience?" Jack the host of the show asks.

"Freak! Freak! Freak!" the audience chants.

Jaden responds with a hypnotizing look on his face.

"You do not look like a freak and you are the best looking superhero we have ever seen," Jaden repeats while waving two fingers at the audience.

The audience and the host's eyes are in a daze. They repeat what Jaden says, "You do not look like a freak and you are the best looking superhero we have ever seen."

The audience cheers and Jaden stands up bowing his head with a huge smile on his face.

Jaden comes back to reality and is now looking at the translucent screen, which says 85% OF BRAIN SCAN COMPLETE.

Jaden is getting bored in the nanoeye facing the screen in front of him. His feeling of nervousness returns. This out-of-the-body experience is confusing him. In a dream, he does not realize he is conscious. However, in this state of mind he is conscious of everything. Being tired and hungry is not a problem for him. This experience feels as if he is in a very detailed, controlled dream. He nervously wonders what the military is doing outside and if they will come in there after him.

Suddenly, he sees the screen jerk back and forth. The screen changes and a big alien symbol shows up in blue. Then it goes smaller, and reads FLIGHT MODE underneath. The screen turns blinding bright and he moves back some in the nanoeye. The screen then goes dimmer and projects an image. Jaden notices it is video images from outside the ship in very detailed clarity. He sees all the military men around and dozens of men in white body suits around the UFO. Jaden concentrates on the screen and thinks about changing the angles of the images. The screen disappears and he is looking on the outside of the ship in a nanoeye. Everything looks huge as he notices the eyes must be at the atomic level.

'Wow, this is like being inside a virtual camera,' he says to himself.

He concentrates on different angles. He sees a tractor-trailer and ropes pulling on the ship he is in. Jaden looks in another direction and he sees Major Robinson sitting in a chair smoking a cigar. He zooms in and sees Robinson's old, wrinkled face up close.

'Oh no, not that guy again, that guy has it out for me. He will take this ship apart and take me apart without mercy,' Jaden says.

He thinks back two days ago to what Robinson told him at his house. *He remembers him grabbing his shirt and pulling him close to his old frowning face, "Listen you little shit! If I find out you're hiding information and not telling me where that object is at, I'm going to make you disappear. Then you're going to wish you were never born. For the last time, where is that UFO you were talking about on the phone earlier today?"*

Jaden remembers his reply, "I already wish I wasn't born, your breath is melting my face. Is this the military's way of pre-torturing someone, by using bad breath methods? Listen, Captain Major Old Sock Breath, I don't know what you're talking about. I don't know anything about a UFO. I thought they didn't exist? I was talking about a UFO show on television to a friend earlier today....." Jaden laughs to himself as he remembers the conversation.

Jaden thinks about the main flight mode on the screen. He quickly leaves looking at Robinson and goes back to the main screen inside the ship. He sees all alien symbols in white over the live video from outside. The alien symbols get smaller, and English words appear underneath them. He reads in red: SHIELD STRENGTH 100%, ANTI-GRAVITY ENGINES 80% CHARGED, MANUAL FLIGHT AND AUTO FLIGHT, SPEED, ALTITUDE, RADAR, GRAVITY FORCES 65%, AIR PRESSURE / BAROMETER 2000 PSI, STAR / SUN SOLAR CONVERSION STRENGTH 60%, 40% SUNLIGHT CHARGE NEEDED FOR GRAVITY FLIGHT BALANCE.

Jaden notices in red: LIGHT REFLECTION / INVISIBILITY.

'Interesting, hmm I wonder....' He concentrates on those words; then they change. Jaden sees SEMI-INVISIBLE, INVISIBLE, INVISIBLE RE-IMAGE, OFF.

'I have an idea.'

7:05 AM

"Oh my God!" Robinson yells. He stands up and looks at the UFO directly.

Peters runs over yelling, "Sir, sir, it disappeared! The UFO has disappeared!"

Robinson and Peters stand motionless with their mouths wide open. John comes over the radio, "Sir, it's still there, but it is reflecting its light somehow, appearing invisible to our eyes. We can still see it

47

on infrared and thermal sensors. We are going to attempt to lift it again."

The chains appear to be holding empty space.

"Have you ever seen anything like that Peters?"

"No, sir, it's like it isn't there. I'm sure the military could really use some technology like that sir."

Robinson starts to talk on the radio, "John, how much longer before it's on the tractor-trailer bed?"

"It is very heavy sir. It seems as if it weighs five times the size; we are taking it slow, a few more minutes…. Hey take it easy there!" John yells to someone behind him.

The sky slowly lightens as dawn breaks. A rooster squawks in the background near the barn as the sun pierces the sky and shines on the little crane lifting the UFO. It slowly shines down onto the invisible UFO and passes right through it.

'Ha ha ha…' Jaden continues to laugh to himself.

'Damn, that was funny. The look on their faces was hilarious. That would definitely make the cut on *America's Funniest Home Videos*.'

The screen shudders again. Jaden turns the invisible option back to off by thought. Jaden knows there are not any aliens on this ship or any aliens he can see. He is guessing the flight screen is in front of him so he can take control of the ship or try to fly it somewhere. 'Maybe some sort of test?' he questions himself. This is very puzzling to him.

'Why else would there be a flight option screen in front of me?'

He wonders if there is an alien here that he cannot see. Whenever he passes a nanoeye throughout the ship, it's mostly black until he reaches outside the body. He thinks that maybe the entire ship is an alien.

'Test or no test, I'm not going where the military is trying to take me and this ship.'

Jaden is looking at the main screen again through the floating nanoeye. He is getting used to being out of his body and operating things as if he is using a personal computer. He changes back to the flight screen.

Jaden sees the same screen he saw a few minutes ago with all the navigation options. He notices the 40% CHARGE NEEDED FOR GRAVITY FLIGHT BALANCE option has gone down to ten percent.

7:10 AM

There is a loud clanging and crashing sound that echoes in different directions. The visible, rectangular-shaped UFO was just placed on the wide load tractor-trailer. The military men and UF1-retrac team are helping to secure it to the trailer with Sgt. Peters supervising the men.

Major Robinson is on the phone talking, "Yes, sir, it will be en route in two minutes. Yes, yes."

Back on the ship the gravity flight balance has gone down to zero percent. The entire screen with alien symbols and English letters on it turns green and starts to flash. He sees two more options on the screen, INITIATE ANTI-GRAVITY ENGINES and VIEW CHANGE. Jaden concentrates on VIEW CHANGE and he is looking outside the ship again. The only difference is all the options that were on the screen are semi-transparent in his view now. He can see the flight screen through the nanoeye also.

This is exciting to Jaden, he feels as if he is in a futuristic virtual reality video game. He realizes he is tied down to the tractor-trailer. He can actually feel the metallic chains as if they are around his real body. The chains feels like small leather belts wrapping around his naked body, slightly squeezing him.

'I have a view all over the ship at any angle. Cool! Let's see, I have some interesting items and options to play with here.'

Jaden concentrates on the INITIATE ANTI-GRAVITY ENGINES to the left of him.

A humming sound is beginning to roar from the UFO. The men tying down the UFO run for cover. The sudden humming sounds make them lose their grips and stumble backwards.

"Oh my God, what was that," Robinson says.

He picks up the radio and yells into it, "Sergeant Peters I want those men back in there to finish securing the chains and I want that tractor-trailer to start its engines!"

The humming sound gets louder. Peters orders the men to get back in there to finish the job. The men try pulling on the chains and ropes. The metal chains and ropes start to lift. The wheels on the back of the trailer begin to lift in the air as well.

"It's trying to get away! Move your men back!" Major Robinson yells into the radio. His voice can be heard without the radio. He continues on the radio in a lower voice, "HCT55 unit, initiate protocol 1."

The men on the ground run and take cover. Fifteen seconds go by and a helicopter is heard hovering nearby. Wind is blowing in all directions from the blades chopping like a high-speed fan. The helicopter stops directly over the UFO with something underneath it. The helicopter drops a metal net over the UFO and quickly pulls away. The net starts to light up with electricity. The tractor-trailer engines turn off and the driver gets out and starts to run. The UFO humming sound goes silent and there is a loud thump. The chains are relaxed and the trailer wheels are back on the ground.

'What the hell was in that net?' Jaden asks. Then everything goes black through the nanoeye. 'This isn't good. I feel like I just closed my eyes, everything is black.'

He tries different nanoeyes and they are all black.

Sergeant Peters runs over to Major Robinson.

"Sir, what was in the net? The sound is gone and the UFO looks as if it lost power along with the tractor-trailer."

"Good old fashioned American technology. The net contains trillions of electromagnetic impulses. Guaranteed to destroy and disable anything electrical or mechanical underneath it."

Sgt. Peters looks down at the UFO with a confused look on his face, and asks, "What about the tractor-trailer?"

"We have time for another one to come in. The backup tractor-trailer should be here in a few minutes. We don't take chances here, Peters. Get your men down there to untie the UFO08 and get it ready to be put onto the next truck."

"Yes, sir," Peters says while running away.

The white-bearded Caucasian driver of the tractor-trailer approaches Robinson. He speaks with a southern accent while waving his hands outwards, "What did you all do to my truck? My watch and beeper stopped working also."

Jaden sees a big alien symbol in red. It gets smaller and he reads RESTART underneath it. Then he reads, PROTECT MODE, PROTECTING JADEN'S HUMAN BODY.

'Damn, I was beginning to shit bricks sitting here in the dark, thinking the entire ship had a blackout.' English words and alien symbols start to scroll by very fast all over the screen.

RESTARTING

'Alright! Cool, the ship is restarting as if Windows 3.11 just crashed.'

The flight screen lights back up and he quickly changes view. Jaden is looking outside the ship and quickly moves between the nanoeyes.

'I'm still tied down. Let's see what this ship can do. I'm getting the hell out of here.' Jaden concentrates on raising the anti-gravity engines to ten percent. He then sees MORPHING FOR FLIGHT.

A low humming sound is heard again outside the ship and quickly gets louder. Robinson turns and looks with his eyes wide open. He knocks over his coffee; it spills all over the small table, and finds its way to the dirt.

"What the hell is this bullshit?" he asks in a disgruntled voice.

The men stop untying and tighten the chains again. The soldiers and Ufl-retrac team cover their ears near the UFO.

"HCT-55 unit 2, initiate protocol 1!" Major Robinson yells over the radio.

Everything is happening very fast. A soldier covering his ears near the UFO has his helmet come off and float upwards into the air. The UFO begins to lift upwards very slowly, lifting the chains and the trailer. The ship begins to glow brightly causing the men to cover their eyes. Light particles can be seen moving up and down the body at high speed as the ship begins to change shape. There is a bright flash as the humming sound continues to get louder. The bright flash and light particles fade away. The body of the ship morphs into a gigantic, metallic, carrot-shaped UFO. Something metallic comes out of the ship's sides on both sides. They pass directly through the chains. The pair extend out four feet from the body and lay flat like floating wings. The metallic wings are about three feet wide and nine feet long. They extend from the middle of the ship towards the small end of it.

Everything seems to be happening in slow motion. Robinson continues yelling in a deep voice. The entire tractor-trailer lifts into the air, and then the cabin area of the truck detaches from the rear trailer and slams to the ground. The loud crash echoes in all directions, shaking and vibrating the ground. The men take steps back. The rear trailer and the UFO are floating nine feet in the air. Small yellow particles begin to come from the bottom of the wings. The soldiers and men in white suits become weightless. They are trying to run, but they levitate in one place and lift with the ship. The men begin to scream and yell, while saliva comes from their mouths and quickly turns to small bubbles. They attempt to grab onto something and another helicopter quickly approaches. Suddenly it goes very quiet. Inside the ship, Jaden feels as if he is stretching his body. Outside the ship, the only sounds are screams and helicopter blades cutting the wind. Peters is holding onto cornstalks with his right hand while trying to keep a soldier from floating away with his left.

"Hold on to my hand tight!" Peters yells as his legs begin to float upwards.

Yellow bubbles float from the pants of the soldier. The soldier Peters is holding onto grabs another soldier's foot and they form a human chain. Other soldiers are not so lucky and spin out of control upwards.

Their arms and legs are out of control. There is a spark of bright electricity around the chains. Major Robinson covers his eyes from the light. Pieces of the trailer, ropes and chains levitate in one spot and leave the UFO. Soldiers and retrac team bodies are still floating fifteen feet in the air. Some are upside down and running while others are screaming trying to grab onto something.

There are men holding on tightly to the frozen cornstalks and have fear in their eyes. The UFO lifts up faster and is about thirty feet from the ground. Robinson extends his neck to look in bewilderment at his prized possession floating away. Suddenly the rear of the ship extends outward like a liquid metal wave. Something comes out of the rear and morphs into a tail. The ten foot wide and three feet deep tail levitates three feet behind the ship. The bottom piece of the silver metallic tail looks like a frown and the top part extends upwards like a smile.

A sniper bullet is shot at the UFO from a distance. The bullet slows down and approaches the UFO. It stops six feet from the UFO and disappears into a small spark of light. Another HCT-55 helicopter hovers over the UFO taking off and drops another net over it. Electricity lights up six feet around the UFO, quickly traveling around it at high speeds. From the ground, you can see a clear energy shield around the ship. The net instantly disintegrates and the electricity fades away. The UFO lifts up faster, slowly turning clockwise. Small yellow particles can be seen being emitted from the tail and wings.

Major Robinson continues to have an astonished look on his face. He can't believe what just happened. The trailer and chain pieces slowly descend to the ground. The helicopter tries to move out of the way. The UFO is spiraling up at breathtaking speed and clips the rear of the helicopter. Four feet of the helicopter tail disappears including the rotor. The engine sputters and the helicopter quickly spins out of control. The dozen or so men floating fifteen to twenty feet from the ground quickly drop to the ground. Pieces of the trailer, ropes and chains also fall to the ground making loud clanking and thumping sounds. Half of the rear and front tires on the trailer are disintegrated. The helicopter sputters and continues to spin out of control towards the ground. The two pilots jump out of the sides screaming; one lands in a pig's sty and the other in a cow's pen. The helicopter crashes into the barn and explodes. Sounds of men moaning on the ground can be heard echoing in every direction. Guns are being shot at the UFO from all directions. Major Robinson's cell phone starts to ring. He keeps his eyes on the disaster in front of him. He rubs his head and continues looking in shock at the UFO getting smaller and smaller. The sunlight reflects on the newly morphed UFO as Robinson's cell phone continues ringing.

America's first comic book/sci-fi themed restaurant.

TORAGON

"BEST SELLER"
2 beef super action burgers with crispy chicken in the middle. Pepper jack, provolone & cheddar cheese. Spicy guacamole, spicy mayo, grilled onions & bacon.

292 Graham ave.
Between Grand & Powers
Williamsburg Bk 11211
718-599-4376

Sweet potato tots   Action wraps

CHOOSE TO EAT HEALTHY LIKE A HERO OR EAT LIKE A VILLAIN

VILLAIN FOOD
Action Burger $6 Double $10.50
Crispy chicken $6 Double $10.50
Cheese steak $6. Double $10

SIDEKICKS
Fresh cut fries, chicken fingers, potato tots, action wings, Nachos, onion rings, cheese steak sticks, sweet potato fries, mozzarella sticks, side salad.

HERO FOOD
Turkey burger $6. Double $10.50
Grilled chicken $6. Double $10.50
Veggie burger $6. Double $10

ACTION MILKSHAKES
Super fudge, mojo, jojo, carmelephant, cupcake kid, strawberry shortcake, peanut shockwave, cheesecake fusion nutella dream, interracial fusior

ACTION SALAD
Brutus - Action Salad
Zeus - Thai.

ACTION WRAPS
Caesar, veggie, zeus, Tuscany, Action classic, Thai, Tuna, Brooklyn, Action-crunch, Euro, Vamptorian, Action fire, Dark energy.

DARCLONIAN   Dark Energy Queen - Crunchy Evil Hot Dog   250+ classic arcade games.   FULL FOOD MENU

2 Action hot dogs, beef chili, red & grilled onions & 2 mozzarella sticks.

What separates us from the competition? Every angus burger is freshly made. We season each burger with over 12 unique herbal spices. Our super action burgers has over 25 spices.

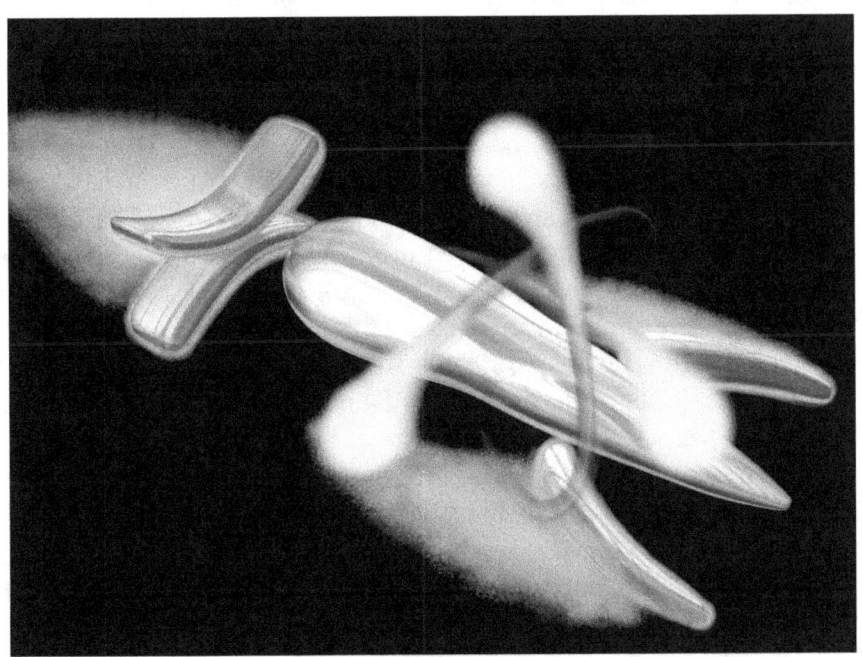

7:15 AM

The wind is blowing from the west at 15 mph onto the UFO making a howling sound. The ship is slowly floating across the sky at 25 mph. Jaden can feel the cold wind all around him as if it is blowing against his face and body. He feels as if he is flying in a dream. He sees the explosion at the barn and feels bad for the poor farmer named Jack that owned the property there. Below him he can see the closed off area with hundreds of military personnel on the ground closing off several areas. There are citizens, police and National Guard troops pointing towards the UFO. The nanoeyes are flying autonomously in different directions. A nanoeye detects a brown-feathered eagle approaching from a distance. Jaden's altitude reads 203 feet.

'Holy shit! What a rush. This ship just morphed like the *Terminator 2* robot. That was amazing watching this ship transform. The wings and tail coming from the body are awesome. It felt like I grew two arms and the tail felt like I just stretched my legs after a long trip. I wonder if my heart is beating fast. Let me check and see.'

Jaden checks his physical body and monitoring screen to see if he is okay. He is still crouching in the fetal position. He can hear his heart beating very fast from the adrenaline rush he just experienced. He feels more comfortable with all this constant multi-tasking and flying the UFO on pure thought. The ship tilts to the left and then to the right instantly. A few minutes pass by as Jaden is flying over the area he grew up. The eagle flies alongside the ship. It makes a hawking noise while turning its neck and head to look at the ship. The UFO stops midair and turns in the direction of the eagle. The eagle continues flying and the nanoeyes continue to circle the huge bird. Jaden makes the right wing extend upwards as if he is waving at the bird.

'Hello, Mr. Hawk. You look so beautiful up close. Your feathers float so nicely through the wind. Don't be afraid, little guy,' Jaden says while the wing extends back down.

Jaden realizes it's a red-tailed hawk and not an eagle. The bird slowly flaps its wings and circles the ship while making loud bird sounds.

'Hey bird, I'm not a nest. There is no place to sit here,' he says while following the excited bird with the nanoeye.

Another red-tailed hawk comes from the national park underneath him. Two mourning doves also approach from below. The hawk reaches the rear of the UFO and one flap of its wings propel the hawk very quickly upwards. The two doves and hawk quickly propel towards the ship out of control. The UFO quickly turns and moves out of the way from the fast moving birds, just missing them. The nervous birds poop as they pass over the ship. Jaden tries to get out of the way, but it narrowly lands on the body.

'Yuck that feels nasty. I can even smell that...no respect for a ship that was just washed...I mean morphed.'

The birds quickly scatter and they gain normal flight. Jaden thinks for a second about chasing them, but he lets them go. He wonders why the birds lost control like that. He figures it must have been gravity related like the military men floating upwards a few minutes ago in zero gravity. He continues forward at a maximum speed of 30 mph. Jaden wonders why he can't go faster.

He wants to go back into his body soon, but he is making the best out of this weird, frightening and exciting experience. The other helicopter is coming towards the ship from a distance. Jaden can flip through the menus and screens much faster now. It is as if he is clicking a mouse on the computer and whatever he thinks of happens

56

instantly. This is much easier than driving a car or playing Super Nintendo. He can see at any angle outside the ship and he can zoom in on anything. He can't wait to tell his friends about this. Jaden wonders what they are doing now.

Jaden sees all the military trucks and police cars blocking off streets. He sees yellow tape closing off areas and a news reporter on the ground from a distance. He zooms in on her.

"I'm Angela Clarke reporting for Channel 6 Local News. Behind me, the military has sealed off the area where some unknown object landed last night. The military has been tight-lipped so far and refuses to answer any questions. Several trucks and helicopters have been seen entering the area. The military said a radioactive meteor landed here yesterday at 5 PM, and didn't give more details."

The camera operator turns the camera up into the air. Miss Clarke turns around and looks up.

"Oh my! There is something flying in the air, just over my right shoulder. Oh my God! It looks like a UFO or something. I can't believe what I'm seeing now," she stands there holding the microphone speechless looking into the air.

The camera operator zooms in on the UFO. "I've never seen anything so shiny and exotic looking like this. The wings look as if they are floating along the side of the body," he says.

"Tell me you're getting all of this, Jerry," Miss Clarke says.

"I didn't blink my eyes for the past minute, ma'am."

The crowd standing behind the yellow tape begins to talk louder. The UFO continues to hover by them making a slight buzzing sound.

"Yes sir, yes sir, I understand. I know the protocol, I'm working on that now," Robinson hangs up the phone with an angry and disappointed look on his face. He takes a deep breath and bangs his hand on the table. He flips the portable table over and radios fall on the ground.

"How the hell did this happen? "Shit! Shit! Shit!"

He kicks the chair and knocks over another hot coffee. Peters and three other soldiers are standing by Robinson in a line, very quietly. Robinson rubs his head and calms down.

"We just went into DEFCON 3. We are also into Operation Unknown Alien Intentions. My bosses are trying to blame this mess on me. We have to take that UFO out," Major Robinson coughs then continues, "Officer, I want you to take care of that crowd and take any video recorders. Relay that message to the men outside the perimeter, and I want you to personally to see that everything is done properly. Then report to me. Anyone giving you a problem, or asking too many questions, arrest them."

"Yes sir, right away."

Robinson turns to Peters, "I need you to go to the Marino family house, question his family and then his friends again. Get any information you can get, he might be a victim or he could be working with this unknown alien terrorist group."

"Alien terrorist group?"

"We don't know what the intentions are of these aliens; that kid could be one of them or a part of them now. That ship is a threat to national security and America. This kid could be trying to kill people or blow up his high school. We don't know. We also don't know what the UFO08 is capable of in weapons," Robinson pauses and pulls out a cigarette from his jacket.

He then pulls out a lighter and flickers it a few times. He sits down in the commander chair.

"I have a light sir," Peters says.

"I got it."

He puts his hand over the cigarette and continues to try to light the cigarette. It lights up and the white smoke flows through the air and seamlessly disappears.

He takes a deep pull and continues, "This might be out of my hands soon..."

The Major exhales.

A man comes on the radio, "HCT2-55 unit still in pursuit of UFO08, flying southeast at 323 feet and at 30 mph. It appears to be flying towards a school and residential area. I have the target two miles in front of me and awaiting further instructions."

"This is Major Robinson. Continue pursuit of UFO08. Do not engage yet, you will be shortly in contact directly with the Pentagon and the Air Force units about to intercept."

"I see two F-15E's forty miles away and a SR-71 Blackbird on my radar intercepting at high speed!"

"That's a copy."

Major Robinson puts down the radio and talks to Peters again, "I can tell this is going to be a disaster; this is going to be a long day. I need you to stay here until Lieutenant Barker gets here and then go to Jaden's family house. Try to get there before the FBI shows up."

Jaden is flying high in the air above his town looking down. He sees his old high school beneath him. He feels as if he is a floating video camera. The fresh air blows across the UFO and Jaden can feel it crossing his body. Everything is so clear and detailed around him. He keeps wondering why he can't fly faster than 30 mph. When he thinks about accelerating or increasing anti-gravity engines, JADEN'S BODY STAGE 1 98% COMPLETE lights up in red. Then he can't see what STAGE 1 means. Words and sentences are still being matched up with alien characters on another screen.

Jaden flies over his old high school.

'This must be first period. Look at all the freshmen walking to class. Let me zoom in on them.'

"You dropped your books!" An older bully knocks down a freshman's schoolbooks from his hands.

"Why did you do that? My mommy paid a lot of money for those SAT books."

"Your mommy huh? Mama's boy huh? Your mommy gave you any lunch money for me?" The older bully asks.

"I'm not giving you my lunch money," the freshman says with confidence, "Who are you suppose to be Nelson from *The Simpsons*?"

Other students stand around and start to watch the entertainment. The older kid gets up in the freshman's face and grabs him by the collar, "You're giving me whatever money you have in your pocket or I'm going to beat your face in."

The freshman looks scared at the bully, but his eyes are behind him.

"Look a UFO!" The freshman yells. The bystanders begin to point into the sky.

"You think I'm that stupid to believe that?" The bully asks while searching the kid's pockets. The freshman stands there in shock pointing in the air.

Jaden is hovering in one place being entertained by the commotion.

'Wow, this is good. Front row seats to a freshman being bullied. This is good, Bart Simpson and Nelson Muntz in high school. This reminds me of my junior high school days of being bullied and kicking the bully's ass. I didn't think these things still happened in high school. Stand up for yourself freshman! I wonder if there is something I can do to help him.'

Police sirens are heard from far away.

"You're a good actor huh? All you have is five dollars?"

The freshman whispers in a scared and terrified voice, "Aliens are looking at us."

"Oh yeah huh? You think I'm stupid?" The bully makes a fist with his right arm and moves his arm back to punch the kid in the face. His right hand stops midair and he releases his grip on the freshman. The freshman falls to the ground and the bully's body floats into the air. The bully begins to scream while his pants fall down to the ground, leaving him naked three feet in the air.

The high school students start laughing at the bully floating in the air unable to move. The freshman runs away with his books. The kids standing around start to run in all directions, screaming and running. The bully falls to the ground with his pants at his knees.

"What the hell! Arrrggghhhh!" He turns around and sees the UFO seventy-five feet in the air near him. He quickly pulls up his pants and he runs towards the school. Local police swarm the area and they escort the kids into the school along with teachers.

'Now that was classic. I used some kind of a tractor beam on that kid. That was hilarious, that kid will believe the next time a UFO is behind him,' Jaden says.

The officers on the ground start to shoot their shotguns and guns at the UFO. The students run into the school screaming and hiding behind trees. The UFO flies away.

"Are you okay son? Are you hurt?" The police officer asks the freshman kid.

The student continues looking at the UFO in the distance and crying. The officer picks up the kid and brings him into the police car. The five-dollar bill lies on the ground covered in blood. The wind blows it away.

PENTAGON, WASHINGTON, D.C. 7:45 AM

"That's right sir, upstate New York in a small town called Stillwater; twenty miles north of Albany. We are currently tracking it on one of our spy satellites with three more moving into position. The UFO08 has already hurt dozens of soldiers and one civilian," General Dudley says over the phone to the Secretary of Defense.

General Dudley is a short bald man in his late sixties. He walks around with a cane and served in Vietnam. Secretary of Defense Oscar

Strongwater is a white man in his early seventies and was appointed to his position by the President of the United States.

"Dudley we need this object taken down with any force necessary. Too many people have seen it and this is getting out of hand. We do not know what this UFO08 is capable of. We need this contained right away. Use as many jets available. Give all jets, helicopters, and tanks the green light to fire. I want everything recorded; I also want Major Robinson's report on my desk by 08:00 hours tomorrow. You even have permission to use the SR-71B and put on standby the stealth bombers."

"The SR-71B? Do you think that is needed?" Dudley asks.

He continues, "There is a fully loaded AC-130U gunship a few minutes away and it should be able to take out the UFO08. It is only flying at 30 mph."

"We don't need to take any chances. The UFO08 could start moving at faster speeds at any moment. It has already changed into an aerodynamic body. This is a threat to national security; we are not taking any chances here. We need our most advanced, fastest and top-secret jet on this," Secretary of Defense Strongwater orders.

"The SR-71B new prototype engine is still in the experimental stage."

"Yes, I know. We need our fastest jets; I want every available aircraft on this. The LRSB online yet?" Strongwater asks.

"No sir, it's currently offline. The LRSB is only active and online in outer space. It transmits on subspace…"

Secretary Strongwater interrupts, "I don't need to know how it works General. Let's try and keep this short and to the point." Strongwater stops talking and coughs a few times.

He continues, "I heard some local citizen could be involved or is being held inside UFO08?"

"Yes, sir, the FBI is on their way to question the teenager's family."

"If this kid is dead or alive, we don't need this story on the front page of Enquire magazine. When the UFO08 is shot down, everything is sent to the labs. No one is to speak to the media and the President has been informed. We will address the media publicly when this is over. If the boy's body is found it stays in the lab, not to be returned to the family. Let the local and state police know this kid is wanted," Strongwater says.

"Wanted for what sir?"

"He is wanted for stealing government property."

"Yes, sir."

General Dudley hangs up the phone with Secretary Strongwater.

"Officer get me on the radio with the AC-130U gunship."

"Yes, sir."

A few minutes pass by. General Dudley walks over to the two-way radio. He walks with his medals shown proudly on his military jacket. The officer hands him the radio.

"This is General Dudley at the Pentagon, who am I speaking to?"

"This is Warfare Officer Cole, aboard the AC-130U gunship from Albany Division, sir."

"Listen Officer, you tell your crew we don't need any mistakes on this. We need this unidentified flying object taken down by all means necessary. It has already injured officers and civilians. It is a threat now to our country!"

"Yes sir! I will inform my crew, we will use all necessary firepower to take down this object...," Cole abruptly clears his throat and continues, "Sir, we mostly fire at ground targets."

General Dudley replies, "The UFO is only flying between 25-30 mph at a low altitude. You are also the closest to the target."

"Yes sir, we will fly higher than the UFO and take it out as if it is a ground target," Cole says.

"Be careful, the UFO08 has an advanced shield technology and might have an offensive system we don't know about."

"Yes sir!" Officer Cole says excitedly. Dudley hangs up the two-way radio.

"HCT2-55 fall back to base, we have live video feed from other sources."

"Yes sir! Reporting back to base." The HCT2-55 turns around.

Jaden is still slowly flying the UFO over where he grew up. He really wants the ship to go faster soon; he knows the ship can do more. It feels as if he is driving a car at the speed limit or flying in a Badyear blimp. STAGE 1 is still flashing red and he knows it has something to do with his speed. Jaden makes it to his neighborhood where he lived most of his life. He floats over his house.

'Wow, I wonder if mom and dad went to work yet. Let me see if I can zoom in here. On second thought, I think I shouldn't do that. I might tractor beam my house by mistake.'

Sirens can be heard in the background as Jaden turns around and heads in another direction. Suddenly his front door opens. The autonomous nanoeye detects this. His mother, Stacey, walks out the front door with a cup of coffee in her hand. Steam from the coffee can be seen coming from the brim of her homemade coffee. She assumed Jaden stayed at his girlfriend's house last night without calling again. Ten minutes earlier, she left a voice mail on Amy's house phone. The UFO turns around.

Stacey is a fair-skinned African American woman in her late forties. She talks with a slight English accent and has a size eight figure. Her hair is short in a Halle Berry early nineties haircut. She has light brown eyes and a small nose. She was raised in England where most of her family is from. Stacey came over to America in her early twenties for a college education. She later fell in love with her husband Tony Marino.

She is wearing a dark brown business suit, a three-quarter black winter coat and opaque tights. Stacey was on her way to work. The keys in her hand can be heard jingling as she slams the door shut. She puts her keys in her bag and pauses. She feels as if something or someone is watching her. Her shadow from the sunlight disappears and she hears a slight humming sound. The sunlight disappears around her as she looks to the sides of her. She slowly turns around and looks up. She sees something blocking the sunlight. She focuses in and sees the UFO levitating in one place pointing right at her, while partially blocking the sun. The sun shines on her face and she puts her right hand over her eyes to block out the sun's rays. Her mouth opens up and a look of fear comes across her face.

"Oh my God what is that?" She yells while dropping her coffee. Her coffee spills out of the cup. Some of it lands on her shoes and lower tights. Her mouth is wide open and she is in complete shock.

'Hi mom, look at my new spaceship! It doesn't need any insurance!'

She quickly opens her bag while looking up at the UFO slowly getting closer to her. Her hands are shaking and she grabs the key and shoves it into the lock. She quickly turns the key, opens the door and slams it behind her. Stacey locks all the locks and runs into the basement. She is breathing heavy. Jaden realizes she couldn't hear him. Stacey quickly takes off her shoes and runs upstairs to her bedroom. She drops her winter coat and bag on the way. She slides under the king-size bed while tearing her tights in a few places. She looks around in different directions to make sure she is alone. Her teeth chattering echoes around the room.

Jaden sees his mother is scared under the bed through the nanoeye. He realizes he freaked her out enough. Local and state police start shooting at the UFO from the ground. The bullets hit the body causing small waves of liquid metal to go in different directions. The bullets feel like hail against Jaden's skin.

They begin swarming on the ground under it and police get on a loudspeaker, "Everyone please stay in your house. This is a police emergency."

Jaden is getting bored and heads in another direction. He feels bad for scaring his mother half to death and now he is freaking out the neighborhood. He still can't get over the amazing feeling that he is flying. It feels like a dream that he can't wake out of. He really wants to see what this ship can do. Jaden knows this can't be the top speed. Jaden flies towards his college. He feels as if the wind is blowing against his face.

'I wonder if Amy is still mad at me or if she is in class already.' He sees students pointing in the air and running. One of Jaden's screens light up and he sees an unknown threat 8000 feet away.

DEFENSE/OFFENSE MODE ONLINE lights up in red letters. Suddenly purple light particle rings are forming in the middle of the ship. The particles quickly stick together at high speed. A huge purple molecule forms together and passes right through the hull of the ship. It extends seven feet outside the ship in different directions and curves back into the body. There are three clear bulbs that resemble the shape of a huge egg on different tracks of the purple molecule. Each bulb is moving around a track of the molecule, slowly passing through the body and back out. The six nanoeyes quickly pass through the huge molecule. 6 NANOSCANNERS ONLINE shows up in red letters. The nanoeyes convert into nanoscanners.

'Cool, look at that. A cool huge glowing molecule. That is awesome!'

He sees different nanoscanner screens with numbers at the bottom of each image. There are more options on each screen now. The options intrigue Jaden's curiosity. The nanoscanners quickly scan the large cargo plane flying towards him. They combine the images together and form one big vision of the cargo plane. The cargo plane has two huge propellers on each side of the wings. Jaden changes his vision and sees the airplane in 3D with an enhanced 360° vision.

UNKNOWN AIRCRAFT, SPEED 315 MPH, ALTITUDE 1522 FEET, DIRECTION NORTHWEST the screen reads. Jaden switches between different nanoscanners. He can actually hear the propellers turning and cutting the air. It actually sounds like a loud fan to his ears as the nanoscanner passes right through the blades. He sees the outside of the plane and changes angles. NO DEFENSE ENERGY SHIELDS FOUND ON CRAFT, 12 CARBON BASED HUMAN LIVES DETECTED, nanoscanners display on each vision.

'Oh Shit! That is the AC-130 gunship! My brother told me about those airplanes when he was in the Gulf War. That is one deadly, dangerous plane.'

Jaden suddenly sees through the body of the gunship in a three-dimensional view. He sees cables, wires, steel, plastic, engines, gas flowing, oil flowing through pipes, eleven male crewmembers and one female crewmember sitting in chairs. He also sees quite a few television screens, hundreds of large cannon shells and thousands of large bullets loaded up. Jaden can see inside of the gunship at any angle or direction.

The crewmembers are breathing heavily and blood is flowing fast throughout their bodies as they each witness the UFO flying before them. A nanoscanner is displaying the bacteria, dirt and sweat on the crewmembers' skin. Trillions of bacteria colonies are growing all over their bodies. They are in many shapes and sizes. He then notices bacteria everywhere in the area growing and moving. Jaden feels nauseous and disgusted. He feels as if he is about to throw up. The nanobots in his body quickly override that feeling between his brain and nervous system. Jaden quickly changes from the amplified vision to another.

'Okay, I feel better. That was the nastiest thing I've ever seen. I've seen that once in lab class, but not all over bodies moving around like that.'

A few minutes pass by.

'This is crazy and unbelievable! I can see everything inside of this gunship from inside of this UFO! I'm controlling all of this with my mind. I'm controlling the nanoscanner when I concentrate on one or it can control itself. The vision is crisp and vivid and is at least three times clearer than my own eyes,' he thinks to himself.

Jaden zooms in closer and he sees the crew briefly without clothes and he can see inside their skin. Their hearts are beating very fast and he can hear them. Beating together as if someone is playing the drums off beat. Jaden looks and zooms in on the female officer.

'Nice body…..hmm…. she looks of European descent. She looks so serious and sexy. Let us see, what we can see here. Superman with his x-ray vision, moving in for a little peak. So, this is what Superman does all day, when he isn't fighting crime.'

Jaden thinks about being on the *Price Is Right* show. He quickly thinks about the previous vision without any clothes on. The nanoscanner is viewing through the seat she is on and shows her sweat soaked back.

'Bob, I think I want to see what is behind door number one.'

The nanoscanner turns around to the front of the female officer.

'Holy shit! She is completely naked! Whoa, this is crazy. Nice sweaty breasts, slim waist, completely shaved, nice suntan line. She looks like she is about 5'2" 109 lbs.'

Jaden is looking so hard that the vision changes to the insides of her body. Inside of her body looks slightly animated, like a cartoon. He can see her entire circulatory system, veins and bone structure. Her lungs are quickly breathing in and out, and he can see the oxygen slowly being absorbed into her blood. She's having an adrenaline rush.

'No traces of breast cancer here officer, you are cleared for duty,' he says chuckling.

He sees her looking very nervous, while sweat drops down her eyebrows. Her eyes are focused on the screen in front of her. Jaden turns the nanoscanner around to see what she is looking at on the computer screen.

'What is she looking at? Shit! She is zoomed in on me with two mini guns and 25mm rounds. Shit, a female Rambo. I'm out of here!'

Jaden quickly changes his view to outside the UFO.

"I'm locked and ready sir!" Officer Jessica yells.

"This is Officer Cole, we see the UFO in sight below us. There is something purple moving around the body and it is about half a mile in front of us. We have a lock and are firing weapons," he says over the radio and continues, "Pentagon you should be receiving your live video feed now."

Four of the nanoscanners fly back towards the UFO at a fast rate. Two stay inside the gunship floating around observing. Jaden tries to communicate to the gunship by thinking about it.

'Hey guys I'm just flying around in this cool ship, I don't want any trouble. I'm not bothering anyone.'

66

They are still locked on him and increasing speed towards him. Alerts of offense and defense icons show up on his screen. Jaden concentrates on trying to get away faster.

"Did anyone hear that crackling humming sound?" Cole asks his crew.

"Yes it came from the radio. The signal came from the direction of the UFO," an officer says.

"Make sure you record it," Cole tells the officer.

"Yes sir."

Cole turns to his crew of eleven, "Fire at will."

" Firing now, sir!" Officer Jessica says while she wipes the sweat from her face.

Everything starts to slow down around Jaden. NANOTIME is seen in the top right hand corner. He sees flashes of light coming from the direction of the gunship as they fire upon him from above. Little beams of light are being shot at him. He sees a barrage of very large bullets and cannons coming at him at very fast speeds. He tries to bank upwards and the light particles are passing by all around Jaden. The first cannon hits Jaden and he feels a painful sting. He tries to move to the right and activates his shields. The sounds of the gunfire and cannons fired are heard two seconds later, "Boom, boom, boom, boom, boom, ta-ta-ta-ta-ta-ta-ta…"

REVERSE SHIELDS ACTIVATED Jaden sees on his screen. Outside the UFO's body and inside the shields turn completely black. Jaden is flying away as fast as he can, still at 30 mph.

'All this technology and this B.S. spacecraft has a maximum speed of 30 mph. I'm a sitting duck.'

The shield catches the gunfire and cannon rounds ten feet from the ship. The force of the cannons makes the ship move in other directions. Sparks of fire are lighting up behind the bullets and cannons, slowly moving with the ship. Everything speeds up again around him and NANOTIME flashes off. Jaden flies upwards towards some clouds to hide. "Boom, Boom, Boom, Boom" The gunfire is riddling around the UFO.

'I can even feel the bullets and cannons hitting the shield.'

The bullets and cannons floating around the shields move closer into the shields then disappear. 'Where did the cannons disappear to? Why does it say NANO-PLASMA ENERGY RECYCLING on the screen?'

The AC-130U gunship continues to fire at the ship as it goes into the clouds. The gunship flies by Jaden in the clouds and stops firing. The UFO is hovering inside a cloud.

'This is stupid; I know they can see me. What would MacGyver do in a situation like this?' He asks himself and then chuckles.

'He would use this cloud and sunlight as a weapon somehow. Then again, he probably would not even be in this situation flying around in this UFO with a 30 mph speed limit! This sucks! I feel like Beavis and Butt-head hiding behind something where I know someone can see me. Let me scroll through these screens, so I can hit this gunship with something.'

"Use the 25mm and 40mm L60 Bofors cannon shells," Cole says. The AC-130U gunship continues firing at the UFO while turning away from it. It slowly turns to the left to circle around, but continues firing at Jaden inside the small cloud. The cannons make the outside shield glow brightly.

BRAIN CONVERSION COMPLETE, OFFENSE WEAPONS 1 ONLINE Jaden sees.

'Let's see, here is a meter, that looks like a strength level. Let me play with this option. I don't want to blow them up completely. I see a few areas on the gunship lighting up on the screen. This is not easy, I have to concentrate on flying, zooming in, concentrate on which nanoscanners to look through and target this big goofy cargo plane with big guns,' Jaden pauses.

'The bigger cannon shells are making this UFO craft move when it hits the outside shields.'

'Fire!' Nothing happens.

'Shoot.' Nothing happens.

The gunship turns around to get another direct shot at Jaden. Jaden flies out of the clouds and towards the gunship. Targets turn green on the screen Jaden sees.

'Duh, I'm not a pirate on a pirate ship. I can't say the command to myself, I have to think it to myself,' Jaden laughs to himself and thinks about firing. The purple molecule around the body lights up brightly and a pink torpedo is fired from the left side of the molecule out of thin air. It passes right through the shield around the UFO and goes in the opposite direction of the AC-130U gunship.

"Sir, something was fired from the UFO08 in the opposite direction," Cole says on the radio.

'Shit, it shot in the wrong direction, stupid UFO. I targeted the gunship in the other direction. Is there an alien Stevie Wonder in here firing the weapons for me?' Jaden asks.

The projectile is moving very fast in the opposite direction and then begins to turn around.

"Weapons Officer, target that pink projectile," Cole says.

The gunship begins to bank left hard. "Sir, the projectile is heading directly towards us, and it's 4588 feet away. It is also speeding up to 500+ miles an hour!" Warfare Officer yells.

"Let the computers take it out," Cole commands.

'Chicken! Where you flying to? Big bad airplane! I shoot a pink torpedo looking booger at you and you're flying away so fast!' Jaden yells at the plane.

Jaden wants to check something out. He concentrates on the projectile and he is looking from the pink torpedo's view. He sees the plane in view, getting closer. The gunship turns in the opposite direction and the computer starts firing at the alien torpedo with its mini gun bullets and 25mm cannon rounds.

'That gunship has such precise aim,' Jaden says.

The bullets and cannon hit the alien torpedo directly. The torpedo breaks up into a dozen little pieces, but still keeps at the same speed at the target.

'Wow! Interesting now I see many different views. I bet this is how spiders' eyes are.'

The gunship continues firing, but without any effect on the torpedo. It gets closer, and the dozens of small torpedoes form back together as one. The gunship does a sharp nosedive and banks right. It starts to release a bunch of flares and continues firing at the torpedo. The torpedo again breaks up into pieces and then forms back together. Jaden continues switching views and he notices fighter jets lighting up on his screen a few miles away. The torpedo breaks into five medium pieces. One hits the mini gun, 40mm and 25mm cannon weapons. The other two remaining torpedo pieces hit two of the four propeller engines. The impact shakes the AC-130U.

"We are hit, we are hit Pentagon!"

The targets that were hit glow pink and then evaporate into thin air. The left side propeller engines do the same. Black smoke starts to pour from the AC-130U in those areas. Liquid gas and oil is pouring from where the propellers used to be. The wings are damaged with two missing propellers but they are still flying with the two other propeller engines on the right side. The aircraft leans to the right. The liquid gas and oil stops spraying and the AC-130U starts flying straight again in the opposite direction.

'I hope they are okay, I don't want anyone to die,' Jaden says in a modest tone to himself.

The gunship's engines are wailing.

'That was a good and interesting shot. That alien booger torpedo just kept going, even though it was shot at. This is amazing and wild. I've never seen anything like that before. This is the best video game and live entertainment I could ever dream of. No controls just thought and concentration.'

"We took a direct hit headquarters. We were fired upon and we need assistance," Cole says to the Pentagon over the radio.

He continues in a disappointed voice, "We lost two of our engines and three weapons. They just glowed and vanished without exploding."

"Stand by AC-130; can you still fly?"

"We can still fly, but losing oil pressure and gas from the missing engines. We only have our 105mm M102 howitzer weapon left that wasn't out when we were hit," Cole says.

"Can you fall back and give long range video footage?"

"Yes, we can give visual support."

"You have backup arriving in your area in less than one minute. We are going to organize a systematic attack on the UFO08. There are two F-15's, SR-71 Blackbirds forty seconds away from you," General Dudley says.

Then he continues, "Two AH-64 Apache helicopters are standing by on the ground, right under the 08."

"Yes, we see them sir on our radar. I will relay the coordinates to the other units. The 08 is giving off very little heat and radar. They will need to set their missiles and weapons to explode before contact or increase sensitivity on self guided missiles," Cole says.

On a small road facing the UFO in the clouds, a young male news reporter is talking into a camera. "This is Paul Patterson, reporting to you from Channel 6 News. It is complete lockdown here in Stillwater. Residents are locked in their houses and told not to come out. People have been hurt on the ground, and behind me is the National Guard with military vehicles. There are two armored Apache helicopters hovering on the ground behind me. There seems to be something hiding in the clouds. An AC-130 gunship was firing at something a few minutes ago. It is hard to see what's going on through the clouds. Over the scanner, we can overhear the military talking about this object as a 08. I have never seen anything like this in my life. My co-worker Angela Clarke was arrested by the military twenty minutes ago. We don't know why many people by and around the farm a few miles from here have been arrested. I was told there was a big explosion from a helicopter from some kind of experiments being done there."

He pauses and drinks a bottle of water. The cameraman points into the sky and gets Paul's attention. They go back to recording again.

"The AC-130 gunship is back. There are also two fighter jets flying in from the east as you can see. The two helicopters are moving towards that mysterious cloud from the south, which something is inside of. They are coming in my direction and …"

General Dudley communicates with the backup units. Cole coordinates with the backup units. The AC-130 flying with one side higher than the other and targets the UFO from over three miles away.

'Oh shit, I see fighter jets and a helicopter below me. They are going to hit me with everything they got, just like a fat kid trying to knock down a stuffed piñata.'

Jaden tries to zoom in and see these jets up close. He doesn't have time to zoom in. He can see them all on his screens. Everything is flashing on his screen and showing threats. Jaden begins to feel nervous and panics.

He flips through all the screens, looking for something he can use. He sees some things still in alien characters, but some are beginning to make sense to him. Jaden slowly flies to another cloud in an attempt to hide. He also sees his body still suspended, lighting up and glowing. A clear eggshell is around his body in a suspended state with half the tentacles still in him.

The Apache helicopters quickly leave the ground.

"Eagle 1, firing sidewinder and AMRAAM missiles," the F-15E pilot says over the radio.

"Eagle 2, firing Maverick and AMRAAM missiles," the second F-15E pilot says.

The two AH-64 Apache helicopters fire their Hydra 70 rockets and AIM-9 sidewinders at the UFO. The AC-130U fires its last remaining 105mm M102 howitzer weapon. Sounds of missiles and rockets being fired fill the air in stereo sounds. Thirty-six military personnel and General Dudley at the Pentagon watch the televisions silently in a large room. A man coughing from the back can be heard throughout the room. They can see different views on the screen from three spy satellites and aircraft cameras. The President and Secretary of Defense in the White House can also see the live video feed. People on the ground are pointing at the cloud and taking pictures of the missiles moving from different directions.

Paul Patterson continues reporting, "... And, the fighter jets are firing missiles at that cloud. The AC-130 gunship is firing from a distance...."

'Oh Shit, with a capital S. Eleven rockets and missiles are coming in all directions directly at me at 1000-1500 mph,' Jaden says in a petrified voice.

Jaden is panicking and tries to fire at the missiles and rockets being shot at him. He can hear the fuel burning from inside and outside the missiles and rockets coming at him at supersonic speeds. A smaller torpedo hits two missiles and rips them into pieces. He can't focus fast enough through the nanoscanners to hit them all. Jaden braces for a painful impact and makes sure the shields are full on. He also thinks about moving as fast as he can, but slowly moves like a turtle crawling 31 mph from the clouds. Suddenly Jaden sees STAGE 1 COMPLETE flashing across the screens in large green letters as the missiles reach twenty feet from the ship.

On the ground the reporter is yelling, "There is a UFO flying towards me about 500 feet up! The missiles are about to hit this flying object!" He yells.

"Are you getting this Bobby?" Paul asks. Bobby the cameraman nods his head, while his other eye is looking at it directly. He admires it and zooms in on the purple exotic looking molecule with the clear egg-shaped balls moving around it.

"It's flying back into another cloud....."

Fireworks of lights and explosions are flickering from the clouds. The sound quickly follows.

"Boom...Boom... Boom... Kabooom."

Loud explosions fill up the airwaves. A small fiery, smoky mushroom cloud forms.

"Boom...Boom...Boom," sounds of explosions take over the airwaves. A different sounding low bass sounding "Boom" is heard seven seconds later about 500 yards in another direction.

Fire and debris quickly fall towards the Earth. Bobby the cameraman starts to backup, while Paul is still talking into a wireless microphone looking towards the camera.

"Oh my god! A fireball just hit the ground ten feet from me. There is more falling right in our direction. It's landing all around me! It is raining UFO pieces and debris."

The cameraman moves behind the news van, along with the other bystanders. Paul is still looking towards the clouds with his back towards the camera.

"It's destroyed! It is gone! That's right ladies and gentlemen; the object hiding in the clouds has been destroyed. The fragments are falling right around me right now as I speak."

"Get out of there!" A voice yells on Paul's earpiece.

Paul turns around to face the camera and he sees that Bobby is gone. The rest of the debris falls on the ground and tumbles towards Paul. He leaps out of the way, but some of it hits him head on, tossing him ten feet away.

"That's right ladies and gentlemen. I have fallen and I can't get up. If anyone hears this, please call an ambulance for me."

PENTAGON, WASHINGTON, D.C.

"Yeahhh! Alright!" Military men are cheering throughout the Pentagon's defense room.

"We got it! It is not there anymore," a first officer says to General Dudley.

"I need this verified, right away," Dudley says to the officer.

General Dudley looks closer at one of the screens and continues, "It looks like a missile has gotten away." The officer asks the pilots to check their missiles' cameras to verify which missile is still flying away.

73

"That is a negative Pentagon, all of our missiles exploded," a pilot says.

The cheers stop and it goes quiet again. The first officer zooms in the satellite at the fast moving missile.

"Damn, shit, damn, son of a bitch," the men in the Pentagon's situation room say at the same time.

"That is a negative General. The UFO08 is still active and flying at about Mach 1.2, northwest. It is giving off a strong heat signature now," the first officer says.

The phone rings, General Dudley talks with a disappointed face for thirty seconds. Everyone in the room is quiet and looking at the screen.

General Dudley turns to everyone in the room and speaks, "We are in DEFCON 2 now, and I need all personnel, Air Force, Marines, and National Guard on duty now. I need the Air Force's best pilots and fastest jets to take this UFO08 down before it gets to a major city and does more damage. I need ground defenses on standby depending on where this UFO08 is heading. I want all spy satellites to track this object down. I also want to see the video of the last attack to see if any damage was done to this spacecraft with our missiles. I am also going to need a sound analyst to decode the sounds that UFO08 is making and has made. Men and women, we must and will take down this 08, this is a big threat to national security," Dudley pauses, while looking at the second officer trying to get his attention.

He continues, "Dismissed."

"Sir, you have two phone calls, Line 1 is John, head scientist from the Ufl-retrac team. Line 2 is Secretary of Defense," the second officer says.

'I can take my antacid after I answer line 1,' Dudley says to himself.

"This is General Dudley."

"This is John Logalbo from the UF1-retrac team. We have reason to believe Jaden Marino is either flying or somehow controlling the UFO08. Also he is trying to communicate with us."

"Ha ha ha! Where did you get this crock of bullshit from Mr. Logalbo? They paying you to be a physicist and a comedian?"

"I have," Dudley interrupts John.

"Where's your evidence? I think some of that UFO08's radiation has gotten into your brain."

"I have proof sir; we have scanned at least one life form still alive on board the UFO08 before it got away. The UFO08 has traveled by

Jaden Marino's neighborhood and school," John is interrupted by Dudley again.

"Maybe the aliens took his mind and memories, and are just going by those places? There is no way he is flying that UFO or learned to use all its weapons and systems in less than twelve hours. Maybe Jaden Marino is an alien himself now and has some alien terrorist thoughts against America. Maybe he was lunch for the aliens on their ship. We just don't know do we?"

John was talking, while Dudley was talking, "Sir, he was flying as if a teenager would be flying an aircraft. He wasn't trying to harm anyone, just defending itself," John tries to get out in one breath.

"Listen, I've heard enough John. It is our job to analyze the UFO08's intent for America. This is what we are paid for. You do your science work and experiments and I will do my job keeping America safe. Do you see me coming down to your deep underground Area 51 alien experiment circus telling you how to probe E.T. or Alf?"

"What if you shoot it down and more of them come? That ship is very advanced; it could be trying to communicate with us."

Dudley interrupts, "Or trying to communicate with its mother ship to kill everyone on Earth. I have a more important phone call on the other line. Will there be anything you need to tell me that is actually important to me now, Mr. John Logalbo?"

"Yes, when the UFO08 takes off or accelerates, it disrupts the gravity around or behind it."

"I will take that into consideration, goodbye!" Dudley says in a sarcastic, angry voice and hangs up the phone. He takes an antacid pill. He takes two more then takes a deep breath and picks up line 2.

Jaden feels the cold wind quickly moving by the body of the UFO as it penetrates through clouds and freezing cold air. The friction against the wind is heating up the outside of the body. Jaden notices the wings are up vertically and energy is coming out from the unattached wings. He has never seen a ship like this and can't believe how fast he is moving.

'Woo hoo! This is flying! Finally some real speed. I knew stage one had something to do with my speed. I don't even feel the vibrations of flying on a regular airplane. It feels like I'm flying like a bird in a dream. I love the orange and yellow thrust coming from the wings and tail.'

Jaden realizes his body was being prepared for this type of high-speed flying. Everything is moving so fast around him. 680 MPH 3790 FEET it reads on the virtual screen. He can see all around him in all directions. The nanoscanners are coming in handy and instantly move in the direction he thinks. Jaden practices switching between them and focuses on the trees and lakes beneath him. The purple molecule goes back into the body and disappears. The wings and tail move when he thinks about turning.

'Where did those jets go? Oh wow, they are way back there. I guess they gave up on chasing me.'

"This is team leader Eagle 1 to Federal Aviation Administration control center," the first F-15 pilot says over the radio.

"This is FAA controls, go."

"We have an escaped unidentified flying bogey heading west."

"We know and we are tracking it on the radar," FAA Control says.

"We are trying to take it down. There are about thirty more jet fighters en route. I'm going to need the air space cleared within 200 miles of this unidentified bogey. I'm also going to need permission for all jet fighters to fly over residential airspace at sonic and supersonic speeds. We are just under the sound barrier and waiting for permission; over."

"Standby Eagle 1, we have to check with the Pentagon, local FAA, local and state police."

The three fighter jets and a SR-71B are flying in formation in the direction of the UFO.

'This is flying! Let's see how fast I can turn and maneuver!'

The thrust of orange and yellow light particles increases. Jaden flies straight down through some soft pillow clouds; the clouds feels like mist going across his face. He can feel the heat being created from the friction of the air. A low thumping bass sound is created from his wake and the air pressure changes around him. A nanoscanner shows the sound waves of the sonic boom quickly moving in all directions around and away from him. Jaden remembers from school when something travels faster than 760 mph (Mach 1) it's moving faster than the speed of sound and a sonic boom is created. A nanoscanner rides the invisible sonic boom towards the ground. Jaden can see naked treetops shaking from his wake of turbulence.

'This feels like I'm playing a flight simulator game on a PC, but in a dream.'

Jaden checks back on his body. He sees it is glowing with something clear surrounding him, as if it is protecting him inside of a cocoon. He checks the screens and sees STAGE 2 53% COMPLETE. Jaden can see images inside of images. He can still see outside of the spaceship, but the screens are blended into the main flying images. Alien symbols and English words are still matching up. He notices the words are of space, stars, and galaxies. The word Andromeda scrolls by on the screen then stops, with an alien symbol. He wonders why it stopped on the Andromeda Galaxy.

Jaden has a flashback to when he was twelve and his father was explaining the Andromeda Galaxy through a telescope to him. However, he cannot hear the words, only the images from the past. Then the image changes to when he was fourteen and reading science books on Andromeda.

'That's crazy! They are scanning everything in my brain.'

Those screens fade away and the flight screen view comes into focus. When he thinks about what direction he is going, a compass shows in the top left corner. He sees that he is flying northwest. The flight screen is setup similar to the flight simulator games he used to play on the computer. But this is so much more realistic, defined and faster to him.

Jaden continues to fly lower towards the ground and comes upon a large lake. He knows this is Saratoga Lake. A nanoscanner a few miles ahead detects sounds of birds, crows hawking and ducks splashing on the half-frozen lake. There are a few boaters on this huge lake.

The ducks and birds detect something coming and fly away. Jaden slows down to about 158 mph and fifty feet above the water. He can smell the fresh lake water and feel the breeze across the ship. Jaden tries to go as low as he can.

'I wonder if a nanoscanner can go underwater.'

He controls a nanoscanner to go below the lake. The ship slows down to a complete stop and levitates ten feet above the lake. An older fisherman in a rowboat sees the UFO and looks as if he sees a ghost. He drops his pole in the water and quickly begins to row.

Underwater it is first completely dark, but suddenly everything is bright as day. He sees fish biting at the worms on the pole floating to the lake bottom. Jaden sees weeds, plants and fish all around. The fish look silver and brown. His vision is as clear as being on the surface. He realizes the nanoscanners can pass through and see through anything perfectly. It passes near a fish and he sees bacteria on it, he also sees oxygen bubbles in the water and a catfish quickly moving. Jaden's attention span is limited and his vision switches to outside the ship. He accelerates towards the boater still quickly paddling away.

The UFO is looking directly at the boater and the man freaks out. The man's blood pressure increases and he begins to yell.

"Aaaahhhhh! UFO is about to get me!!! Somebody help me!!"

Jaden chuckles to himself, but thinks the old man might have a heart attack if he messes with him. He flies off and quickly accelerates. He admires the water coming out of the lake behind him.

'The water underneath me is beginning to float upwards in small balls. Hmmm... Let's see how fast I can go over the water.'

Jaden speeds up and the water behind him flies up thirty feet. Then it turns into suspended bubbles for a few seconds and then falls back into the lake. He is creating a straight line across the lake and reaches 741 mph. A sonic boom is felt and heard all around him. Another man on a small fishing boat drops his fishing pole, begins yelling aloud while holding his ears. Water splashes in his face and all over him. The thumping boom echoes across the lake, breaking ice along the shoreline and causing huge waves on the lake.

'I love doing that! That was amazing!'

He feels as if he is a smaller Concorde jet. Some of the lake is frozen near the edges and Jaden flies over it. A fifteen-foot wide portion of the ice is being ripped up in slow motion and then the pieces fall back down onto the ice. He sees trees and land approaching very fast.

'I'm thinking and reacting so much faster. My reflexes are so much more enhanced. Let's see what else this ship can do.'

Jaden is flying at 812 mph and approaches the shore at an altitude of nineteen feet. He starts dodging between the trees. Jaden hits a tree, but his reaction automatically activates the shields, ripping the tree branches off.

'When I was about to hit that tree, it was as if I had a reflex reaction of something about to hit me. Then the shield came on by itself, as if I was trying to protect my body.'

Jaden pulls above the trees and back into the air.

'Shit, that was fun! Hell yeah! I'm getting used to this.'

He flies straight into the air pointing straight into the clouds at 1024 mph. He levels out and starts to fly south above the clouds. He again climbs in altitude.

'I'm flying like Superman! Daa, da, da, daaa....' Jaden hums the Superman theme.

'I need some theme music. I would love to fight Superman now. Chase him through the air and catch him with my tractor beam, with his made in Japan, super tight suit. While I have him in my beam, I'll fire some Kryptonite alien booger torpedoes at him. Oh man, that would be hilarious... Wow, I must be taking a lot of G's, turning like this.'

Jaden ascends to 13,700 feet and stops. The wings automatically turn downwards and horizontal. He is levitating. The cold wind blows on the ship and Jaden feels it blowing across his body. The cold feeling goes away and he feels warm again. The temperature is -50°F around him. He misses the cool purple molecule and wonders why it disappeared.

He changes his views from different nanoscanners. Three of them constantly stay around the ship while the other three wander. A few minutes go by and Jaden quickly speeds up again. He descends while increasing speed to 533 mph and then breaking the sound barrier. The nanoscanner behind the ship picks up the loud sonic boom sound waves.

'I know that major highway. That is the Interstate 87, that highway goes to New York City I believe. I haven't been there in years. I can always come back by my neighborhood later when school is over. Hmmmmmm.'

Jaden descends to about 1000 feet, slows down and follows the highway south. A sudden booming sound quickly passes the spaceship. Jaden flinches and the shield automatically goes around the ship. He can actually see the sound wave heading towards the ground. Jaden realizes what it was and the shields disappear.

'I love this view. Flying is a lot of fun, those cars look like ants moving in formation. That is the Hudson River alongside the highway.'

"This is the FAA Control Center to team leader 1, over."

"This is team leader 1, FAA Controls, go," the F-15 pilot says over the radio.

"You have full clearance to fly above Mach 1 to take out the bogey. The airspace is clear 300 miles in all directions. All airliners and personal aircraft have been forced to land at the closest airport. The local and state police are aware you will be breaking the sound barrier over residential areas. There have been already hundreds of calls of that bogey creating sonic booms throughout the area," FAA Controls says.

"Thank you FAA Controls, we will try to take this object down as fast as we can. We have fifteen jet fighters here and ten more on the way, over."

"Good luck and Godspeed to you all. FAA Controls out."

"Team leader 1 to my squad and the other team leaders; we have full clearance to take down the unknown. We have been given the okay to break Mach 1 and beyond. Shoot to kill, please keep in mind we are flying over residential areas. Be careful where you fire a missile; the debris could land on a house or school. There are citizens and civilians down there. Any questions?"

It is silent for a few seconds and then the SR-71 Blackbird pilot speaks, "Team leader 1 are there any records of so many jet fighters flying over residential airspace at above Mach 1 speeds? Wouldn't this create supersonic booms and chaos for people on the ground? Over."

"I'm sure this would create some concern for people on the ground and no this has never been done over residential areas at such a low altitude. But that's not for us to worry about. Our main priority is to bring this object down as quickly as possible before it hurts other people. Any more questions?"

There is silence.

Flight leader 1 clears his throat, "Well if there aren't any more questions, the bogey is south seventy-five miles near the 87

Thruway. We will synchronize our attacks as best as possible. All pilots good luck and afterburner on."

All the jet fighters turn on their afterburners and loud sonic booms are heard in all directions. A small, puffy fog of smoke is seen near the tail of each jet fighter as they break the sound barrier. They fly in formation at 875 mph towards Jaden flying the UFO by pure thought. The thumping sound echoes towards the ground in all directions, breaking glass and windows. Thousands of dogs are barking in the area. The loud sounds confuse elderly drivers and simultaneous car accidents happen. Hundreds of cars on the ground are shaking and animals run for cover. The bulbs in stoplights and streetlights directly below the aircraft explode.

Jaden is flying closer to the ground at about 200 feet and 156 mph. The highway south and north has two lanes. There are two vehicles driving at 49 mph blocking both lanes. The SUV is in the right land and the car is in the left. There are trucks and cars tailgating behind them flashing their lights.

'Let's see what is going on down there. Let me use my natural human investigating techniques along with some alien nanoscanners.'

He uses two nanoscanners to move closer towards the SUV and car slowing down traffic. Jaden gets upset seeing a female driver in the car eating a donut and drinking coffee while she drives with her right leg. Another female driver is in the SUV in the right lane. She is arguing with someone on a cell phone.

Cars and trucks are blowing their horns behind them.

"The speed limit is fifty miles an hour! I can drive in any lane I want to! Obey the speed limit assholes," the lady in the passing left lane says while taking a bite out of her second donut.

"Cruise control at forty-nine saves lives," she mumbles to herself while licking her fingers.

Jaden can hear the other lady's conversation.

"...I think she should be expelled from the PTA and arrested for sleeping with that 15-year-old male student. If she can't get some from her own 50-year-old husband that's not my problem. This is not the state of South Carolina....."

Jaden flies closer to the ground and behind the two drivers slowing down traffic. A nanoscanner passes through the car's body and Jaden sees the engine's pistons moving up and down. Everything looks animated and in 3D. Hot engine oil and radiator fluid circulate into different compartments around the engine. The nanoscanner exits and circles the car.

'I have something for these two road hogs,' Jaden says to himself.

The other drivers see the UFO flying in front of them and slam on their brakes. Jaden goes as close to the ground as possible and HOVER MODE appears on the flight screen. He is three feet above the ground hovering at 48 mph. The cars and trucks behind him stop completely while the two women drivers continue at their same speed. Jaden thinks about bright light and a bright beam of sunlight is emitted from the front of the two wings. The drivers in the opposite direction slow down to see the UFO flying above the highway. Some slam on the brakes and there are accidents.

"I don't care how bright your lights are, I'm not moving! Flash all you want! Asshole," the lady in the car says while she wipes her mouth with a tissue and drinks some more coffee.

"Some asshole in a big silver truck is flashing their brightest lights behind me, Karen," SUV lady says over the phone.

The huge purple molecule appears around and through the body of the UFO. Jaden fires a very small pink torpedo, the size of a hotdog towards the female in the car. It passes through her slightly open window and hits her donut causing it to vanish. She drops the coffee on her leg, and fumbles with the steering wheel.

"What the hell was that?" She says while swerving all over the road and into the right lane.

SUV lady sees this and moves towards the right shoulder dropping the phone into her lap.

She yells out the window, "Bitch! Learn to drive! What are you drunk? You almost hit me!"

The lady in the car looks at her hand in disbelief. She leans over and manually rolls down the passenger side window and sticks her middle finger out the window.

"Who you sticking your fat middle finger up at? You overweight buffalo, with your loser Buffalo Bills team stickers on your windows...." The SUV driver yells out the window while looking back and forth at the road. "That is why your loser Buffalo Bills lost four Super Bowls in a row. They can't catch or win and you can't drive!" She yells while reaching down to pick up the phone.

"I represent the average American, you Euro-toothpick. Thick is always going to be in. At least my team made it to the Super Bowl," the lady in the car yells.

The jet fighters quickly fly overhead and pass Jaden. A few seconds later, constant sonic booms are heard and felt on the ground like very loud bass thumps.

"They are shooting at me! Aaaahhhhhh," the lady in the car yells while she speeds up.

"I have to go Karen, I heard five loud gunshots, I think that large truck behind me is shooting at me. Call 911! I got to go!" She speeds up and hangs up the phone.

Jaden sees the jet fighters flying by above and realizes they do not see him this low to the ground. The purple molecule forms from the body of the ship.

"Team leader 1 to pilots, do you see the bogey on your radar?"

"That is a negative sir."

Jaden felt those loud sonic booms passing by him. He realizes they are loud and scary from the ground.

'Okay let me get out of here this is boring, flying behind these two arguing road hogs. But, I have to leave with a bang. This is for all the drivers who suffer behind drivers like you two.'

Jaden slows down and stops. He then speeds up and wings turn vertical. He flies ten feet above the ground and accelerates over the two vehicles. The two drivers start to scream in panic as their car and SUV lift up from the back in slow motion. The coffee floats in midair as the vehicles flip forward and land upside down. Their bodies float as they put their hands towards the ceiling in anticipation of falling downwards. The vehicles slowly slide upside down and onto the rooftops. They continue to scream and grab onto the ceilings. Jaden sees an overpass coming up very fast with an 18-wheeler stopped there. He pulls up fast and slices the top rear of the trailer. Jaden creates a sonic boom in the process that travels back towards the ground shattering car and home windows. The women in the vehicles continue to slide faster while all their windows break. The zero gravity leaves the area and their bodies fall towards the ceiling of their upside down vehicles. The strong sonic boom also shatters windows on vehicles driving in the opposite direction. Birds are seen flying away in all directions.

The ship shows up on radar again. The loud sound travels from the ground upwards. The jet fighters change direction and bailout left 90 degrees descending towards Jaden's ascending upwards position. The UFO takes off like a missile launches from the ground. Jaden reaches 4822 feet at 1050 mph in two seconds. Constant sonic booms are heard in the air and over the ground. The emergency call center is flooded with phone calls. People are calling reporting bombs are going off.

"Pentagon to teams. Be careful, the UFO08's trail disburses energy that disrupts gravity for an unknown distance. This can cause confusion with the onboard computer circuits in missiles and your jets' systems."

"That is a copy sir; we are engaging this threat now, with caution."

Jaden flies into some clouds. Four of the F-15 jet fighters step up pursuit. A trail of white smoke follows the tail and wings of the UFO. The other fifteen jet fighters stay behind and observe. Jaden slows down and stops inside the thick clouds. He checks to see what he is up against. Nanoscanners go out from the purple molecule in all directions and instantly scan each jet fighter.

The flight screen Jaden is seeing shows each jet fighter's ship in 3D animation. He can see their missiles and guns showing a color of red. The gas tanks, fuel lines, electronics and the pilots are in yellow. The screen also shows their speed, altitude and gravity forces around them in blue. He sees the jet fighters' gravity is reading sixty-five percent. He finds it interesting that the gravity forces around the ship he is in is between zero and ten percent. The nanoscanners show the materials their hulls are made from on the periodic table.

'Four against one huh? I have an idea… let me check my flight menu again.'

He reads in red letters: SHIELD STRENGTH 100%, ANTI-GRAVITY ENGINES 95% CHARGED, MANUAL FLIGHT, SPEED 201 MPH, ALTITUDE 5126 FEET, ENEMY RADAR 19 THREATS, EARTH GRAVITY FORCES 65%, AIR PRESSURE / BAROMETER 2000 PSI, STAR / SUN SOLAR CONVERSION STRENGTH 99.5%, 40% SUNLIGHT CHARGE NEEDED FOR GRAVITY FLIGHT BALANCE.

The flight menu has items in blue: LIGHT REFLECTION / INVISIBILITY, SEMI-INVISIBLE, INVISIBLE, INVISIBLE RE-IMAGE, OFF, STAGE 2 61% COMPLETE.

'Let's have some fun.'

The UFO flies out of the clouds directly in front of the four jet fighters. They quickly arm their missiles. The UFO banks right and up. It accelerates faster up to 540 mph. Three of the F-15's fire two missiles each. The missiles travel at a very fast speed towards the UFO. The missiles travel right through the UFO flying on a straight path. They explode at a distance on the other side of the UFO.

"Did you see that flight team leader 1? The missiles flew right through the UFO; I can't believe what I just saw!" Pilot 3 yells.

"Target was a miss but they all detonated on the other side of the UFO08. The heat signature was generated about seventy feet in front of the threat," team leader 1 says.

The jet fighters begin firing their 20mm machine guns. The bullets look like fast moving fiery lights being shot from all directions. The bullets go straight through the UFO, slowly flying in a direct path as if it wants to be shot.

"We are not hitting the target at all. The target is now turning upside down and right side up. It is doing complete circles, as if it's playing with us," pilot 2 says.

"It just disappeared back into some clouds," pilot 3 says.

"Are you getting this team leader?"

"Yes I am, I'm watching. I've never seen anything like this before,"

'That re-image option was cool! It showed what I was thinking the UFO should be doing, while I was flying nearby invisibly. The nanoscanners got together in front of my fake UFO image and created a slight heat source. That was awesome and it was so easy to use these options. This UFO turned my thoughts into action instantly. I'll fly with regular invisible now,' Jaden says to himself.

REFLECTING LIGHT FROM ALL ANGLES continues to flashes on the screen. Jaden accelerates out of the clouds.

"The UFO08 is still inside the clouds," pilot 2 says.

"Does anyone have a visual?" Team leader 1 asks.

"No visual, nothing on the radar," pilot 2 responds.

The team leader 1 pilot knows the UFO is around here somewhere, but can't figure out where it is.

"Team leader 1, I'm flying faster with less power. It feels like I'm floating and my controls are less responsive. My computer system is saying 'Unknown gravity force,' " pilot 4 says nervously.

Team leader 1 continues to think to himself and then he comes up with the idea to turn on his infrared/ heat sensors. He sees the UFO swirling around one of the F-15's.

"F-rank1504 the target is right in front of you, twenty feet, flying backwards and doing swirls! Turn on your infrared, thermal imaging and heat sensors!" The team leader shouts to pilot 4.

The image of the UFO quickly appears on the young pilot's left eyeglass screen. Fear and panic spreads throughout his body as he jumps back in his seat. He swallows some saliva down his dry throat and his heart rate increases. He is looking at the advanced spaceship up close. He freezes up for a few seconds.

The pilot panics and starts to fire his M61 Vulcan cannons from the wings.

"Aaahhhhhh!" He yells as he bails to the right. The UFO turns back forward and accelerates quickly. The first few 20mm cannons hit the body of the UFO while the rest are deflected by the shield that just instantly formed. The hits on the body are interpreted to Jaden's body as being hit by paintball rounds.

'Ouch, that really stings.'

"The UFO08's body is generating heat as it passes through the air. Set your computers to constant changing heat signatures. The computers will automatically adjust at lower and higher speeds. The UFO08 also reflects all radar when invisible," team leader 1 says over the radio.

Eight more jet fighters accelerate and join up. "This is team leader 2, we are here to assist. We are about to coordinate all of our missiles and gunfire at the target at the same time."

'Okay the gig is up, that was fun while it lasted.'

The UFO goes visible again. One of Jaden's screens is showing heat being generating outside the ship. It is showing the ship cutting through the air and creating heat.

'Let's see what these American jet fighters and this UFO can do.'

The UFO accelerates and creates a bright light from behind its unattached tail and vertical wings. Unknown magnetic energy is keeping the wings and tail floating in one place on the sides and rear of the UFO. The speed of the UFO reaches 977 mph in seconds and a loud thundering sounding sonic boom quickly follows the ship. Team leader 1 and three other pilots on his team put on their afterburners and step up pursuit. The UFO descends at break necking speeds. All twelve jet fighters descend and try to catch up to the UFO. They each launch a missile at the UFO. Jaden can see the twelve missiles traveling behind him at around 2600 mph. Jaden increases speed up to 1880 mph and the Hudson River quickly approaches. Jaden quickly brakes in two seconds to a complete stop eighteen feet above the river. The wind and sonic boom crash into the river. Water flies in different directions as if there was an underwater explosion. The UFO levels out and Jaden quickly accelerates again in the opposite direction over the water. The missiles try to change course, but slow down a little and burst into the river. Several powerful explosions explode and feel as if it is happening in slow motion. Water flies in different directions. Twenty foot waves form and crash into the shorelines on each side of the river.

"Shit! Did you see that? That UFO just took at least twenty-five G's on that complete stop at that speed," a pilot yells over the radio. They all continue talking about that.

PENTAGON, WASHINGTON, D.C.

"No human body can survive twenty-five G's, there's no way that kid can be alive in there," General Dudley says to his first officer.

"Maybe they changed his body into something else? The UFO08's actions are like a young teenager playing with our jet fighters."

"It's possible, but we need a precise hit on this target at once," General Dudley says in a firm voice while hitting the table with his hand. The officer relays the message to the jet fighters.

POUGHKEEPSIE, NY

'Oh my God! This is like playing a futuristic virtual reality flight video game. No controllers and everything is at the speed of thought. In fact, this is faster than the speed of thought. I feel like I am thinking much faster than I usually do. I can multi-task like a 386 personal computer, see many things at different views and do the impossible. This is crazy; I have to show my friends and family later. This is the best thrill I've ever had.'

Jaden continues flying down the Hudson River south at 750 mph at nineteen feet above the water, creating a stream of floating water behind him. He is intrigued by the small cloud forming around the ship from the sonic booms.

Team leader 1 quickly flies behind the UFO, firing cannon rounds at Jaden. The water flies up behind the UFO and floats in the air for a few seconds, looking as if it is suspended in midair. The jet fighter flies about forty feet above the river behind its target. The cannons get caught up in the shield and disappear. The UFO starts to turn left and right, and then upside down in an attempt to dodge the fast moving cannon projectiles.

'I can actually see the 20mm cannons flying towards me. It's like the nanoscanner sensors are detecting them for me and I'm able to move before it hits me.'

Two additional jet fighters fly one hundred feet above them and begin firing. Most of the cannons create a huge splash in the water. The UFO continues spinning in circles at a very fast speed while flying straight. The cannon fire passes right between the wings. Constant sonic boom sounds spread out in all directions in the area. "Boom, Boom, Boom."

The two jet fighters flying above the UFO fire missiles. The UFO stops spinning and accelerates quickly. Using his nanoscanners Jaden sees a small bridge quickly approaching. The missiles approach quickly from above and get within thirty-two feet of the UFO. It continues to spin while dodging the cannon fire. Jaden goes under the bridge, stops completely and nose-dives into the river. Water splashes in all directions. The missiles quickly pass by and are hit by the water. His human body feels the cold sensation around his body from the 35°F water. The jet fighters quickly pass over and pull upwards.

'Wow, this water is cold.'

The cold feeling goes away and Jaden hears the sounds of being underwater. He can taste the brackish water through the body of the UFO. The current of the river is pushing the UFO south. The wings change direction and are straight out at a horizontal angle. Jaden can see a few fish quickly swimming away. The ship comes out of the water backwards with its nose towards the river. There is no water dripping off it and it doesn't appear wet. It levitates up beside the bridge.

He flies above the bridge backwards, while the cars on the bridge slam on their brakes. There are four simultaneous fender benders in both directions on the small bridge. The missiles crash into the river without exploding. The people in their cars on the bridge are amazed at the UFO flying above them straight into the air backwards. Jaden sees them watching him forty feet below him.

'Look at me humans! I'm doing a nose stand over the bridge. Once in a lifetime trick. Throw your dollars into the air, don't be cheap. I don't work for free,' Jaden says sarcastically.

The people are looking with their mouths wide open. He starts twirling in the air clockwise and then comes back down the other side of the bridge and goes back underneath. The wings change directions back to vertical with the body and to the sides. He takes off at a very fast speed. People get out of their cars and try to look down, but he is gone. They see all the jet fighters in the air going after it. The people on the bridge point at a completely black jet that they never seen before flying by.

'Okay, that was too tough for the jet fighters. I guess follow the leader was out of the question. What is this coming up behind me? Hmmmm… a new black jet fighter? Let's see what you're made of.'

He begins to probe the SR-71B Blackbird that is trying to catch up to him. Team leader 1 tries to re-circle.

"This is team leader 1 to Blackbird 1."

"Blackbird 1 go."

"Blackbird 1 you cannot fly directly behind the UFO08, the trail of the UFO08 disrupts the gravity from 0-20%. It will mess with the gyroscopes and computers of your jet fighter."

"That is a negative team leader 1. My computer system and gyroscopes are very advanced. I was watching and analyzing your teams go after this UFO08 for the past twenty minutes. I reprogrammed my flight computers to adjust in zero gravity, increasing my thrust power and controls handling. I'm taking this threat down."

'Impressive,' Jaden says to himself as he overhears the communication of the pilots.

The Blackbird SR-71B comes up behind Jaden flying 455 mph. Bright yellow particles come out from the wings of the UFO and it accelerates up to 920 mph flying over the river. The Blackbird accelerates behind the UFO also using its advanced afterburners. The Blackbird begins firing rounds at the UFO. Jaden quickly dodges the bullets by spinning again. Some of the bullets hit the UFO.

'Man that really stings. I guess I can't use the shields while doing that.'

'I'm going to take you down,' the Blackbird pilot says to himself.

The pilot has a black beard, brown eyes and a full helmet over his head. The white middle-aged pilot has a look of determination in his eyes as if the UFO did something to him personally.

'Let us see what you got, Mr. Black Jet, with the cool aerodynamic shape,' Jaden says.

The Blackbird fires bullets at the UFO while the other jet fighters fly above and observe. The UFO pulls up sharply and begins to fly straight up at a 90° angle. The Blackbird pulls up slowly and the pilot grunts from the G-forces he is taking. The heavy pressure on his body increases his heartbeat. Blood slowly circulates to his brain as he struggles to pull up on the joystick. He feels light headed. The pilot turns upside down at an angle back towards where the UFO is flying straight up. Jaden slows down for the Blackbird. The SR-71 Blackbird flies into the UFO's gravity wake and flies straight up into the sky vertically. The Blackbird's afterburner ignites and it tries to catch up to the UFO.

"That Blackbird pilot just took at least ten G's on that pull up. That UFO took at least forty G's. That pilot has to be careful not to blackout," team leader 1 says to his team.

"I guess he knows what he is doing to be flying a top secret SR-71B that I didn't even know existed," pilot 4 says over the radio.

The UFO accelerates straight up at 1266 mph and 11,999 feet. The sounds of a high-powered engine can be heard above the clouds. Orange light particles are exhausting from the wings of the

UFO. The SR-71 Blackbird continues to fly 508 feet behind the UFO while firing bullets again. The UFO begins spinning and dodging the bullets. The UFO's bright orange light is blinding the Blackbird pilot. The glass around the Blackbird's cockpit darkens. The pilot continues to accelerate as the UFO also increases speed. The UFO hits 2256 mph and reaches hypersonic speeds. Thumping sounds can be heard rippling down to Earth in a 200-mile radius. They are at 59,000 feet still flying straight up at a 90° angle. The outside body of the UFO is at 808°F, while the air temperature is at minus -170°F. The wings and nose of the UFO change to a light red color. The nose of the Blackbird lights up slightly red also. Their speeds begin to multiply, as the oxygen gets thinner. They hit 7489 mph and then 10,433 mph. The Blackbird continues to fire frozen bullets as the UFO continues dodging them.

PENTAGON

"This is General Dudley to Blackbird 1, come in Blackbird."

"Blackbird 1, if you can hear me pullout. You are reaching your maximum ceiling height. Pullout, that is an order," General Dudley repeats over the radio for a third time.

The SR-71B Blackbird cannot hear any radio transmissions. The pilot has no idea how high up he is.

"How is the Blackbird able to fly straight up like that?" Dudley asks his first officer and then continues, "No one can survive that many G's flying straight up into the sky like that at that speed."

"Remember he is flying in zero gravity. G forces do not exist in zero gravity. It is like flying in space, but with oxygen all around. Similar to our zero gravity training chambers," the first officer says in a calm voice.

'Come on you Top Gun Tom Cruise look-alike pilot, you slowing down on me. Keep up!' Jaden yells.

"I got you, you bastard," the Blackbird pilot says in a low confused voice. He locks onto the UFO with a smile on his face. He fires a missile; it accelerates slowly towards the UFO trying to catch more momentum. The missile speeds up considerably and gets within twelve feet of the UFO. A bright orange flash is seen exploding like a lightning strike on a dark night from the rear tail of the UFO. The pilot hears an explosion. The UFO disappears from the Blackbird's sight. The missile explodes, but doesn't create an explosion. The UFO quickly accelerates and reaches 26,555 mph. The sky turns dark around the Blackbird as it reaches 114,000 feet. The pilot is breathing heavily through his oxygen mask and begins to feel dizzy. The Blackbird loses its flame and engine thrust. It slows down considerably and floats upwards out of control rotating in different directions. The pilot blacks out and lets go of the flight stick. It is completely silent around the pilot. The computer screen flashes STALL, NO CONTROLS, S.O.S., 1% THIN OXYGEN. The Blackbird loses the zero gravity wake from the UFO. It continues to fly upwards while spinning out of control. Ice is quickly forming around the Blackbird.

Jaden continues to fly straight up at 34,000 mph and hits 520,666 feet. There is a red and orange tail stretching miles behind him. Jaden's screens light up flashing: STAGE 2 70%. His thrust begins to slow down automatically. Jaden realizes he is about to go into space and the ship is slowing down on its own.

The SR-71B Blackbird slowly begins falling towards the Earth. Jaden hovers horizontally at 615,000 feet looking around. He looks outside the UFO in all directions.

'I love how the wings change to horizontal automatically when I'm hovering. That is so cool. I'm on top of the world!' He continues, 'Eat your heart out Mr. Englewood.' Jaden thinks back four years ago when he was in high school.

"Mr. Jaden Marino! Do you think you are on top of the world?" Jaden's social studies teacher asked him.

He grabbed Jaden in the hallway in-between two classroom doors by his shirt.

"I know it was you that put that boot on my car's wheel yesterday afternoon."

Jaden replied with a smiling face, "Maybe you owe tickets. How can a kid give you a city car boot?"

"I don't owe any tickets you little bastard!" He yelled and continued, "I know it was you. You were the only kid who got a D on my social studies test two days ago. You were the only person who argued with me for twenty minutes for his grade. You are the only student that gets away with things because your father is the principal," Mr. Englewood said while accidentally spitting.

"Say it but don't spray it," Jaden said in a humorous voice, while he wiped his face and turned his head.

"Mr. Englewood, is that my Pops walking down the hallway?" Jaden asked.

Mr. Englewood took a step back and released his tight grip from around Jaden's shirt near his neck.

"Maybe the city gave you a D, for disabled," Jaden said while chuckling.

"You think you're funny huh?" He asked.

He continued, "Just because your daddy is the principal of the school doesn't mean you can get away with whatever you want. You have to earn a grade in my class. You can't skip through life not paying your dues. Life isn't a joke. What are you going to do when your daddy isn't around?"

"I can handle things without my Pops' help..." Jaden is interrupted.

"Listen you little shit, I'm going to take you down. You're going to amount to nothing once you're out of high school. You'll never be an astronaut; they don't accept people who never work hard for anything. You'll be lucky to gas up or remove human waste from an airplane in the future," Mr. Englewood said in a low voice.

"Maybe one day I'll save the world or do something great that no man has ever done before."

"Only thing you're going to do great is make the perfect taco at Taco Bell or dry my son's BMW at the car wash. You certified loser and horrible comedian. You think because your father is the principal your grades can be adjusted and you don't have to work hard. We shall see who will be left back and I'll make sure social promotion doesn't save you this time."

"I heard your wife left you back because you can't get it up, ha ha," Jaden laughed and continued, "Maybe they will make something that fixes that in the future."

Mr. Englewood's face turned red and his face frowned.

"You leave my ex-wife out of this. You think you're funny huh? We'll see how long you're on top of the world attitude lasts. Your arrogance will be your downfall," Mr. Englewood paused and took a deep breath. He moved closer to Jaden.

"Maybe you should volunteer for the Marines now and go overseas to the Gulf War. They need some know it alls. So you can come back in body parts like your dead brother. Maybe then. . . . ."

He paused as he looked at Jaden's face increase with wrinkles. Jaden's eyebrows went down into his face. His light skin turned red. His right fist curled up into a ball and Mr. Englewood stepped back. Jaden quickly went into his Tae Kwon Do stance. He threw a right punch into Mr. Englewood's chest. Mr. Englewood took two uneven steps backwards as Jaden spun around with a roundhouse kick into the older man's face. Mr. Englewood turned to the left and fell down grabbing some lockers on the way to the floor. The locks on the lockers rattled in sequence. A teacher walking down the hallway blew a whistle and rushed to the scene. Students came out of their classrooms to see what is going on. Someone grabbed Jaden and the images get fuzzy and then fade away.

Jaden is looking outside of the UFO while hovering in one spot. It is completely silent around him and he is at the beginning of space. He is flabbergasted by the view at this height.

'I can see the planet curving in all directions and everything is so small below me.'

A nanoscanner continues to fly upwards towards space at a high speed. He is looking through them and he sees something lighting up and slightly reflecting in space. The nanoscanner flies faster towards this object that is turning into three or four objects sitting above the earth.

'What the hell?' He asks as the nanoscanner gets closer.

'I can't believe this! These four satellites are right over me! I'm being watched by military forces all over the world probably.'

He gets a closer look at one of them. Jaden is amazed at all the little moving parts inside of the first satellite. He reads what is says on it: TOP SECRET, PROPERTY OF MASA. He checks what the other satellite says: TOP SECRET, PROPERTY OF UNITED STATES GOVERNMENT. CIA.

'These have to be spy satellites. I can actually see the radio waves coming and going from them. This is amazing!'

'Made in Taiwan, China and Japan? At least the government has received some good labor and parts for a good price. This third satellite far to the right looks a lot older, let's see what this says, property of Russia? They watching me too. This is crazy, but very interesting.'

Jaden switches back to outside the UFO view.

'What can I do now? I have an idea.'

94

Jaden quickly accelerates forward at a fast speed. He switches his view back to the satellites and sees thrust coming from outside the satellites as they move in his direction.

'They are really watching me and following me.'

Another nanoscanner flying in autonomous mode shows its vision smaller inside of the vision Jaden is already seeing through to get Jaden's attention. The vision changes and he sees the SR-71B Blackbird flying out of control towards the Earth with frost all around it. He can see into the Blackbird's cockpit and notices that the pilot is unconscious. There are beeping sounds and lights flashing all over the place. The aircraft is shaking and flipping in every direction.

'Shit! That pilot is going to die! I forgot all about him. I have to do something.'

More nanoscanners quickly descend towards the out-of-control Blackbird as it falls through thick clouds. Jaden dives down in the direction of the Blackbird and accelerates as fast as he can. The yellow energy particles are being emitted from the wings of the UFO. The entire outside body of the UFO turns bright red as it heats up. He is flying downward at 32,053 mph. The UFO is lighting up like a meteor as it enters the upper atmosphere.

'My altitude is 478,000 feet. The Blackbird's altitude is. . .'

Jaden tries to see the altitude on the SR-71's flight computer screen. He sees it is at 29,899 feet. Jaden hits the lower atmosphere and the increasing oxygen slows him down considerably. The yellow energy coming from the wings of the UFO turns to a bright, whitish-orange color. The SR-71 is at 19,038 feet. Jaden slows down to 5407 mph and continues to lose speed even though he is trying to go faster. He is confident he will catch up to it, even though he is at 67,193 feet.

The other nanoscanners reach the SR-71 and scan everything on the aircraft. Jaden sees other jet fighters firing warning shots by the SR-71, but the pilot is still unconscious. A nanoscanner scans inside the pilot's body and sees very little white smoke coming from his lungs. Jaden sees an animated image of his heart beating irregularly. The pilot's body is at 95°F and is shivering. The pilot's altitude reaches 12,998 feet. Jaden can see the SR-71 zoomed in through the clouds from the UFO's view. He quickly catches up to the SR-71 and slows down to the SR-71's falling speed of 590 mph. Four loud simultaneous sonic booms created from Jaden's high speed pass him and the SR-71. The powerful shock waves rattle the Blackbird like an earthquake waking and bringing the pilot to consciousness. The supersonic booms continue towards the ground. A trail of white smoke follows the Blackbird's wings. The pilot wakes up disorientated and confused.

'How can I stop this jet from hitting the ground?' Jaden asks as he uses his imagination.

The other F-15's begin firing cannons and bullets at Jaden as he gets close to the SR-71. The shields go on instantly around the UFO.

'I'm on your side you flying dicks! I'm trying to help your pilot!'

Six nanoscanners fly about ten feet below the SR-71 Blackbird jet. The powerful cannons continue to hit the outside shield while causing the UFO to move from the force. The UFO begins to release a translucent energy to the six nanoscanners and a ring of light particles begins to glow under the aircraft. This technique is greatly reducing the gravitational forces around the Blackbird. The UFO's energy slows down the SR-71 to 121 mph, but it continues to fall towards the ground. They are now 1568 feet from the ground.

'This guy is still going to smack the ground. I have to do something else.'

The computer is asking the pilot to eject. His radio is still not working as he tries to use it. He tries to eject, but his screen communicates to him a failure. The escape hatch over him is frozen. The UFO fires a translucent green beam at the SR-71 from the purple molecule. The green beam spreads out and covers the entire jet fighter. The green beam is slowing down the Blackbird significantly and straightens it out horizontally. The pilot sees the UFO over him and realizes what it is trying to do. He tries to fire the engine, but it does not turn on.

'This must be a tractor beam or something. This ship read my mind and translates that into the best possible action, cool,' Jaden says.

Jaden wonders why the UFO can't pull the jet upwards with the tractor beam. The SR-71 is still falling towards the earth at 75 mph at 789 feet. The other jet fighters stop firing at the UFO as they finally figure out the bogey is trying to save the SR-71 from crashing. The pilot still tries to start the jet engines, but they are dead. Billions of microscopic nanobots leave the purple molecule around the ship and ride the green waves towards the SR-71. They enter the foreign aircraft and quickly move around the fuselage. They find ice all around the engine compartment and the fuel lines. The nanobots heat up the internal parts in the Blackbird.

The nanobots push fuel into the engines and remove particles of ice in the hydraulics of the Blackbird's tail. The SR-71 is seventy-three feet from the ground and is approaching a residential house in Nyack, NY. The pilot tries the engine again and it sputters like a broken down car. The landing gear comes out. There is a crowd of neighbors pointing towards the sky in the quiet suburban neighborhood. There is an elderly man covering his ears with his hands standing near his 6-year-old granddaughter. His ears are ringing from the powerful supersonic boom that attacked the neighborhood less than a minute ago. There are also broken home windows and broken car windows on the street and sidewalks.

The young girl points towards the sky and tries to get her grandfather's attention. The grandfather sees his granddaughter's hair floating into the air and is speechless. Broken glass, dirty snow and debris begin to float upwards.

"Look granddaddy look, Superman is inside of that spaceship saving that Air Force jet from crashing into our roof. Superman has a spaceship now!"

"What did you say, Cathy? I can't hear anything you are saying! My ears are ringing."

The sputtering engines get the older man's attention and he looks up. He is in complete shock and stands with his mouth wide open. His hands are still over his ears.

"Watch out Daniels! It's going to crash into your house! Get out of there!" A neighbor across the street yells.

The grandfather is in shock and can't move. The little girl is smiling and pointing at the rescue. "Come on Superman alien, you can do it!" The little girl yells.

F-15 jet fighters can be seen flying near the clouds from a distance. The Blackbird pilot becomes very nervous as he is within several feet of the house beneath him. Sweat is running down his face as he turns his head from side to side looking out the oval window over him. He closes his eyes and prays for a second. He nervously presses the engine start up button for the last time before impact and holds the button pressed in. The engine on the right ignites first. The SR-71 leans to the left and then the left engine ignites and it levels out. People are running down the street covering their ears. Hot yellow thrust shoots out from the rear and 150 decibels echo in all directions. The powerful vibrations from the engines cause birds to flee in a nearby park. They quickly flap their wings in an attempt to leave the area. The trees aligned on the sidewalk also vibrate and the snow falls from the naked tree branches simultaneously. The vibrating sound rattles the already broken glass in homes, causing more fragments to fall. The pilot feels a sense of relief as his aircraft gains momentum. The thrust heats up the snow on the roof of the house. The little girl covers her ears and her grandfather pulls her away from the scene. The SR-71 slowly moves forward and the people in the street can feel the heat from the thrust. The wheel from the right landing gear hits the chimney of a brick house. Bricks fall towards the ground and some people start running. The stalling alarm goes off in the cockpit and the SR-71 quickly takes off at a 20° angle. Debris lands in the street as water comes down from the melted snow. The radio starts working again and the green beam from the UFO disappears. Jaden follows the Blackbird as it's flying twenty-seven feet from the ground and over a park area. The nanobots and nanoscanners float back towards the ship. The Blackbird flies faster and gains altitude. Just as it flies away, Jaden is hit with three missiles from different directions. He activates the shields too late and takes a direct hit. The force from the powerful missiles spin the UFO out-of-control and towards some trees below. It loses some of its anti-gravity lift. The UFO lightly crashes into a wooded area. The wing and tail go into the body of the ship. The ship rolls in some mud like a carrot stick. Snow falls from branches of nearby trees.

'Shit, that hurt like hell. That felt as if I was hit by a car and I flew over the windshield. Man, why do I have to feel the pain when something hits the body with something?'

Three Blackhawk attack helicopters approach where Jaden went down. A tank also approaches knocking down small trees.

'I have to get out of here, let me check the screens. Okay diagnosing damage complete.'

ANTI-GRAVITY LIFT IS ONLY 10% OPERATIONAL, LOWER ATMOSPHERE THRUST ENGINES 20%, SHIELDS OFFLINE, BODY INTEGRITY 100%, NANOBOTS REPAIRING ANTI-GRAVITY ENGINES, THRUST ENGINES, AND ANALYZING SHIELD'S RPM MOLECULES SEQUENCE .

'I have only one nanoscanner to use. The others are helping the nanobots with repairs.'

Jaden thinks quickly and he tries to take off.

"This is Blackhawk 1 to base; the UFO08 is taking off over Mountain View Nature Park with smoke behind it at 12 o'clock in front of me. I believe it is damaged and I'm opening fire."

"This is SR-71 Blackbird to base; the UFO08 just risked itself to save my life. Is there another option besides destroying it?" The pilot asks.

"This is General Dudley; you have your orders to destroy the target. SR-71 if you feel you suddenly have a change of heart because E.T. saved you from being a splattered fly you can relieve yourself from duty."

"Sir, this UFO08 ship has very advanced technology. It repaired my ship in seconds. We should at least try to communicate with it some more. It isn't attacking anyone."

"Blackbird SR-71, can you clear the airwaves, we have a job to do. You need to come in for repairs and be debriefed," General Dudley says.

The Blackhawk helicopter fires its cannons and rockets. The rockets and cannon fire go right through the UFO slowly taking off into the sky.

"This is General Dudley, everyone use their infrared and heat sensors. I repeat! Infrared and heat sensors only, do not use regular vision and lock. Does anyone see the UFO08?"

The UFO disappears into thin air.

"That is a negative sir!" The Blackhawk helicopter pilot says.

General Dudley gets off the two-way radio and talks to his officers in the room. "I want a team at the crash site right away. What town is that?"

"Sir, that is Rockland County, NY," the first officer says.

"Make sure that SR-71 pilot returns to base ASAP, I think that UFO messed with his brain and turned him to the dark side."

'Man, I barely got away.'

Jaden is flying four feet above an 18-wheeler on the highway in invisible mode.

'Flying around the trees and using just a little thrust got me to the highway less than a mile away. That decoy worked again for me. The nanoscanner created a sense of heat and smoke in the decoy, very cool.'

Jaden is going over a long bridge called the Tappan Zee. He recognizes the area and he knows this is towards NYC. The fresh breeze from the river flies across the UFO. He sees a view of the city through thick clouds and fog to the south. The 18-wheeler makes it across the bridge and slows down at the tollbooth. Jaden keeps flying forward at a low speed. A spot check is setup on the other side of the toll. One of the National Guard troops at the spot check is using infrared binoculars. He spots slight heat coming from the invisible UFO flying over the cars and spot check. He radios in and gives the location while following it as it passes over him. A few National Guard troops open fire with their M-16 machine guns.

'Man, they see me now. Those bullets feel like bee stings. Let me check the repairs.' Thrust engines are at fifty-five percent and anti-gravity lift engines are at twenty-five percent. The shields are still offline. Jaden increases speed over the highway. He is balancing the amount of engine thrust and anti-gravity thrusts manually. The tail comes from the rear. Blackhawk helicopters fly over the bridge.

Jaden reaches 225 mph and is fifty feet above the 87 Thruway heading south. Jaden decides to fly higher and into the clouds. The nanoscanners detect eight F-16 jet fighters quickly approaching.

'So you jet fighters want to shoot me down after I help one of your pilots huh? I have something for you.'

Jaden checks the screens for weapons. He focuses on the same weapon he used on the AC-130 gunship. He scans the jet fighters and targets their missiles and guns.

'I don't want to blow them out of the sky or kill them. I want to see what they will do without any weapons to shoot at me.'

"Team leader to squad, the UFO08 is in the clouds. It looks like the missiles and gunfire hit it directly. I don't think its shields are working. I can see it flying in the clouds to the south of us at 1600 feet. Its radar signal is stronger, so I know this is it," team leader 1 says.

Four of the jet fighters approach from the east, another four approach from the west. Two from the north and two from the south also join the fight. They arm their weapons to detonate before impact.

Two pink torpedoes come from each side purple molecule. The torpedoes begin spinning around as they increase speed. The torpedoes change direction and head towards the ground.

"Something was fired from the UFO08, I repeat, something was fired from the UFO08. It is glowing pink and is heading towards the ground. Everyone fall back and take evasive action," team leader 1 says.

101

The alien torpedoes break up into dozens of smaller torpedoes and go in different directions towards each F-16 jet fighter.

They all put on their afterburners and begin evasive maneuvering. Each alien torpedo maneuvers with the jet fighters and quickly catches up. They drop flares in front of the alien torpedoes, but they keep coming faster. The alien torpedoes hit each jet fighter's missiles and guns causing them to glow different colors, and then disappear. An empty area remains where the jet fighter's missiles, cannons and machine guns used to be.

"Team leader 1, the alien torpedoes had no effect or damage on my craft," pilot 4 says.

"F-4 have you," team leader 1 is interrupted.

"I'm firing on the UFO08 now; it just moved from the clouds. I have a lock I'm taking it," pilot 4 says. ERROR, ERROR is shown on his flight screen.

"F-4 pilot, I thought you were taking the shot?"

"I have all weapons errors on my flight screen."

"I was trying to tell you before you cut me off that the alien torpedoes destroyed every jet fighter's missiles and guns including yours."

The foolish pilot swallows the spit in his throat and looks at the UFO flying away.

"This is General Dudley, team leader 1 and another pilot continues to following the UFO08. There are too many clouds for the satellite to continue tracking. The rest return to base for plane analysis. A second wave is on its way. We will be changing up our offensive strategy."

11:30 AM SOUTHERN WESTCHESTER, NY

Jaden accelerates right by the defenseless jet fighters and heads south towards New York City.

'That was amazing how those little alien boogers took out only the weapons and didn't damage the rest of the ship. It was like they were vaporized.'

He flies under the heavier clouds and notices it is beginning to pour down rain. The rain slides smoothly over the UFO's shiny body. The bubble rain floats around slowly in different directions behind the UFO. Jaden flies over the Hudson River while a few jet fighters still try to follow a few miles behind.

'So many beautiful tall buildings. I haven't been down here in years. So many people and cars.'

Jaden flies over near north Manhattan. He quickly accelerates over the East River and heads south towards midtown. The rain is pouring down harder and harder. Shields are back online and so are the engines. Jaden flies closer towards the East River to thirty feet. He is flying by the cars on the F.D.R Drive Highway at 55 mph while approaching midtown. Jaden goes under the 59th Street Bridge and something catches his attention. He does a complete stop midair. The UFO begins to come up the bridge while facing downward. As the UFO comes over and on top of the bridge, cars crossing it begin crashing into each other. People get out of their cars and point towards the sky. The UFO flies towards the tramway crossing from Manhattan to Roosevelt Island. The cold rain falls onto the tram roof. Jaden levels out horizontally in front of the tramway and zooms inside with a nanoscanner. He sees some young schoolchildren looking out of the windows. Jaden flies closer to the tramway while slowly moving forward.

"Kids! Kids! Stop running around. Stay in one place," second grade school teacher Motley yells to her ten students on a field trip.

"Miss Motley, Miss Motley," a student calls to her teacher while walking over.

"Yes Kim?"

"Look at my hair, it's floating in the air," Kim says.

The schoolteacher looks at the child's hair in amazement with her eyes wide open. Kim starts to laugh and point at the teacher's hair. Miss Motley looks up as the hair on her wig starts to stand up and float upwards. She quickly grabs her wig and holds it down. Another student named Berry jumps up and touches the ceiling.

"Teacher! Teacher look how high I can jump!"

The student jumps up and down slowly, higher and higher. The other kids watch in amusement.

"Wow! Look at Kenneth and Berry!" They yell.

"Stop jumping Kenneth and Berry this moment!" Miss Motley yells while holding her wig.

Berry stops and holds onto another student. Kenneth bangs his head on the ceiling. He falls to the ground and starts crying. The assistant teacher comes from the back and tends to the student crying. The other kids by the tramway window start to point upward.

"Look at the alien ship! It's right in front of us!" One of the students yells. The kids move back towards the other side of the tramway with a petrified look on their faces. A couple on the tramway sees the UFO also and moves towards the opposite side. The kids start to scream with frightened looks on their faces. They jump back to hold on to their teachers' legs. The kid that was crying on the floor stops crying and moves towards the opposite side with the assistant teacher. One student walks towards the UFO levitating on the side of the tramway. The other kids begin crying and screaming.

"I want my mommy!"

"It's going to kill us!" The young students yell.

"Kim! Come back!" Miss Motley yells while holding the other kids.

The curious student stands by the window in amazement, while her hair is standing straight up. The UFO does *something* and then disappears. The student's mouth and eyes are wide open. The curious student is grabbed from behind by her teacher and pulled closer towards the other side.

'Interesting, seeing those young students' reactions. One kid wasn't scared at all and was very brave.'

Jaden flies upwards and towards Manhattan still invisible. The sky gets darker and darker. He sees jet fighters flying overhead. Jaden flies towards the buildings on 59th Street. Jaden sees all the people on the ground walking with their umbrellas open as it pours on them. The people on the ground look like ants to him. They are walking around in different directions not knowing he is floating above them. Rain is floating around the UFO as it slowly goes down the streets at 30 mph.

'I have to go by the city speed limit. Ha ha.'

He turns north on 5th Avenue. Seven nanoscanners go out and start to look around inside of buildings. Jaden is flying over Central Park.

'I wonder what is going on inside these buildings.'

'Boring. Boring. I see boring people just sitting at their desk doing normal office work.'

Jaden is flying over Central Park. He sees a few people jogging and walking their dogs with umbrellas.

'Hey! Clean up after your dog!' Jaden yells.

'Some people just don't care if their dog leaves soft landmines behind.'

He concentrates on the dog's landmines and sends a small torpedo towards it, vaporizing it. He leaves a little hole in the ground also as small pieces of concrete fly into the air.

'Hey I'm not perfect! What's another pothole in this city with millions of them?' He asks.

'I'll clean this city up! One poop at a time!' He yells in a sarcastic tone.

The dog looks up into the air and begins barking.

'So you can hear and see me huh, little doggy?'

It begins to rain harder and lightning flashes across the dark, cloudy sky. The nanoscanners are scanning through buildings and different floors. One nanoscanner is only scanning voices and sounds without any images. The lightning temporarily disables its video transmitting capabilities.

Inside of a close by office building in a janitor's closet, the nanoscanner overhears a conversation. Jaden smells perfume, sweat and vaginal wetness. It quickly grabs his attention. Jaden also smells deodorant and coffee breath.

"How many more times do I have to keep doing this until I get my promotion and next raise?" A female voice asks.

"Don't worry baby, your name is on top of the list. That should be done around Christmas time, I promise," a male with a deep voice says.

"You said that last Christmas."

"You're wasting time. Why don't you pull that little skirt up and panties down. You can sit right here."

"You don't feel bad doing this knowing your wife is at home?" She asks while sitting on him.

"Oh baby, my wife doesn't feel like this. That old wrinkled 100 lbs more than you Patsy. I don't feel bad at all. I wish I could trade you in for her. You still taking your birth control every day right?" The man asks while kissing his secretary in the cleaning closet.

"Oh yeah...I'm still taking them every day....Right there, oh, oh," she moans.

The nanoscanner is transmitting the audio conversation. Jaden sends the other nanoscanner to the same location. He hears the moaning sounds.

"Are you finished already, sir?"

Just then lightning strikes very close to the office building. The audio transmitting nanoscanner temporarily loses its connection to the UFO and floats upwards to another floor. The audio comes back....

"Tell me Charles, why should we go with this new writer's books?" An older man asks.

"This book 'Quickflash' has the action, adventure and romance you have been looking for. It's like a futuristic James Bond. I see great potential with this book and it is very creative. The second book, 'Terry's Nightmares' is an exciting book for teenagers..." The agent says in a publishing meeting as he is interrupted.

"What was the author's name again?"

"Vlane Carter. He is very creative and is definitely going to be a successful writer....."

'What the hell am I listening too? What happened to the moaning sex sounds? That malfunctioning nanoscanner must have gone into a board meeting or something.'

The damaged nanoscanner goes into a working nanoscanner. Jaden is outside the building still invisible moving up the building's floors. A strong wind flows down the side of the office building. He uses all of his nanoscanners to find that interesting room he was just listening in on. He finds the cleaning closet again with the moaning sounds coming from it. Now he has images to go along with it.

'Alright! This is a show! This older guy is breathing hard as if he is about to get a heart attack. Nice legs and body Miss Secretary. Damn it's over though. Minute man is finished,' Jaden says.

"Do you hear a humming sound Ben?"

"No," the excited boss says while pulling up this pants.

"Look, Ben my panties are floating in the air behind you, so is my hair!" The secretary yells.

'Hey! That's not safe! Where's the protection...' Jaden yells while he is interrupted.

Two missiles hit the UFO from below and another two rockets hit the UFO from above simultaneously. The shield goes on instantly, absorbing most of the blast. There is a huge explosion, while the UFO flips in different directions and crashes into the building on the ninth floor. The ship rips through steel and concrete like paper. Glass explodes into thousands of different directions. The shield strength quickly goes down. The explosion creates a huge fiery hole in the side of the building on four floors. People and debris are instantly incinerated. A very low flying stealth bomber is seen flying down the avenue. A silent flying helicopter also flies by. People in the streets are pointing up, looking at the stealth bomber and the explosions on the side of the building. A huge fire quickly spreads.

'That really hurt, those jets caught me off guard. I was too busy being a peeping-alien-tom. The shield came on automatically like my body reacting to something about to hit me. The ship braced and protected itself just like me doing the same thing as though something is about to hit me.'

Jaden sees fire and smoke all around the ship's energy shield. The nanoscanners can see perfectly clear through the smoke and fire. Jaden sees bodies burning and people trying to run down the stairs. The two people having sex are unconscious lying on top of each other.

"I've fallen and I can't get up!" An older lady yells out with dirt on her face and debris over her.

"Help me! I can't breathe! Something fell on me!" A trapped and injured person yells out.

The building sprinkler system begins to spray water over the fire. However, it has little effect.

Jaden checks all his screens to make sure everything is okay. He sees that everything looks normal. He slowly flies through the fire while papers and debris fall around the ship. Jaden notices the nanoscanners can move freely back and forth through the energy shield. Sparks are coming from the lights as the power goes out in the building. People are hiding under desks, in lounges and running down staircases with clothes over their mouths and coughing. People are screaming. The fire alarm is blaring throughout the building. Jaden can see the molecules inside the fire consuming everything around it like a virus or a hungry leech consuming its prey. Lightning continues to strike in the sky while it continues to rain. The rain goes inside the building. Jaden's nanoscanners detect several jet fighters flying above, two Apache attack helicopters hovering above and military trucks with rockets on the ground below. Jaden sees people trapped in different rooms around him. He chooses to see if he can do something about the fire he feels he is somewhat responsible for. He can feel the heat from the fire as if he is in a very hot sauna. It smells like wood and chemicals. The UFO is still hidden inside the fire from the outside.

"There is no sign of the UFO, sir. It's just fire all over the place, nothing could withstand a simultaneous blast like that, sir. It was a direct hit," Apache pilot 1 says to General Dudley over the radio. He continues, "Sir, that was over 10,000 lbs of TNT".

"This UFO08 is stronger than you think, soldier. All units standby, continue scanning anything that moves," General Dudley says over the radio.

Jaden concentrates on the fire and the molecules it is made of. He zooms in and sees trillions of atoms jumping around spreading and mating with oxygen atoms. The purple molecule shoots beams in different directions to disrupt the gravity around the fire. The fire takes up a spherical shape and nanobots attack the mating atoms.

A fire ladder from the street begins to extend to the ninth floor. A young firefighter with a water hose on his back quickly climbs the ladder.

"Sir, the fire around the explosion is turning round like a sphere," the first helicopter pilot says.

"That is what fire does in zero to low gravity. The UFO08 is still active. Wait until it comes out of the fire before taking another shot at it," General Dudley tells all units.

"There are people on the ground and people stuck on higher floors banging on the windows for help."

"You have your order," Dudley replies.

The young firefighter begins spraying water on the spherical fire. The water turns into little balls and floats forward.

The UFO's outside shields begin to glow and a clear shock wave of energy is spreading all around in different directions instantly putting the fires out.

One of Jaden's screens says: MATTER, ATOMS AND OXYGEN ATOMS DISRUPTED.

The young firefighter looks in disbelief as his water floats into millions of one-inch bubbles. He sees the entire fire disappearing before his eyes on all four floors from the little water he sprayed. Firefighters, police and people on the ground begin to cheer for the young firefighter. He turns around and waves at the crowd smiling.

The rain slows down as the heavy clouds pass by towards the east. The UFO quietly flies out of the building invisible.

'Oh, thank you everyone! Thank you! It was all the UFO; advanced E.T. technology,' Jaden proudly says to the cheering crowd below him.

"Hit it now!" Dudley yells.

The helicopter pilot sees the fireman below the UFO and stalls. The wings on the side of the spaceship turn vertical and Jaden slowly flies up the side of the seventy-story building.

Another fast, low approaching stealth bomber flies down the avenue targeting the UFO slowly flying upwards.

"I have a lock on the UFO08, I'm taking a shot," the pilot says.

"STB03, do not take the shot, too many civilians on the ground and witnesses watching now," the helicopter pilot tells the stealth bomber pilot.

The stealth bomber flying fifteen feet above the cars in the street tilts upwards 90° and fires a missile at the UFO. Jaden's nanoscanners detect the fast moving stealth bomber and he takes evasive action. The UFO quickly accelerates up the side of the building. A strong force of air follows behind the UFO. A roaring sonic boom is created, echoing the loud boom downwards. The windows begin to break into millions of pieces that float in the air. They dance together making small clashing sounds and mix with bubbles of rain. The missile quickly crashes through the pieces of glass. The light rain and glass slowly dance together a few feet from the side of the building. Glass from other buildings in the area near the UFO begins to shatter as the sound travels in all directions. The buildings swirl back and forth, as the spaceship continues straight into the cloudy sky. The missile follows the UFO into the clouds. The glass quickly falls towards the ground as people run for cover. The firefighter on the ladder quickly runs into the floor where the fire was to avoid the glass. The shock wave freaks him out as he covers his ears from the sudden boom.

The UFO quickly does a 180° turn and heads back towards the ground. The missile continues upwards. Jaden is getting upset at these aircraft firing missiles at him.

'Where did that cocksucker stealth bomber go to?' He asks.

The nanoscanners are moving around autonomously while going where Jaden might want them to go. They are learning Jaden's habits and things he usually looks at.

'There he goes, flying south down 5th Avenue.'

Still flying invisibly, he tries to catch up to the stealth bomber trying to get away. Rockets are shot from a military truck driving down the street. He quickly dodges the rockets shot at him. Jaden comes up behind the stealth bomber flying low down the avenues. It picks up speed as the UFO's heat signature is detected. The nanoscanners quickly analyze its stealth technology.

'Interesting material the body of this stealth bomber has. Let's see, what can I use on you?' Jaden asks, while he searches one of his weapon screens with alien symbols all over it.

'Hmm...Let's see what this does.'

Jaden fires an unknown alien weapon towards the stealth bomber as the bomber pulls up from flying low. A small orange projectile torpedo is shot from under the purple molecule. It travels at high speed and misses the stealth bomber. The projectile disappears into thin air. The stealth bomber does twists in the air and heads west towards the Hudson River.

'How did I miss that little bastard?'

Many more jet fighters approach Jaden from the clouds in all directions. The stealth bomber pilot ejects from his aircraft and parachutes towards the ocean. He can't comprehend why the pilot ejected even though he missed it. Jaden speeds up and continues heading south in Manhattan.

'What a view this is! I can see everything like it's a sunny day. I always wanted to do this!'

Jaden flies in between the World Trade Centers. He always wanted to do that and everything feels like a dream coming true for him. To Jaden's right he can see the stealth bomber crashing into the river creating a huge splash. The UFO slowly approaches the Statue of Liberty and stops.

'Looking kind of green today, huh Miss Liberty? You have trillions of dirt particles all around your body Miss Liberty.'

Jaden thinks about what that last alien weapon actually did. He thinks back and replays what just happened as the orange projectile went off. He zooms in and looks in slow motion.

'The projectile completely missed. But the exhaust from the stealth bomber went off.'

He zooms in on the ground in the area and he sees streetlights going out and cars shutting down. This intrigues Jaden and it gives him an idea.

110

Suddenly a bolt of lightning strikes the UFO directly.

'Shit! What was that?' The electricity dances around the shields and goes into the purple molecule. It feels like a massage on his shoulders. The electricity slightly charges his weapon systems. Jaden concentrates on the army of aircraft coming towards him. He notices an alien character on his screen that reads: THREAT LEVEL 49%. He speeds up to 204 mph and heads up through the clouds.

"Team leader 1 to Pentagon, the UFO08 was just struck by lightning and just flew into some low clouds. The UFO08 is no longer a civilian threat. We will fire all weapons at once."

Thirty-four jet fighters are spread miles across the sky targeting the UFO from all directions. Jaden can hear their engines roaring towards him. Stealth bombers, stealth F-117's, F-15's and many other jets speed up towards the UFO. Jaden stops above the clouds while the jet fighters approach within a few miles. Jaden gets the UFO to act as if it is damaged by going constantly visible and invisible. The UFO is also emitting dark vapors.

"We can see the UFO08 on satellite now again. The object looks damaged. All units fire all missiles at target," General Dudley says over the radio.

A young officer whispers to the General, "Sir, if you fire those missiles over nearby residential areas and destroy the UFO08, it could explode like a nuclear bomb and kill people below. Staten Island, Brooklyn and Jersey are below the UFO08."

The General steps back, puts his right hand on his shoulder and looks the young officer in the eyes, "That is the chance I'm willing to take. Accidents happen every day; my job is to stop this UFO from making a mockery of the United States government. This wouldn't be the first government cover-up. I'm sure the White House will come up with something good."

The young officer walks off and Dudley looks back up at the large monitor screens.

One news helicopter is flying below the clouds circling as a military helicopter keeps them flying below the clouds.

"There is definitely something going on above the clouds ladies and gentlemen," a news reporter in a helicopter says in front of the camera.

Jaden uses the nanoscanners to go out in all directions around him.

'Damn that's a lot of jet fighters....1, 2, 6, 34?' Jaden asks.

'Thirty-four jet fighters? This is crazy. Okay, let me concentrate. Let's see if the king can outsmart you pawns, knights and bishops. Hmm. . . . one chess piece against thirty-four.'

Each jet fighter fires two missiles each at the UFO sitting in one place above the clouds at 3200 feet. The missiles cruise through the air from all directions, then speed up as they fly through a zero gravity zone. It's quiet in the Pentagon office as everyone is looking at the monitor screens. Someone's pager goes off, but it keeps beeping.

The news reporter can see two surface to air missiles coming from the Staten Island Ferry. He can hear the missiles in the clouds. The anxious news reporter gets the pilot to fly around the military helicopter and into the clouds.

Three orange larger projectiles are shot from the UFO and very quickly go below the missiles and into the clouds. The clouds light up orange for a few seconds in all directions then turn back to grey and white. An invisible shock wave spreads through the clouds and in all directions. The sixty-eight missiles lose thrust and continue to float forward facing different directions.

"This is News Chopper 10 and we are in the clouds to see a glimpse of the stolen military jet the military claims it is trying to take down. Could they be terrorists? We are about to get a ..."

The camera goes off and the lights flash inside the helicopter. It starts to shake and the engine sputters. It is all white around them inside the clouds as they spin in all directions. The pilot's control screens are all messed up and he does not know which way is up or down.

"Holy shit! We are going to die!" The news reporter starts to scream into the non-working camera. The news helicopter begins to float upwards out-of-control. The military helicopters below the clouds lose control and head towards the river.

The missiles float aimlessly in different directions. One explodes causing more to explode. The explosions turn into a huge sphere of fire. Another twelve missiles continue upward and some fall to the ground slowly spinning out of control. Some of the thirty-four jet fighters try to bail out and bank in different directions, but it is too late. They are caught in Jaden's trap. They all lose power, controls, and thrust. They float up and then flip upside down in the direction they turned. Each jet continues to float out-of-control in the direction they turned before they lost power and controls. Several pilots parachute out of their aircraft as four jet fighters crash into each other. They parachute upwards and continue to go upwards in the zero gravity area. The other twelve jet fighters that were floating upwards slow down as they go outside the zero gravity zone. The pilots inside of the zone are still trying to get control of their jets. The jet fighters that banked downwards continue towards the ground, but speed up as they leave the zero gravity area. Those pilots eject out of their aircraft and open their parachutes.

The news helicopter that was in the clouds continues to float out-of-control upwards with its blades slowly spinning. The passengers are screaming at the top of their lungs. It comes out on top of the clouds and in the middle of the chaos. The news reporter is lightly holding onto the handles. He can see all the jet fighters floating in different directions and some parachuting out. He looks to his far left and sees the UFO floating in one place. Even though he is spinning in different directions, he keeps his eyes focused on this exotic UFO just sitting in one place.

"My God!" He yells in a shocked voice.

The jet fighters floating upwards outside the zone change direction and speed up as they fall downwards. They slow down again as they go back into the zero gravity area. Half of the jet fighters parachute out of their aircraft and float upwards.

'Damn this is funny and entertaining. Look at how stupid everyone looks, floating in different directions yelling and screaming in their cockpits. The force of the parachutes opening up and zero gravity is propelling the pilots straight into the sky,' Jaden says.

Jaden heads under the clouds. He sees jet fighters crashing in all directions and heading down in slow motion. Lightning bolts are striking to the east. Pilots are parachuting towards the water in all directions around him. Jet fighters are raining from the clouds. Everything is happening in slow motion for everything else, but fast for Jaden. There is a pilot falling near the Statue of Liberty that gets his attention. He quickly moves closer to the pilot and levels out. The Caucasian pilot in his early thirties is holding on tightly to his parachute with both hands and staring into the clouds as if he saw a ghost. Jaden notices the pilot is petrified, as the nanoscanner gets very close. The Statue of Liberty is facing the pilot and UFO. Jaden concentrates on his head and he sees what the pilot is thinking. Chemical messages and small impulses of electricity are moving all around his brain. Jaden sees images of the pilot's kids, wife, and dogs. Images of his past, of dying and his life up to now.

The pilot is shaking all around his body and his eyes look as if he is seeing a ghost. He has images of himself being in a coffin. Those images go away and an image of a gun appears. The scared pilot pulls out his handgun with his right hand from his jumpsuit. He holds onto the rope of the parachute with his left hand. The nanoscanner leaves his brain and is directly in front of the freaking out pilot. His mouth is wide open and fires his bullets at the UFO only twenty-one feet in front of him. Everything is happening so fast for the pilot.

"Pow, pow, pow."

The bullets stop a few feet from the UFO's body and sit midair. The nanoscanner spins around the pilot as he continues to fire.

114

Pilots and jet fighters can be seen crashing into the water and exploding on land in the background. Jaden moves forward as the wings flash and turn vertical. The pilot continues to fire his gun as he aims at the moving away UFO.

"Pow! Pow! Pow! Pow!"

Jaden feels bad for freaking out the pilot. Orange and yellow exhaust shoots from the wings and tail. Jaden takes off north at breathtaking speeds and quickly gains altitude. The gravity in the area returns to normal. Stealth bombers, helicopters, jet fighters and parachuting pilots quickly fall towards the ground and river.

The UFO flies back into the clouds and turns west at 1475 mph. Trails of cloud lines follow the spaceship. The nanoscanners keep up with the ship.

'Let's see how fast I can get to the west coast. I want to fly down Hollywood Boulevard and then tea bag the Hollywood sign.'

Nothing is following behind the UFO. He reaches 2809 mph and continues to increase speed. Suddenly a grey and black camouflaged SR-71C Blackbird comes from below and begins to tail Jaden.

'That's a nice color, never seen you before. Let's see if you can keep up.'

Jaden increases his speed and reaches 5102 mph. The UFO is pushing the thick, hot air out of the way, as if it was cutting through water. The high speed is creating strong winds to the sides of the UFO. Wakes of sonic booms move in directions behind the UFO and Blackbird. The Blackbird keeps up and gets closer. Jaden tries to go faster. He feels the outside of the UFO getting hot as it creates friction against the air.

'How can I go faster?'

A few minutes pass by. Jaden is constantly changing altitude as he goes back down to 1700 feet.

He scrolls through some screens. He sees ANTI-MATTER LIGHT ENGINES OFFLINE.

Jaden tries to put them online, but they flicker and stay offline. As Jaden is concentrating on the light engines screen, he quickly switches his attention to what is going on outside the ship. He sees a large airliner heading towards the ground trying to land on a runway directly in front of him. Jaden changes direction as the airliner instantly appears in front of him. The UFO turns upside down at the last second. He flies under the belly of the airliner with hundreds of passengers on board and just misses the extending landing wheels. Jaden sees big buildings and recognizes the Sears Tower. The SR-71 Blackbird flies up higher just missing the slow airliner. Jaden flies above the buildings at 4177 mph. The powerful wind shaking feels worst than an earthquake. To the pilot it felt like strong turbulence. Their radar screens light up for a few seconds. People on the airplane look around at each other with confused looks.

The UFO's powerful supersonic wake catches up to the airliner and hits it with such force that it rips off the flaps on the wings. The landing gear just finished fully extending and windows crack and shatter. The cabin windows explode outwards and the loud engines fill the airwaves. The powerful jolt feels like a car crash. The aircraft lifts up from the rear and begins to nosedive. The airliner tilts left and right. The brave pilot fights the forces as his adrenaline kicks in. The co-pilot wakes up and looks around in shock. The passengers panic on the full 737 airplane. The two airline stewardesses lose their balance and fall to the floor. An older man in first class has his glass of wine splashed into his face. The first class passengers' oxygen masks drop from overhead first. Passengers scream from the sudden explosion sound. They automatically think they were hit by a missile as the lights flicker onboard. All their belongings on their laps float into the air as they hold on to the seat in front of them. A second sonic boom hits their craft. They feel the aircraft continuing to lean upwards. The pilot increases the dual thrust with his right hand. The loud engines can be heard throughout the cabin at 150 db.

"Oh my God!"

"Terrorists!! We going to die!" A man yells as he covers his ears.

"Pan Am bombing!" Another man yells.

There are more screams and yelling. A stewardess crawls into the bathroom to cover her ears. Passengers can't hear anything except the sounds of the engines on the wings. Young kids are screaming hysterically. The co-pilot radios into the tower. An Arab man with a turban on his head is praying and moving his body back and forth in the back row. A nervous white teenager sees this and points at the man.

"Terrorist!!" He yells, but no one hears him over the loud engines.

A religious female crosses her heart with her hand and puts her head between her legs. Female passengers' hair is floating over their heads. Luggage falls from overhead as people think they are going to die. Passengers cover their ears from the sudden change in pressure and oxygen masks drop from above in the coach section. Babies are screaming hysterically and people urinate on themselves. An older man grabs his chest. A female holds her baby in her arms and puts the oxygen mask over the baby boy first. She also covers his ears from the loud roaring sounds. The pilot struggles to gain control of the aircraft only 500 feet from landing. The plane slowly levels back to horizontal. The airliner quickly accelerates and bypasses the airport landing.

Jaden watches the airliner with a nanoscanner and sees that it is circling around to land. He witnesses the damage he caused, but is relieved it's still going to land safely. Snow is on the ground in Chicago. Jaden sees the SR-71 pilot is far over him and he increases speed and altitude. He catches up to the SR-71 and is flying in front of it. He gets up to 5203 mph and tries to get the anti-matter light engines online. The pilot tries to get a lock onto the UFO. They go online and his nanoscanners disappear in front of him. The wings move closer to the body of the ship. The light engine power level goes to 0.1%. The outside of the UFO begins to glow yellow and it lights up as bright as the sun. All the sunlight in the area reflects into the UFO and it gets darker all around. The shields going around the UFO disappear and a vortex matrix shield forms 3000 feet in front of it. The SR-71 slows down and gets away from the UFO. Clear energy waves are being drawn in all directions towards the UFO. The sky around the UFO goes completely dark. The UFO flashes like a camera, then there is a very loud bang and it disappears. The force and powerful wind pulls the SR-71 and it spins forward out-of-control.

12:45 PM

"Where did it go? Does anyone see it?" General Dudley asks.

"Sir, it is off the radar and it disappeared. The satellites aren't picking up anything," the second officer says.

"Try the LRSB."

"That is a negative sir, it isn't online yet."

"Damn! Shit!" Dudley yells. He takes a deep breath then continues, "That damn UFO08 has to be somewhere. It's probably still on Earth somewhere. Activate all spy satellites all over the world to find this spaceship."

"Sir, the phones are ringing from law enforcement all across the country. They are saying there was a loud explosion from the sky and windows were broken in millions of people's homes. Car windows and businesses have broken windows also. There are 100,000's of citizens complaining of ringing in their ears. There are tornadoes reported forming from the sky in different mid-state cities," the second officer tells the General.

A satellite expert walks up to the General.

"You need to look at this sir," The red-eyed General Dudley walks over to the satellite expert and reads his paperwork.

"Look at the clouds. They were floating eastwards at 12:30 PM. At 12:31 PM the clouds in this 200-mile radius are now floating westwards, creating tornadoes and deadly thunderstorms. In addition, a strong sound disturbance is spreading all over the world at Mach 100 speed from where the UFO08 was last spotted."

The General is speechless and doesn't know what to make of it. Fifteen minutes pass by and the military is still trying to locate the UFO that disappeared.

"Sir, North Korea is stating there is something flying straight down into their air space from 500,000 feet. They are saying it's glowing yellow and have tremendous heat. They don't know what to make of it," the second officer says aloud in the office.

"That's it!" He yells. He gets up and looks at the screens. "That's the son-of-a-bitch! Move all satellites to that location."

'What happened? Where am I?' Jaden asks.

Everything is bright yellow outside the UFO. Jaden feels intense heat all around his body. He feels as if he is baking in the sun and sauna at the same time. He wonders if he flew into the sun.

Jaden switches to a nanoscanner and sees the ship heading down. He cannot control the ship anymore. He checks the screens: manual controls are offline and autopilot is engaged. He wonders what is going on and he reads that stage 2 is 99.9% complete.

His altitude is 190,038 feet, speed 2309 mph. It is dark all around the ship. He realizes he is somewhere where it is nighttime. The nanoscanners quickly reach the ground and Jaden sees military aircraft with red stars on them taking off. Huge surface to air missiles are aimed upwards ready to be fired. He notices the colors and a red star flag. Jaden notices he is in North Korea and sees thousands of angry Asian people pointing and looking up at him. A nanoscanner turns and looks upwards towards the UFO from the ground. The ship looks like a bright shooting star. The UFO slows down and stops midair at 31,001 feet. Surface to air missiles are fired from the ground. Jaden begins looking through the screens.

'Preparing for space journey?' Jaden asks and continues, 'This isn't good. Okay, you can drop me off at home now. I had fun in the futuristic UFO, but you can drop me off back in New York?'

A minute passes by and Jaden continues to look through the virtual screens trying to see what is going on. Part of Jaden is curious about space and traveling wherever the ship will take him. But more of him is afraid of the unknown and what these aliens want with him. Panic sets in, as he has no control of the ship he is in. What is controlling the UFO is puzzling to him. He thinks about talking to someone there, but nothing happens. He is a prisoner and passenger on this exotic UFO. The yellow bright glow around the ship slowly fades away by the very cold air. Jaden checks on his body.

'Oh wow! Look at my body.'

His body is semi-transparent in a cocooned fetus position. His organs can be seen glowing different colors. He can actually see his heart slowly beating through his lungs. Jaden takes a closer look and he sees his veins and millions of little nanobots of different sizes moving through his bloodstream. He wonders what those nanobots are doing. Just then, one of the screens shows stage two complete. It quickly changes to STAGE THREE 15%. The percentage number slowly counts up.

Twenty-four North Korean jet fighters are approaching the UFO. Jaden continues to check out the different alien screens as he tries to make sense of it.

'Wait a second,' he pauses, 'Some of these screens are in alien symbols, but I understand what they mean. Cool!'

He can see 20-30 alien characters inside of one symbol and they come out in 3D.

MICRO OXYGEN CELLS 100%, PRESSURE AROUND HUMAN BODY 100% NORMAL @ 1000 FEET SEA LEVEL, ANTI-MATTER / MATTER STABLE 100%, LIGHT ENGINES 80%, SHIELDS STRENGTH 75%, MATRIX VORTEX SHIELDS 20%.

'These Korean bastards are firing at me. Man, I want to take out all their missiles and jet fighters.'

The jet fighters get to about 3000 feet away and fire their missiles. The front of the UFO points upwards towards space and accelerates. Creating a small sonic boom, the missiles quickly change direction and follow. The jet fighters fire their machine guns and cannons, but they do not hit anything. The UFO continues to increase speed. The missiles explode in the air like fireworks behind Jaden.

'78,000 feet, 6231 mph, oh shit!'

'The outside of the UFO heats up again. The UFO also begins to shake as it passes through the upper atmosphere and freezing cold temperature at -175°F. The air outside the ship gets thinner and the shaking slowly goes away. The ship greatly increases speed. The UFO reaches 430,081 feet at 9808 miles an hour. Then 17,089 miles an hour at 780,088 feet as it reaches the beginning of space in lower orbit.

OPEN BAR! $30

Every Fri & Sat 11pm-2am
UNLIMITED 16oz LIQUOR DRINKS:
Black Island ice tea
Rum & Coke, Vodka & orange juice, Cranberry &
Vodka. Selter & Vodka, Selter & Gin, Ginger ale &
Vodka, Ginger ale & Tequila, Coke & Whiskey,
Diet pepsi & Tequila, pineapple juice & Vodka,
pineapple & Rum.
SHOTS (Rum, Tequila, Whiskey, Vodka).

The first of it's kind: "ACTION BURGER"

COMICS, BURGERS, SCI-FI, BEER & FREE VIDEO GAMES.

Chapter 3: 30 minutes to Jupiter

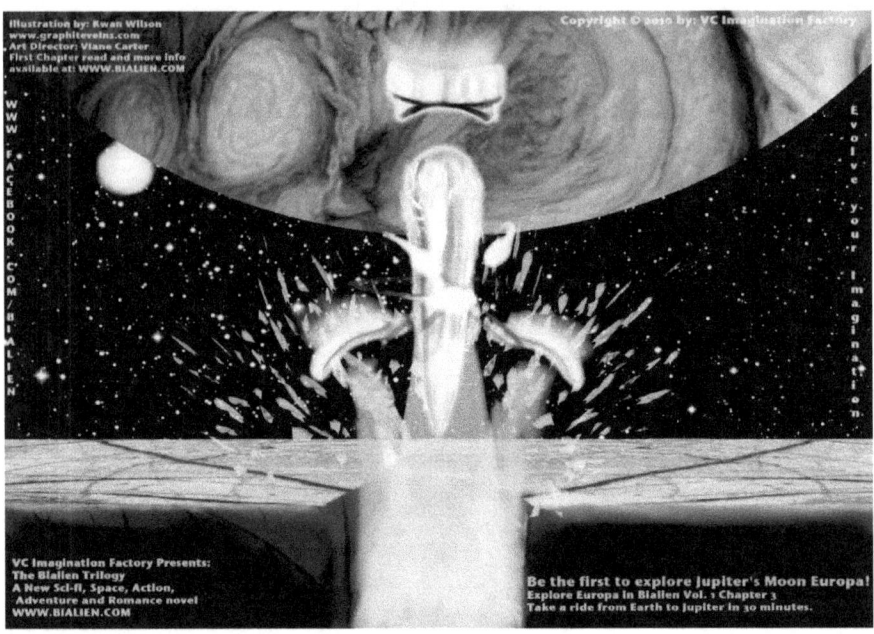

The ship passes tons of space debris as it passes through lower orbit and higher orbit. The nanoscanners detect hundreds of pieces of debris floating aimlessly around the planet. There are pieces of satellites, non-functioning satellites, engines and metal floating in orbit around Earth.

A very large screen comes up by itself and displays a map of our solar system.

'Oh wow, this is cool.'

The planets are all moving slowly around the sun. There is a planet flashing on the screen with a line drawn to it.

He slowly counts, 'Earth, Mars and Jupiter. Looks like we are going to Jupiter for some reason. This is exciting, but scary. I wonder how long this might take. I hope it doesn't take years.'

This is very amazing to Jaden as he sees space close-up and so many stars clustered together. The view is amazing from the dark side of Earth. This feels like a crazy dream to Jaden. This is freaking him out, but at the same time, it is capturing his curiosity. His imagination is going wild. The Earth is getting smaller and smaller behind him. Jaden is past where the satellites are. The altitude on the screen has been turned off and the speed reads 108,000 mph.

The sun is coming out and shines on the UFO leaving Earth's orbit. Jaden checks his screens that show both images outside and info about the ship. The smell of fresh air is gone. When Jaden thinks about smelling the outside of the ship it feels like his nose is trying to breathe in a vacuum hose on a vacuum cleaner. An eerie cold feeling goes around Jaden's body as he looks into the blackness in front of him. The moon suddenly comes into view towards the right.

LIGHT ENGINES 100% READY, OPTIC-WARP DRIVE ONLINE, YELLOW ANTI-MATTER / YELLOW MATTER STABLE 100%.

The ship changes direction and heads towards the moon. Messages continue to show up on the screen. The nanoscanners disappear in front of the UFO. The two tailpieces on the rear of the UFO separate by a foot. Light is drawn into the UFO from all directions and it begins to glow. LIGHT ENGINES POWER STRENGTH 1%. There is a slight flash of light around the UFO and it quickly accelerates. A long trail of exhaust comes from the tail and between the two upside down tails. Small amounts of yellow exhaust come from the two side wings.

Everything is moving faster around him. He sees Earth behind him getting smaller and the moon getting bigger. OUTSIDE EARTH'S MAGNETOSPHERE COSMIC RADIATION PROTECTION ZONE, HULL OF SHIP 100% STABLE he reads on the translucent virtual screen. The huge sun is shining so brightly. 1860 MILES PER SECOND can be seen on the screen.

'This view is amazing; I never thought I'd be in space. I hope I have enough oxygen. That's a long ride to Jupiter. The nanoscanners are in front making sure my path is clear. There are six of them!'

Jaden gets three of the nanoscanners to scan the moon. The nanoscanners are able to move much faster and give information that is more detailed. They scan around the moon very fast.

'Did we ever land on the moon?' Jaden asks.

The nanoscanners show there aren't any leftover presences of any man-made materials. It reads: VIRGIN MOON AND ZERO HUMAN PRESENCE.

'I've heard rumors from people saying we didn't land on the moon and conspiracy theories. But I'm sure there is some explanation,' Jaden pauses and stares at the moon. The UFO passes the moon very quickly.

He notices it took only two minutes to reach the moon. The speed to him is amazing. He wonders if the ship can reach the speed of light or faster.

Soldiers and military personnel are walking around quickly in the huge underground Pentagon area. Disappointment is in the air

"Sir, we don't know. The LRSB is online now. It's tracking the UFO08. It left our orbit a few minutes ago. It just flew by the moon in less than three minutes," General Dudley says over the phone. He listens, and continues talking, "It's working well, and is still hidden inside the UFO08, sir."

"The President is going live in forty-five minutes to talk to the nation about what happened today," Secretary of Defense Oscar Strongwater tells Dudley over the phone from the White House.

"Sir, remember the radio telescopes all over the world are also picking up the loud radio frequencies and noise the UFO is making as it flies through our solar system. The Metrewave Radio Telescope in Pune, India has already detected the UFO08's radiation trail and radio wavelengths. The ship has light speed capabilities and is traveling at a fraction of that speed now. It is moving faster than any meteor or asteroid in our solar system," Dudley says.

"General Dudley, what is a radio telescope?"

"Sir, it is like a telescope, but it picks up radio waves and noise in space. It's like an advanced radar capable of picking up different radiation and object transmissions. If that ship jumps into warp or light speed, radio telescopes around the world are going to light up."

"That just shows what I know. I need to brief the President; I'll call you back in a few. This is a big disaster; we need to do what we do best and get this covered up as soon as possible."

SPACE 340,981 MILES FROM EARTH

Jaden is amazed at the planets in full color slowly spinning and moving around the sun. The UFO on the alien map is moving slowly towards Jupiter. The moon continues to get smaller and smaller behind the UFO. On one of the screens, the numbers count down from ten. The light engines charge to ninety percent. The ship begins to glow brighter as the light thousands of miles around the ship comes towards it. It gets very dark like an eclipse. A very bright flash of light flashes in all directions. The ship moves like a blur and he barely feels it. The flash can be seen from Earth with the naked eye. The speed is shocking to Jaden; it's like nothing he ever saw on television. He sees the light he created is in front of him and is moving away. The sun also begins to get smaller.

'This is very fast! Very fast! I'm going at warp speed! I'm going faster than any human being!'

124

The screen shows 178,000 miles per second.

'I'm going a little under the speed of light. I think the speed of light is 186,000 miles a second,' Jaden pauses then continues, 'Thank you *Star Trek* episodes. I'm going boldly where no man has gone before.'

The ship is causing radio telescopes around the world to detect unknown radio frequencies, microwaves and x-ray signals to go crazy. The light that was in front of the UFO slows down and stays in view. The ship reaches 186,101 mps. The outside body of UFO is glowing bright like a small nova. The ship is leaving a long energy exhaust in its wake. The small light the UFO is creating is passing in front of the ship like a wave. Jaden is intrigued that he is able to use nanoscanners to zoom in on Mars from inside the UFO. Jaden notices that Mars is on the other side of the sun and is too far away.

'That's interesting where the planets are; the screen here is showing each planet rotating.' Minutes go by and the vortex matrix shields go online. Jaden sees the nanoscanners ten million miles in front of the UFO passing through the main asteroid belt. Energy from the purple molecule is beaming in front of the ship. A strong concentration of shields is forming in a cone shape in front of the UFO, extending hundreds of miles in front of it. Jaden quickly figures out it is there to destroy or block anything in front of the ship. The nanoscanners pick out the best path through the asteroid belt. The UFO changes its direction slightly with thrust from the left wing. Jaden sees rocks and very large asteroids floating around and barely moving. Jaden feels as if he is in a front row seat in a 3D movie, but without the glasses. The view is unbelievable and mind blowing to him. He feels as if he is flying through space.

The UFO slows down to 100,000 mps. The UFO is passing through millions of tons of rocks and asteroid debris. A fast moving rock the size of Rhode Island gets into the path of the UFO. It is caught in the vortex matrix shields and the UFO goes right through the newly created hole.

'Wow! That happened so fast.'

Jaden replays what just happened in slow motion.

The ship clears the last of the asteroid belt and continues towards Jupiter at 169,000 mps.

PENTAGON, WASHINGTON, D.C.

"Yes sir, we are now tracking it using the Hubble Telescope. It is giving us the best images of the UFO08," General Dudley says over the phone.

"That damn UFO08 has technology we really could have used. It flew right through the asteroid belt without incident. It looks like a very fast moving comet," Oscar Strongwater says.

"It does sir, but we can't get a clear image of the UFO because it is moving so fast, we can only see the light it's creating."

"Keep tracking it, the President and I are having a private meeting after he is fully briefed on this situation."

OUTER SPACE

Fifteen minutes pass by and the brown, white and grey planet quickly approaches. The planet gets bigger and bigger. The ship enters Jupiter's powerful magnetosphere. A humming sound can be heard coming from the planet through the nanoscanners. Jaden sees hundreds of moons and asteroids circling Jupiter. The ship jumps out of warp speed and continues on warp impulse speed. It continues towards the Red Spot on Jupiter at one percent light engine power. Jaden remembers his father telling him about the Great Red Spot of Jupiter when he was younger. Jupiter has thousands of storm systems. He also remembers his father telling him that two planets can fit inside of it. The nanoscanners return towards the ship, pass through the molecule, and continue towards the hundreds of asteroids and moons surrounding Jupiter. Jaden is amazed with everything he is seeing. There is so much for him to see at once. He feels as if he is a kid again in a large amusement park, with so much happening around him.

The thrust impulse wing engines go online and the light engines go offline. The ship passes the closest, brightest moon with volcanoes on it and the ship continues to go towards the Great Red Spot on the night side of Jupiter.

'If I was in my body now my mouth would be wide open. The size of this planet is beyond amazing. There are storms, clouds and so much happening at once. The planet is moving so fast. That was a cool moon, wait a second, that moon is called Io. That means the Galileo spacecraft is around here somewhere. It just got here three months ago; I remember watching this on TV. '

The UFO gets closer and closer. Jupiter's size is breathtaking to Jaden up close. The pressure outside the ship greatly increases as it passes through very thick, bright red clouds that look very colorful. The clouds smell like rotten eggs to Jaden. Stronger anti-gravity energy comes from the molecule and covers the entire ship. The molecule's energy balls are quickly moving in and out of the ship collecting ammonia, methane, hydrogen and helium atoms. There is a violent storm taking place around him with 1200 mph winds. Gravity is constantly being disrupted around the UFO. The ship passes through the storm with slight turbulence. Jaden uses a nanoscanner to find MASA's Galileo spacecraft that should be near a moon. The powerful winds, forces and turbulence have the anti-gravity engines at forty percent power. The front of the ship turns red from the heat as it passes through 15,000 miles of clouds filled with ammonium hydrosulfide and water drops. It gets darker and darker as the sunlight can't penetrate this far into the planet. The ship quickly approaches oceans and oceans of steamy, solid white clouds. The pounds per square inch (psi) reach a staggering 900 million psi outside the ship, and it continues to multiply. Jaden can see the outside temperature on his screens exceeding 9000°F.

Suddenly the wings on the side turn horizontal as if they were airplane wings. Jaden notices an alien character on the screen that he translates into MPB -MATRIX PLASMA BEAM ONLINE. The wings begin to emit blue beams in front of them, while yellow thrust continues to come from the rear of them. The wings slowly rotate clockwise around the body while emitting a blue light. Concentrated blue beams of energy are shot a mile in front of the ship. Jaden notices this is creating a tunnel through the steamy compressed hydrogen clouds. The ship enters the newly created tunnel. It turns completely dark all around as the ship cuts through thousands of miles of thick clouds. A cold, eerie feeling comes over Jaden. Goose bumps are actually forming on the skin of Jaden's cocooned body. Yellow thrust suddenly comes out of the rear of the side wings that are still rotating. They light up the area around the ship. He changes his vision and looks through a nanoscanner far in front of the ship. His mouth is wide open at what he sees. He sees bright blue light coming from all directions from a liquid metallic hydrogen ocean. Blue Javian lightning bolts strike upwards from the vivid colorful ocean. The constant thunder sounds like loud explosions. The nanoscanners are detecting all kinds of energy particles and atoms moving in so many directions around the highly compressed area. Jaden can't believe what he is seeing. There are oceans of metal boiling with bubbles exploding hundreds of miles upwards. The shape of the ocean looks like huge lava waves moving out of sync. The crushing, humming and exploding sounds quickly become very loud and annoying.

The UFO finally makes it down to the area. There is a very close energy shield two feet around the body of the ship. The purple molecule and moving energy balls are sticking out of this shield area. The wings stop spinning and switch to hovering mode, the MPB also goes offline. Jaden sees the outside temperature is exceeding 19,800°F. He checks on his body to make sure he isn't roasting. His body screen shows his internal temperature at 98.6°F with a cocooned area temperature of 78°F. Suddenly blue lightning attacks the UFO from all directions and Jaden quickly changes his vision. The strong, colorful Javian lightning bombards the outside shield and quickly jumps around in all directions. The ship glows lightning blue as the energy goes into the purple molecule's energy balls. To Jaden the energy feels as if he is getting a massage in the Jacuzzi.

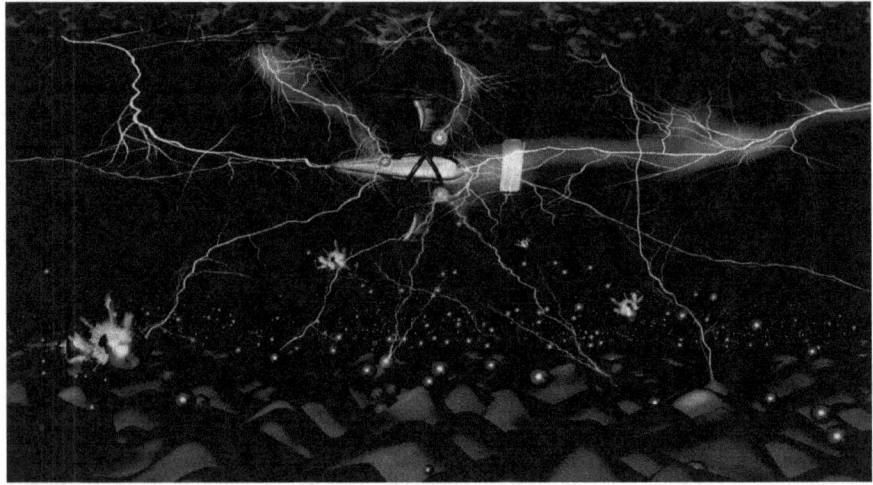

The matrix vortex shields, optic-warp drive, and other systems begin to quickly charge. The pressure reaches a staggering 2.1 billion psi. The ship then suddenly dives down into the hot 22,000°F metallic blue ocean. Jaden feels as if he jumped into an ocean of hot castor oil. He sees x-ray lightning particles jumping in every direction. The sounds he hears are like a loud jet engine, explosions, a whale cry and a rumbling earthquake muffled together. The ship quickly comes back out of the blue abyss. The metallic liquid floats around the shield and goes into the energy balls and then into the outside hull of the UFO. The lightning doesn't strike the ship anymore. The ship quickly accelerates upwards. Jaden can't believe this mind-boggling experience.

The lightning continues to dance around the shields. The ship turns around, points upwards and takes off through the thick, liquid hydrogen clouds. A wake of clouds followss the ship. The MPB goes back online and the ship creates another tunnel towards the surface. The ship is moving faster as it rides out the compressed hydrogen's exploding forces. Five minutes pass by and Jaden can see the powerful Red Spot get larger and then smaller as he leaves the atmosphere. Trails of white smoke trails behind the ship.

'Okay, everything is fully charged, I wonder where we are off to now?'

The UFO accelerates around the side of the huge 11 times bigger than Earth planet. Most of the nanoscanners wait at a large white and grey moon orbiting Jupiter. Jaden doesn't recognize or remember this moon.

The matrix plasma beams go online as the ship quickly approaches this obscure, isolated moon the size of Earth, just outside of Jupiter. The moon is light blue with dark tan and red veins that stretch thousands of miles across the surface. A few spots on the surface resemble dunes of ice. Floating debris and rocks that get in the way of the ship evaporate into harmless particles. A nanoscanner locates a slight crack in the ice. The purple molecule shines a bright beam in front of it. The angle of the wings allows the MPBs to aim directly in front of the ship. The ship flies straight towards the surface and the MPBs touch the surface first. Jaden gets a little nervous; he fears whoever is controlling the ship is inside of the moon. He knows this isn't Jupiter's moon Io. The blue beams from the wings create a circular hole in the ice as the ice quickly approaches. Millions of small clear pieces of ice float in different directions around the beam's energy and depart from the surface. The thin beam from the molecule is shining directly into the hole and between the MPBs. The sun can be seen from a distance near Jupiter. Enormous Jupiter is directly behind the spaceship and fills up the entire view over the icy moon. The tail of the ship separates further and floats about eight feet behind the body. Millions of stars are in the background and darkness of space. The UFO dives into the tunnel of the hard, icy crust.

Jaden is curious to what is beneath the surface of this moon he is unfamiliar with. The quickly spinning MPBs on the wings are destroying miles of solid ice. The tunnel is very dark in front of the artificial light. Millions of pieces of ice are dancing together behind the UFO. The ship quickly reaches an ocean of liquid water. The sound of a car crashing into the water echoes up the tunnel. A loud splashing sound follows the crashing sound. The salty water quickly floods upwards towards the surface. It freezes the tunnel in seconds. The MPB turns off and the molecule glows in the darkness while still providing a powerful beam of light. The wings turn from a pointing outwards position to 20 degrees pointing towards the tail. The tail shrinks slightly in size. The ship moves much easier through the salty, dark water.

The completely dark water is showing bright as day through the molecule's front lights. Jaden doesn't understand the need for the bright lights because he can already see in the dark through the spread out nanoscanners. Thousands of fish come from dozens of miles away seeking out the light. The ship continues to dive as Jaden sees purple fissures creating heat and bubbles. Black smoke is coming from some of the hydrothermal vents. The ocean floor continues to drop as if he is going down into a canyon. There are quadrillions of green glowing extremophile bacteria slowly moving around the vents' geothermal energy. The uneven floors dip down miles below like a cliff. The invisible thrust from the wings turns the water into a slightly pinkish color.

Hundreds of small alien fish the size of a man's hand swim up looking at the UFO, but they stay away from the bright light. Most of the animals get out of the way of the light since they have never seen anything so bright. Jaden's is stunned at what he sees. He could never imagine underwater life on an alien planet in the solar system. He has never heard about this in school or anywhere in science books. The fish form a circle around the ship. They are emitting a green light around their body simultaneously as if they are trying to communicate. The grey fish have two spiky, white, long fins on each side of their bodies that helps them to swim. The fins resemble sharp Q-tips and carry small gills on each of them. They resemble parrotfish with two eyes on the side of their faces, and a third eye in the middle. The UFO is collecting samples of the rich mineral saltwater with seventy percent oxygen in it.

PENTAGON, WASHINGTON, D.C.

"The LRSB is not transmitting sir," the second officer tells the General.

"Where did it last transmit?" Dudley asks.

"Somewhere on the outside of Jupiter."

"I know this thirty million dollar piece of shit transmitter didn't just stop working!" Dudley yells while he slaps the desk putting his head down and grabbing his hair.

"Jupiter could be affecting the signal. The Galileo Orbiter craft has been updated to try to locate the UFO in its proximity."

JUPITER'S MOON EUROPA

'This is amazing. I didn't know there was an underwater ocean on a Jupiter's moon. This is crazy! My know it all astronomy professor Dr. Samuels should be here to see this.'

130

Jaden switches between different nanoscanners spread out in different directions. There are plants, fissures, algae vines, and miles of underwater mountains. At a distance on top of the mountains are huge, colorful, glowing coral reefs, the size of elephants. Thousands of small fish are swimming around them. They extend in all directions, less than a mile beneath the ice. The smell of the ocean reminds him of being at the beach when he was younger. The 32°F degree water against the outside of the ship is transmitted to Jaden's brain when he thinks about it. His mind interprets the signals as brain freezes and cold chills around his body. Jaden can taste the very concentrated amounts of salt, algae, and acidic water through the hull of the UFO as well. As he gets deeper, everything around him is emitting some kind of dim green light in the dark. The little grey fish quickly scatter into many directions as they sense something. THREAT LEVEL 11% shows on the screens. The UFO turns off its bright light and thrust engines. The glowing molecule also disappears. The ship uses pro-gravity energy to continue to sink like a rock. The nanoscanners detect large alien sharks approaching from below, as the ship continues to sink. They quickly scan each of their bodies analyzing cartilage, oxygen levels, muscle, and brain structure. The data quickly passes by on each nanoscanner's vision screen.

There is a school of fifteen alien sharks approaching in an orderly fashion from the left. Jaden is able to see the insides of their bodies in animated vision. The sound of the insides of their bodies sounds like a balloon quickly being twisted near his ears. The twenty-foot long sharks resemble the shape of a shark on Earth. The grey-bodied shark with green glowing scales around its body has two huge pointy horns as noses on its heads. They stretch out three feet each. Inside of the double horns is a clear protective area where dozens of small, black, reflective eyes sit. The rows of eyes are on both sides of the cone noses. Under the noses is a huge mouth with hundreds of six-inch long razor sharp teeth inside. On each side of the sharks near the head are round, double layer fins that stick out five feet in diameter. The fins look circular like stingray bodies. There is another small set of fins towards the midsection and a long narrow tail. There is a huge muscle in the tail that allows it to change from horizontal to vertical when it changes directions. The UFO continues to cruise downwards. The nanoscanners detect the group of sharks communicating with each other using a magnetic radar system in the tips of their noses.

Jaden changes his vision to outside the ship. He sees the wings imitating a fish. The side wings are sticking out straight and flapping backwards like a fish. The wings then disappear into the body, reappear in a straight out position, and repeat the sequence. Jaden sees some of the sharks approach the ship and surround it. The ship levels out and faces the majority of the huge sharks. The wings stop moving and sit at an outward 90-degree angle. He sees that they have a confused look on their strange faces. Jaden thinks the ship is going to try to communicate with the organized sharks. He can't believe how organized they are, as if they have some sort of evolved intelligence. The ship's body lights up in a sequence like Morse code. The confusing sequences are making the sharks get closer to Jaden and slowly freaking him out. He has a bad feeling about this communication.

The sharks quickly attack the ship from all directions. The ship jerks in different directions from the sudden force. Two attack the wings on both sides. The double noses turn sideways and their huge jaws comes out from underneath and swallows the wings simultaneously. Another attacks the nose of the ship and grinds its sharp teeth on the silver metallic hull. Another two attack the rear tail, trying to pull them apart. Another pair attacks the hull of the ship from the rear. One slides down the bottom side and the other on the top like a snake, in opposite directions. Their bodies wrap around the hull and lock into each other's tail. They pull into opposite directions passing each other side by side squeezing the hull. When their faces split apart to open their large jaws, their vision changes to directly in front of them.

'What the hell?'

There are hundreds of other alien fish watching from a distance. Jaden is caught off guard from the sudden attack. Jaden feels the biting and squeezing against the ship. The wings feel as if a huge snake with small teeth is nibbling on his arms. His feet are experiencing the same thing, up to his knees. His midsection feels as if two pythons are trying to squeeze him. Jaden also has the feeling of a huge leech over his head, squeezing and scratching his skull. The gross feeling he is interpreting makes him feel like throwing up. Jaden still doesn't have any control, but he wishes he did.

'Get off me you little shark rats! I'm not a meal!'

Jaden tries to mess with the weapons screen, but it's offline. He wants to blast these bastards around him so bad. Jaden figures the ship is doing some sort of experiment or taking a non-violent approach.

The UFO continues to float downwards with these sharks continuing to bite and pull. The sharks on the wings are trying to pull the wings off. But the powerful, invisible magnetic energy between the body and the wings keeps them from moving. The sharks wag their tails in different directions in an attempt to come off with a piece of the ship. The entire wings are in the sharks' mouths as they continue to pull and bite. The sharks on the tail continue trying to pull a top and bottom side of the tail apart. The angry sharks coordinate and swim the ship towards the left. But the ship counters that action. A nanoscanner detects a seventy-five foot mother alien shark quickly swimming towards them a half a dozen miles away. Jaden can't believe how organized the sharks are. This reminds Jaden of a Tom and Jerry episode where Tom had crabs biting him all over his body and he was jumping around yelling. The pain increases around Jaden's body.

Suddenly the sharks with the pit bull jaw grip over the wings and tail begin to glow pink. Jaden is surprised that the thrust isn't hot or bothers the sharks. The ship continues to head downwards, gradually increasing speed. Brighter pink thrusts come from the wings and tail as the ship increases in speed. The side wings point towards the rear, while the sharks continue to hang on. The shark on the nose falls off first. The sharks on the tail lose their grip and spin in circles from the ship's powerful downwards tidal wake. The sharks around the midsection of the ship do the same and join the tidal wake. The sharks on the wings are slowly being pulled off from the increasing force of 200 mph. A screeching sound is heard on both sides as the sharks slowly lose their strong grips. There are hundreds of different fish moving out of the way from below. A whirlpool spreads behind the ship in all directions. Jaden feels as if his arms are slowly being scratched by two cats. The sharks fall off one by one, and spin in the tidal wave whirlpool. A relieving feeling passes around Jaden's body. The zero gravity wake quickly spreads outwards and pulls hundreds of animals into the ship's direction. The whirlpool reaches the top of the ocean.

The nanoscanners detect dozens of miles of milky white, glowing strings floating aimlessly in all directions, below and around the ship. There are all types of fish swimming around the glowing strings providing a dim light.

The huge mother shark continues to head towards the ship at an amazing 90 mph. Jaden sees it through the nanoscanner as if it wants a big meal. The threat level goes up to 18%. Jaden is in disbelief as he sees all of this before him. Another nanoscanner detects the ocean floor three miles in front of the ship. Jaden sees some lime glowing starfish, thirty feet in diameter with four-foot long spikes and thorns around them. There are glowing seaweed vines 80-90 feet long extending from the ocean floor. Fissures, alien crabs with twelve arms, glowing eels with wings and square-shaped stingrays parade the ocean floor. They begin to scatter as they hear something coming from above them. There are giant glowing worms on the ocean floor the size of a big screen television. There is glowing endolith all across the ocean floor in rocks, shells and coral. There are dozens of brown scallop shells that resemble lasagna ruffles on the floor. The alien scallops have dozens of glowing eyes all across its shell. They also have thousands of small teeth that extend across the opening of the two shells.

The wake behind the ship gets bigger as it dives past 300,000 feet. The ship slows down and turns as it reaches a rocky bottom. The whirlpool resembles an underwater tornado from a distance as it slams into the ocean floor. There is a loud crashing and exploding sound as the whirlpool hits the rocky bottom. The whirlpool is glowing green and white from the extremophiles and millions of collected strings. The ocean floor shakes violently as a shock wave travels in all directions at 5600 mph. Debris, sharks and other animals spiral down the whirlpool colliding on top of each other as if a train was just derailed. A cloud of dust moves from the impact area as if a bomb just exploded.

Miles in front of the ship there is a huge twenty-foot glowing jellyfish with a yellow body floating towards a collective of thirty of them to form a glowing 400-foot circular congregation of connected jellyfish. They slowly connect together from all directions as if they were seeking shelter. The UFO continues to scan millions of different alien life forms as it moves across the high-pressure ocean floor. Jaden is speechless as he tries to take in everything he is seeing. He is zooming in on the pitch-black ocean floor. There are dozens of red snakes with little legs and hard, narrow, glowing shells on their backs. They spread out in many directions as they sense danger approaching. There are dozens of fifteen-foot wide clamshells in a group. The majority of the five-inch fish have one eye in the middle of their heads and skinny bodies. The creatures also have 10-20 small fins moving on the side of their eyes across the side of their bodies. Their bodies are repeatedly glowing together as if they are sending Morse code to each other. The UFO begins to glow and light up at the same pace the alien fish are.

The ship turns down and goes through a tunnel that leads miles deeper. The wings move into a forward position and closer towards the body. The dark tunnel gives Jaden the creeps as green light from the vines disappear. The vines extend across to each side of the solid rock tunnel. The ship rubs against a few vines. The ship passes the vines and enters an area in the tunnel where 100,000's of little thin hairs are extending across the tunnel, blocking the pathway. The hairs move and rub around the body of the ship as if they were tasting it. A nanoscanner detects something alive hiding in the walls of the tunnel. The ship passes without incident.

The pressure oddly decreases as the ship goes lower. There is a huge open area that resembles a large cave. The nanoscanners are picking up a mountain half a mile away. It looks like the mountain is alive with carbon-based cells and membranes. The ship goes in that direction. The nanoscanners detect something alive inside. Jaden sees shreds of glowing, digested material that resembles feces around this huge mountain that extends a mile high. The UFO, still in autopilot, scans the side of the mountain and materials. The nanoscanners detect something moving very fast inside the mountain. Suddenly something large reaches out of the opening to the mountain and grabs the UFO. The UFO is pulled quickly inside of the mountain by a sticky, large tentacle tongue. Jaden panics as the UFO turns off its thrust engines and the wings and tail morph back into the body. The ship does not do anything as it is quickly propelled into the mountain and what looks to be a mouth. Jaden freaks out as he can feel goose bumps jumping around his skin. The sounds of being inside of a body can be heard. Huge hairs push the ship down what appears to be a throat. The throat area quickly attempts to squeeze the ship. Jaden can feel the pressure of the cellular walls squeezing him as if a big person was hugging the life out of him. Panic sets in as a slimy material coats the ship.

'I'm claustrophobic!' Jaden yells in a panicked tone.

The high pressure squeezing has no affect on the ship's hull. The area opens back up and the silver carrot shape UFO lands in what appears to be a huge stomach area full of acid.

'Oh shit, this is gross. I've just been swallowed by a slimy sea creature! This is disgusting! This is beyond disgusting!' Jaden has the feeling of wanting to throw up, but can't. The nasty acid liquid feels as if it is all over his skin. Goose bumps return to his human body. Squishing, farting and digesting sounds are all around him. He tries to ignore the smell and sounds he hears around him. The smell is worst than road kill. Jaden knows he is protected inside the ship and tries to calm down. But he can't figure out why the ship went along with being captured. The nanoscanners put together a 3D image of a large, grey, squid-looking alien animal quarantined inside of this huge underwater mountain. The humongous animal has hundreds of very long tongues that look like tentacles that extend to different holes in the mountain. Jaden's fear turns to curiosity as he looks at the 3D images on his screens. He has never seen anything like this. The strong stomach acid tries to digest the UFO along with other half-digested alien creatures.

STAGE 3 COMPLETE flashes on the lower part of the screen.

'Oh great, stage three was to be eaten by an underwater alien monster on a moon far far away.'

Jaden investigates what is inside the Mortal Kombat pit of death he is inside of.

'I can't believe all the things sitting in this animal's stomach. It has eaten thousands of fish animals. Ha! Ha!'

Jaden continues to laugh as he sees a few half digested alien sharks beneath him. He continues to laugh as nanoscanners detect three more alien sharks coming down from different throats.

'Looks like you sharks couldn't attack Mr. Godzilla Squid here.'

The sharks fall into the huge stomach and they start going crazy as the acid burns their skin. They quickly try to swim back towards the throat, but it closes up. The sharks together begin biting one closed off throat.

'Where you sharks going? Sit and stay awhile, let's play a game of UNO. Don't leave! This acid sauna feels good after awhile; it's good for your skin. You don't want to give this squid indigestion while you stay at the roach hotel; I mean squid motel. You'll get used to the strong acid in no time, just like your friends below did.'

Jaden tries to entertain himself while trying to not think about the disgusting situation he is in. The sharks are quickly ripping away pieces of the throat with their sharp teeth, but slow down as the strong acid digest their skin and inside mouth area.

'You should have called your big mama to come rescue you. You don't look so bad now.'

There is a thumping sound from a distance outside the mountain. A nanoscanner quickly detects the mother shark that was coming towards the ship earlier a few miles above the mountain. She crashes into a tunnel she is too big for. Jaden admires the huge size of this enormous creature. He notices she has eyes on the side of her body and vertical and horizontal gills.

'Looks like your mama is here for you, but her big ass can't fit in the tunnel.'

Jaden thinks of some mama jokes from high school to entertain himself, while the sharks a few feet above him slowly stop moving and sink into the abyss.

'Yo mama is so fat, the last time she saw 90210 it was on a bathroom scale. Yo mama is so fat she can't jump to conclusions.....'

He laughs to himself, but can't think of anymore fat jokes for some reason.

'....Yo mama is so ugly she entered an ugly contest and the judges said: sorry no professionals. Ha! Yo mama is so stupid, she took the Pepsi challenge and chose Jiff peanut butter.'

'Okay that last one was kinda corny and very junior high school.'

The ship is analyzing and scanning everything inside of the monster. Jaden tries to get manual control of the UFO, but it does not work. He wants out of this monster squid; he had enough torture.

'Oh man, let me fire some weapons inside of this giant squid monster and give him some nasty tasting indigestion. I'll let it know what American fast food taste like after a few hours in someone's stomach,' Jaden says in a humorous voice.

Jaden wishes the UFO would at least put up its shields so he doesn't have to taste, smell and hear the insides of this animal. Jaden wishes he could wax the outside of this UFO with this squid's insides.

Suddenly the ships anti-gravity engines go on. The wings and tail morph from the body. The tail and wings are in their normal flight position. The UFO fades semi-invisible and an unknown alien symbol shows up on the screen. The unknown alien symbol has numbers counting down from 8 seconds next to it. The huge purple molecule forms around the body. The UFO begins to move through the stomach not in a solid form. It passes right through the skinless, eyeless, finless sharks and other dead creatures. The ship leaves out of the giant squid's stomach and through the solid mountain.

'Holy exogorths, how is this ship doing this?'

The UFO quickly clears the large, solid mountain with two seconds left and is back in the deep ocean. The UFO goes visible and takes a solid form. The giant squid makes a loud belching sound.

'You're excused!'

The UFO points upwards and accelerates towards the tunnel.

'Alright, let's get out of this dark E.T. octopus monster land. This scene just reminded me of a scene in *Star Wars V: The Empire Strikes Back* when the exogorth space slug tried to eat the Millennium Falcon, but ten times more gross.'

A long, tongue tentacle quickly reaches out to grab the UFO again. The yellow tentacle wraps around the rear of the ship's tail. There is tension as the tongue pulls back tightly with a strong force and slows down the UFO. The ship measures the force at 100,000 pounds per square inch. More tentacles come from other directions to assist in recapturing the first dinner to leave the squid's stomach. The ship gently increases speed as more pink thrust comes from the wings.

'What is this tug of war? Shoot those tentacles with something!'

The tentacle is torn from the alien squid as the ship quickly propels upwards, just missing being grabbed by the other high-speed tentacles. The ship reaches the tunnel while dragging the 3000-foot long sticky tentacle still wrapped around one side of the tail. The wings move to a forward position and closer to the body. The ship quickly moves through the tunnel passing thousands of hairs. Suddenly a huge animal that resembles a Venus flytrap snaps out from the right wall and completely swallows the ship. The ship doesn't stop and rips the mouth from the walls. The wings morph through the animal's body and continue to provide thrust up the tunnel. The wings are now five feet from the UFO's body. The yellow glowing mouth with thorn teeth continues to squeeze the ship's hull. Jaden feels another bear hug as the animals begin to annoy him.

'Catching a ride huh?'

From a distance, the ship looks like a silver dildo with a glowing, yellow rubber tightly around it. The tentacle on the rear resembles a long piece of toilet paper being dragged on someone's foot.

Jaden sees the mother shark at the end of the tunnel, swimming back and forth over the exit, with an army of sharks nearby.

'Oh shit, big mama shark heard my insensitive mother jokes.'

The UFO quickly exits the tunnel and the seventy-five foot long mother shark times the exiting ship and opens its huge mouth.

'Oh no!! Not again!' Jaden yells as he sees thousands of huge teeth before him.

It swallows the ship and the flytrap animal still gripping the UFO's body. The blunt force and speed of the ship makes the shark propel upwards. A loud impacting sound echoes in all directions. The ship goes right through the shark's stomach and stops in the lower intestines area. The animal cries in pain as it bites down on the still moving tentacle protruding from the shark's mouth. The rubbery tentacle refuses to break away and pink thrust comes out between the shark's teeth. Jaden gets disgusted again as he is inside of another alien life form. He feels like the hand inside of a sock puppet. He can't help but laugh as he and the ship drag three things towards the surface. The wings morph through the shark's body and are twenty-five feet away from the UFO on both sides. The powerful magnetic energy in between the wings is messing with the mother shark's navigation and communicating capabilities in its nose. The army of smaller sharks tries to catch up to its leader, but can't catch up to the ship's 159 mph speed. They are caught in another tidal wake. The mother shark is wagging its huge tail in an attempt to stop from going up at such a fast speed. The ship fights the direction changing force from the alien tail.

'You not so tough now, huh big mama Jaws?'

The pink light particles from the wings shine brightly against the shark's glowing skin. The ship reaches 315 mph as it quickly moves through the water causing another whirlpool. The Venus flytrap animal dies from the change in pressure as the ship reaches ten miles from the ice surface.

'Goodbye, genetic modified fish from The Simpson's power plant lake.'

The ship slows down as the wings begin to rotate around the entire shark's body. The matrix plasma beams go online. With the wings fifty feet away from each other, they concentrate their beams on an area twenty feet in front of the shark's tail. They penetrate the ice creating a much bigger tunnel, 115 feet wide. A tidal wave of water rushes behind the ship. The loud sounds of a bottle filling up echoes behind the ship. The sudden change in temperature begins to affect the still alive shark. The UFO breaks through the surface in a huge explosion of water. The sunlight shines over the shark's body. The water begins to freeze behind the ship and a hundred foot frozen crystal geyser quickly forms.

The ice quickly freezes the entire tunnel with debris and other smaller sharks trapped inside. The yellow tentacle continues to drag from the shark's teeth. Jupiter is very bright towards the left of the ship. Two small moons can be seen from a distance near Jupiter. The small Sun shines from the right side of Jupiter. Jaden is so happy to see Jupiter and the sunlight shining towards him. A small atmospheric pressure around the moon makes everything frozen around the UFO. The ship vibrates from the shark's final silent groan as the temperature in space drops to -454°F. The vacuum of space sucks the air from the shark. The water begins to boil in the shark's mouth. Oxygenated blood rushes to the dying animal's brain as the body quickly freezes from the outside in as if it was floating through liquid nitrogen. The carbon-based animal is frozen solid and its insides expand around the ship, crushing it tighter.

'Hasta la vista baby!'

A flash of light comes from the animal's mouth and the ship quickly accelerates to 60,000 mph. The shark breaks off into thousands of frozen pieces, along with the flytrap animal and tentacle tongue. A strong feeling of relief and freedom comes over Jaden. The wings move closer and stop three feet from the body as they emit a bright yellow thrust.

'Oh wow, I'm so happy to see this large colorful planet again. What an experience,' he says cheerfully.

Feelings of remorse quickly come over him as he thinks about the shark dying that way, but it quickly leaves him as he feels that's what it deserved. The ship changes direction to leave Jupiter's orbit.

'There goes the Galileo spaceship orbiter. I knew it was around here,' Jaden says while zooming in towards it with a nanoscanner.

Jaden notices it is pointing towards him in the UFO. The antennas are pointing towards Earth's direction. Jaden reads the insides of the orbiter: WELCOME FELLOW ALIENS. WE COME IN PEACE. GREETINGS FROM HUMANS ON EARTH. Then there is a map and diagram of where Earth is. There are records and other things buried deep inside of it.

'What a Catch-22, as soon as these curious aliens find this orbiter and reach Earth, the government will put them underground in Area 51. I see why aliens would want to come to Earth to attack us. Most of the time we encourage it or ask for it.'

Jaden can see the invisible radio waves being transmitted towards Earth. He suddenly remembers when the Orbiter left Earth's orbit in 1991 it couldn't fully open its high-gain antenna and it was forced to use the low-gain antenna. Two sets of nanoscanners get to work and enter the high-gain antenna that looks like a half opened golden umbrella. The nanoscanners quickly find the problem and dispatches nanobots to create artificial microscopic lubricants inside the deployment motors. The high-gain antenna fully opens like a golden umbrella. The nanobots go back into the nanoscanners and 134 kilobits a second of data transmits from the antenna at the speed of light.

The light engines charge and go online. Jaden smiles as he realizes he changed history and seriously helped MASA with its spaceship orbiter that couldn't properly send pictures and data to Earth.

A much larger map comes on the screen.

'This is radical! I can see millions and millions of stars. This is the Milky Way Galaxy.'

Jaden can zoom in and out to different parts of this large map and notices a line. The ship uses a little extra power to escape Jupiter's powerful gravity forces. He zooms into where he is now.

'The line points to the ship going into the…into the…' he pauses and follows the line.

'The sun?' He asks. Just then, the UFO goes into light warp speed.

The ship races with the invisible radio waves streaming towards Earth. The solid line goes into the sun and then broken lines can be seen heading towards different stars. They end at the center of the galaxy. Jaden is puzzled. He looks around the screen. On the side of the map it reads: GALACTIC BULGE / CENTER MILKY WAY GALAXY 28,459 LIGHT-YEARS."

Then it reads underneath it: 35 EARTH MONTHS.

'Thirty-five months?' Jaden asks, 'That is impossible. That doesn't make any sense. Oh no, I'm going to be older.'

Jaden zooms out and he sees Andromeda Galaxy glowing. He zooms in on Andromeda and sees more solid lines leaving Andromeda's Galactic Bulge center. The lines then point to a planet in the middle of Andromeda's Galaxy. The planet is also spinning around its own star.

The UFO passes the Asteroid Belt and clears it, avoiding hitting anything. The UFO slows down out of warp between Mars and the Asteroid Belt. The nanoscanners are in front of the ship and around it. So many things are on the screens that Jaden is trying to understand. On one of them it says: ANALYZING SOLAR WINDS STRENGTH, ANALYZING OPTIC-WARP POINT OF SUBSPACE ENTRY.

'What the hell is all of this stuff?' He asks.

'Now I'm getting nervous.'

The UFO enters light speed again, but this time at maximum speed. The light engines are at 100%. The bright waves of light the UFO just created are in front of the ship and stay in sight. The ship's speed reaches 185,900 mps as it heads directly towards the glowing sun.

PENTAGON, WASHINGTON, D.C. 2:31 PM

"Sir, the LRSB just came back online eighteen minutes ago. It transmitted a signal from near one of Jupiter's moons. Photos of the UFO08 just came in from the Galileo Orbiter. The high-gain antenna mysteriously began working. Using the Hubble, we can now see the UFO08's light and wake traveling at the speed of light with a trajectory course to the sun. It should be passing Earth's orbit around the sun in nine minutes. It should reach the sun in 16 minutes," the first officer says.

"That is interesting. Look at that thing move. Maybe it's going to destroy itself or blow up our sun. Who knows? We have a lot of explaining to do, there is going to be a big investigation from every agency on this planet. The Russians are asking questions. Anyone with a telescope can see this UFO08 flying around lighting up our solar system. We also had to delay the President's worldwide speech about this event, until we see what this UFO08 is about to do now," Dudley says.

Jaden stares at the bright yellow sun, not knowing what his fate is. He thinks that maybe landing on the sun is some kind of transporting method.

'Man, this sucks. I hope I don't die; I don't like looking the sun in the eyes. I guess the ship is returning to the planet where it is originally from. Some 2 ½ million light-years away from here. I'll be dead before getting to the third star from here. This sucks, I'm never going to see my mother, father, girlfriend or friends again. I'm going to die of old age traveling through space,' he says in a panicked voice.

Jaden looks at his body again through the nanoeye. He sees his body glowing invisible and visible again as it sits in an embryonic cocooned state. His lifeless body is not breathing, but he can see and feel his heart slowly beating.

'My body looks like I'm in a giant womb, hooked up to an artificial umbilical tentacle.'

The UFO passes Earth's orbit in a blur of light. The ship starts to shake and rumble like turbulence on an airplane. The sun gets brighter and brighter. There are five nanoscanners hundreds of miles directly in front of the UFO. They begin to spin around in circles very fast creating a colorful rainbow spectrum of light. An arched trail of white light that resembles a quarter moon stretches from the wings to the tail on both sides. The UFO reaches 186,100 mps and more energy and light go into the UFO from in the area. The UFO passes the orbit of Venus. The ship continues on a straight path towards the sun, while just passing Mercury's orbit.

Jaden's vision through the nanoscanners in front of the ship is unviewable. They spin around creating a very small hole in space. He notices something flashing on the screen: SUBSPACE OPTIC-WARP PATH 98% STABLE.

The vision outside of the UFO is very bright, like high beams in his face. The temperature outside the UFO goes past 7000°F. Jaden goes into shock as he feels he is about to die, the sun getting so close is freaking him out.

The UFO reaches 186,222 mps, its maximum speed. The UFO starts to rotate clockwise and goes semi-invisible. The purple molecule emits exotic infrared energy around the ship. The small quarter-sized circle resembles a hole. The blinding bright sunlight in front of Jaden allows him to focus on the completely dark hole that is slowing down towards the ship. Jaden thinks the hole must be some sort of pathway somewhere.

Everything seems to be happening in slow motion. The ship begins to glow very brightly as if it were using the sun's rays and radiation as an energy source. The UFO reaches a few 100,000 miles from the sun. There is a bright flash of light as the ship goes faster than the speed of light. The spaceship breaks down into quadrillions of microscopic molecules as they quickly move through the nanoscanners' circle. There is another bright explosion from both sides of the Sun's surface as the subspace hole closes. Coronal filaments, loops of mass ejections, magnetic arcades, ultraviolet typhoons and x-ray hurricanes explode from the surface of the sun. Solar flares travel in all directions and towards the solar system.

People are running around the office very fast and phones are constantly ringing.

"Sir, the space station detected a powerful solar flare coming towards Earth in the next 5 minutes," the first officer tells the General.

"Pardon my ignorance, but what is a solar flare?" He asks.

"Sir, a solar flare is high concentrated energy erupting from the sun's surface and goes out through our solar system. Earth's magnetosphere field protects us from regular solar flares. But the powerful ones effect things on Earth like beepers, cell phones and satellite transmissions."

"Thank you soldier, is there any trace of the UFO08 or signal from the LRSB?" The General asks.

"No sir."

"Keep monitoring, I have a conference call with the chief of states and the resident."

The first officer turns on the main television in the large room.

"This is Betty Miller live from BNN worldwide television. Something has happened in upstate New York today. Early this morning there were reports of the U.S. government chasing something in the area. People have been saying it was a UFO, but the government says an experimental jet fighter was stolen and the government was trying to shoot it down. They didn't say if they were successful or not. The President is giving a public address in a few minutes; we will switch to that live. We will now switch to reporter Jerry Cuttings that is live in Middletown, New York at a local hospital."

"Thank you Betty, there has been a rush to the emergency room like this one all over the northern states in America. Thousands of elderly people rushed the emergency rooms, as some had heart attacks and trouble breathing. This is due to the loud sounds that were coming from the U.S. Air Force jets flying at sonic speeds over land. The FAA approved flight at these speeds to shoot down an experimental government jet that was stolen. People have been panicking, going crazy and thinking we were being bombed or under attack. Many vets came to the hospital having flashbacks thinking they were still in a war."

The reporter walks over to someone in a hospital bed.

"Sir, tell me what happened to you today? What did you hear?"

"I fought in the Vietnam War twenty-five years ago. I was driving down Main Street earlier today when everything went to hell. I heard a missile fired and loud booms that can be felt on the ground. I looked up and it was all happening above the clouds. I could see some Air Force jet fighters speeding across the sky as if it was an air show. People started to panic and I my heart started to race. I thought we were under attack. I know the sound of missiles being fired and jet fighters maneuvering in the air. I felt like I was in Vietnam all over again. I saw Vietnam jet fighters firing back. Everything was happening so fast and I couldn't breathe. I got out of the car and collapsed on the ground. I began to crawl, holding my heart. People started to ask me if I was okay. I looked up at them and they looked like those Vietnamese bastards," the grey-haired man says.

"Okay sir, I hope you feel better thank you for your time," he says while pulling the microphone away.

The Vietnam vet grabs the microphone back. The startled reporter looks at the man with a look of confusion. Their eyes lock as a cold chill moves down the reporter's back. The cameraman takes his eye from the eyepiece and looks at the reporter.

"I'm not finished talking," the man says in an eerie voice. He continues, "I fought for this country twenty-five years ago and I can't even get normal medical coverage! I can't get a job, can't get any respect and nobody cares about vets!"

The reporter takes back his microphone and walks away from the angry Vietnam vet, sitting by himself on a hospital bed.

"This is Jerry Cuttings, reporting live from Middletown, New York."

"Thank you Jerry, seems like you made a new friend at the hospital. We now go live to Stillwater, New York where reporter Dennis Matthews is standing live in front of the alleged suspect's house," the news anchor says.

"Thank you Betty. Early this morning, government officials, men in white clothes, MASA and the FBI have been questioning a family outside this small town. It has been a complete circus here as the Marino family has been questioned throughout the day. The police and government officials are looking for this 19-year-old male named Jaden Marino for questioning about a missing government experimental aircraft missing early this morning. Here is a video earlier of the mother, Mrs. Marino being driven away in a black government truck," Dennis says.

"Mrs. Marino do you know where your son is, or why you're being asked to go with these men?"

"I don't know where my son is, I don't know what's going on. Jaden come back home if you hear this," Mrs. Marino yells while looking confused and being escorted away into a black SUV.

"That was earlier today, we have Major Robinson coming out of the house now. Major, can you tell us, how a 19-year-old teenager was able to steal a top-secret government experimental plane?" he asks in front of the other news reporting shoving their microphones into his face and flashing their cameras.

He stops and looks into the camera with a dead serious look. He takes a deep breath. Sgt. Peters stands behind the Major. Cameras continue to flash like a movie star is present. There is complete silence as Robinson clears his throat.

"I don't know how he was able to steal a government's aircraft at the time. Teenagers steal trains, cars, boats and airplanes all the time these days. He is wanted for questioning. It's possible he might know the person who did it or could have had help," he says as he looks at the news reporter in the eyes and not the camera.

"People in the area are saying there was a UFO involved and there are many witnesses," the news reporter says.

"There was no UFO involved, our new experimental jets might look like a lot of things, but there was no UFO involved here today," Robinson says.

"Why was the Air Force given clearance to break the sound barrier over residential land? That is illegal over residential land. Didn't they know that would cause massive panics in the area?"

"That's something you'll have to ask the FAA and Pentagon. I don't have time for anymore questions," he pauses.

Major Robinson looks directly into the camera, "This teenager's name is Jaden Marino. He is 5'9" 160 lbs, fair skin with blue eyes and curly hair. He is bi-racial and was last seen wearing a black and blue NY Giants jacket, blue jeans, and black Jordan sneakers. He is wanted in connection to this investigation. If anyone sees him, they should report him to their local police or FBI ASAP at 1-800-555-5FBI."

Major Robinson walks away and Peters follows. They all yell out questions simultaneous.

"Okay sir. Well what now?" Peters asks

They walk into a black government truck and news cameras continue flashing pictures. They quickly drive off while other military SUV's follow.

"Thank you, Dennis. This is BNN news and we have full coverage from today's strange events. There were reports of three dozen Air Force jets and numerous missiles crashing and exploding around the area of lower Manhattan. Many just landed in the water without exploding. Witnesses report aircraft falling from the sky like rain by the Statue of Liberty today. The low clouds camouflaged the activities of what was happening above. There were dozens of military boats pulling jet fighters from the water all afternoon."

"Four jets crashed into Staten Island, one hitting a house and another landing on a supermarket. There were reports of serious injuries there. Missiles landed in Bayonne destroying a business and a row of stores.

Three aircraft crashed into different parts of west Brooklyn. One F-16 landed on a I.T. business building on 39th Street in Sunset Park, destroying a few back offices. Another one landed on the elevated BQE Expressway. The last one landed in a park off 76th Street in Bayridge. The rest crashed into the East River and Hudson River. Witnesses say the air fighters were falling towards the ground as if they ran out of gas. Other witnesses reported there was gunfire and missiles fired above the clouds. There were also reports of power going out in cars, streetlights and homes for hours in this area. There were many more complaints of loud booming sounds from New Jersey to Chicago. From Chicago to California a very loud explosion sound spread south and north of Interstate 80. People along this highway reported seeing tornados forming from the sky and clouds changing direction from east to west. An undetermined number of people were reported having ringing in their ears. North Korea has suspected the United States of shooting something into its airspace. They are in full tactical alert and are in defense mode."

Peters and Robinson sit in the back of the black government SUV talking as they are driven towards a military airport.

"The Pentagon says the UFO08 flew out to Jupiter at the speed of light and then it flew right into the sun destroying itself. Isn't that crazy sir?" Peters asks Robinson.

Robinson shakes his head and smokes a cigar.

"I wish I had a Cuban cigar, nothing like the taste of a Cuban cigar. They used to let us smoke Cuban cigars at Guantanamo Bay when I was in charge down there years ago. It was so nice playing by your own rules," Robinson says while he zones out

Peters continue talking about the UFO incident in the background. Robinson pulls out a lighter and lights a cigar. He opens his window next to him. The smoky haze of smoke flies out the window as he exhales. Major Robinson is day dreaming back to when he was sitting on the beach, with his sandals on, giving out orders smoking his Cuban cigars. He thinks about the taste of those cigars compared to the Dominican cigars he is smoking now. Robinson continues to mumble to himself smoking his cigar.

"...the speed of light, sir. This isn't fiction, or *Star Trek* or *Star Wars*; this is a real ship traveling around our solar system at that speed...." Peters continues to talk to himself.

"...the sand was so white, I was working, but I was on vacation..." Robinson says in a mumbling voice zoned out.

"If that kid is still alive, he would be the fastest flying human in the world!" Peters yells.

"... I want to retire on that beach, Peters..."

Peters is so excited, he doesn't notice Robinson not listening to him.

Robinson continues with eyes in a daze, "I wish we could invade Cuba and kick out the dictators. Why can't we put in a leader we choose, like we did for Haiti last year? America could greatly profit from the Cuban economy, the tax alone on those cigars...."

"The World Wide Web has pictures of the UFO and people are talking about it in chat rooms. Sir, are you listening to me?" Peters asks in a louder tone.

"Peters! What are you talking about? World Wide Web?" The Major asks.

"The Internet sir, it's getting more popular every year. It's going to be the new way of people communicating in the coming years."

"I heard about that, I don't believe it's going to amount to anything. You're wasting your time investing your paychecks in Yahoo and AOL stock. What the hell is a Yahoo? The government would control all of that in the future and control what is on the Internet."

"I don't know sir; private sectors are jumping to get online. I think Yahoo has a catchy name."

"That damn UFO ruined my promotion. We have a lot of explaining to do this evening Peters."

"I know sir, we can just tell the truth. We did our job as best we could."

Peters turn on the medium-sized TV to BNN.

"I can't believe military trucks have satellite TV in them. This is unbelievable."

"Yeah it is, but soon every citizen will have something like this in their cars and trucks. I wish the government would come out with something then keep it for themselves. Citizens always get our past down technology. Peters! Turn that up."

The television has scrambled signals as trees block the satellite's signal. Peters increases the volume by using a remote control. Robinson taps his cigar on the top of the open window. The ashes blow into the wind with the white smoke. The picture then comes in clear and the volume is very loud. Peters quickly turns it down as Robinson gives him a serious look. He then focuses on the 10-inch television screen behind the driver's armrest.

"… twelve people died, because of today's freak events," the news anchor pauses and listens to her earpiece.

"We will be going live in just two minutes, ladies and gentlemen for the President's speech in Washington. We now have Sandra live in Ballston Spa, New York, as she has the suspect Jaden's best friend in front of her. Sandra you're live," anchorwoman Betty says.

A few seconds goes by and Sandra talks into the camera.

"We are in front of a local autobody shop. I have suspect terrorist's best friend James White in front of me. Mr. White is your friend a terrorist and do you know where he is?"

James is a chubby, Caucasian, teenage male that is wearing a backwards NY Jets football hat. He has a few freckles on his face and chubby cheeks. He stands at 5'8", 215 lbs and has brown eyes. He talks into the camera with a smile on his face while the reporter puts the microphone under his mouth.

"My friend is no terrorist. He is nothing more than a pretty boy geek. I've been his best friend for the past ten years. Jaden where you at man? Stop hiding from the police and turn yourself in and clear your name," the teenager yells while smiling into the camera.

Another teenager walks up and yells into the camera, "Jaden is sticking it to the man! Fight the power Jaden. Don't give up! I'll be at the pizza shop later playing *Street Fighter Hyper* edition!"

The teenager quickly runs away. The news reporter is caught off guard and looks startled.

James has a smile on his face as Sandra puts the microphone to her mouth.

"Do you believe what the government is saying that he stole or helped steal a government experimental plane?" She asks.

"No way! He can barely drive good, he doesn't know how to fly a plane; he can barely beat me in *Flight Simulator, Doom 2* or *Mortal Kombat 2* arcade games. Come to think about it, I remember him telling me yesterday or the day before that he found a UFO...."

"Which day was it?" She asks.

"I have no idea, I was high at the time, I thought he was messing with me. That California ganja had me on cloud nine. I thought I was dreaming when he was telling me all that stuff over the phone."

"Is there anything you want to tell your friend?"

James looks into the camera, "Jaden stop hiding out wherever you are, before you fall behind in your school work again. The government towed your car and people are looking for you. Your mother and father are worried sick. Your girlfriend Amy is also looking for you..."

An older hippy looking man runs up to the news reporter and James. He is out of breath and breathing hard. He sticks his head between them and grabs the microphone.

"The government is grabbing up dozens of people, man. Some kind of conspiracy is happening. They grabbing up anyone who saw the UFO. They tried to put me in a van, but I ran and jumped in my Jeep. I took the back roads, but I knew they were still somehow following me..." the hippy man says while his white smoke breath reflects against the bright lights of the camera.

148

Black vans with flashing lights in the fenders approach from each direction on the small business street.

"Shit! Here they come! The Area 51 pigs! Save yourself!"

The out of breath man runs and the cameraman follows him running down the street. James sees unmarked police vans coming down the streets, tosses his bags of weed on the ground under the news reporter's feet, and takes a few steps back. The video is cut and back at the studio news anchorwoman Betty is looking into the camera with a serious face.

"We somehow lost that video feed. That was very interesting information we just received. Something odd is really happening all around New York today. We are going live to Washington, D.C., where President Clifford is giving a live speech to the entire world about today's events."

The BNN news channel switches to the President of the United States in Washington, D.C. The small auditorium is full of news reporters, cameras and bright lights.

"Good evening fellow Americans. Today was a day of long events. Today we were under attack by an unknown terrorist group. They stole a top-secret government plane and tried to use it against us. He or she was flying loose over New York and across the United States. We are not going to stand by while fellow Americans die and get hurt, due to a group of selfish people that don't like what we stand for. It could have been an inside job, but a full investigation is on the way. I gave the Air Force permission to fly at sonic speeds today to take out this threat..."

People around the country are glued to their television screens.

"... I know there were thousands of Americans that didn't know what was going on and are suffering headaches and ringing ears. However, we had to act fast. The top-secret plane was destroyed and we are looking for the few involved. The threat level has been raised and the threat has been taken out. Are there any questions?" President Clifford asks.

All the news reporters raise their hands at once. The President points at a reporter.

"Where is local news reporter Angela Clarke? Angela and her cameraman were investigating where this incident started early this morning in Stillwater, New York. Now they and a bunch of other people disappeared without a trace, where are they?" The older news reporter asks.

The President drinks some water and speaks, "I don't know of any people missing, and I don't know anything about the whereabouts of Angela Clarke. Maybe you should fill out a missing person report for her and those missing people in 24 hours," he chuckles.

"We have proof the government is rounding citizens up in black vans," the reporter shouts.

"Next question," the President shouts.

The President points at the next reporter.

"How is a local teenager, Jaden Marino, involved in this missing government top-secret plane? He, his friends and family don't have any connections to a terrorist organization. Is he considered a terrorist also?" A news reporter asks.

"I believe he was involved with an unknown terrorist group. Teenagers in college join many organizations and groups. This could have been one of them. You never know who might be crazy or a terrorist these days. There is also a chance he died in the plane crash when we shot down the stolen plane. If anyone sees him, turn him in. Next question," the President says with a straight face.

A chubby, young, white man with glasses stands up, with photos in his hands.

"Good evening President, I'm Michael Morris. I have proof that there was no governmental experimental plane involved and there were no terrorists involved. That this experimental plane was actually a UFO you were trying to shoot down. This has cover-up written all over it. Here are the photos of this UFO being chased by the Air Force. There are also witnesses that saw this alien plane being fired at."

The room is filled with people mumbling to themselves and flashing photos at Michael Morris. The President chuckles.

"Mr. Michael Morris, let me see those photos."

A secret service man grabs the photos and takes them to the President on the podium.

"There's no such thing as UFOs?" Mr. Morris asks in a laughing voice.

"Where did you make these photos up at?" The President asks.

"I didn't make them up; they were photographed by a photographer in upstate New York, outside of Stillwater."

"I can see the Air Force jets in the background, but that image looks like something that was made up. There are no such things as UFO's. If there are witnesses that saw this UFO, they should call the FBI and tell them what they saw. They would be more than happy to investigate these findings. Next question."

"I also have witnesses in Europe that reported seeing a UFO through their telescope flying at the speed of light in space...." he is interrupted by the President.

"Next question!" He yells, and then continues, "Does anyone have a question that doesn't involve accusations of an imaginary UFO flying around?"

"Yes, you!"

Peters turns off the television as they reach a checkpoint to get into the military airport.

"That was crazy," he says.

150

"That Michael Morris has always been a troublemaker. He put together this cover-up very fast. I'm sure him and his photos won't be making it out of the White House tonight," Major Robinson says.

"Sir, I've been to Area 51 recently in Nevada and went into some restricted areas over the years. I saw some things that were very puzzling. Did we actually land on the moon in 1969?" Peters asks.

Robinson looks up at the driver, suddenly looking up in his rearview mirror at him.

"Sergeant Peters, certain questions should never be bought up. If you see something puzzling it is good to keep it to yourself and use your imagination."

The SUV stops 100 feet away from a military helicopter sitting by itself. The driver runs and opens the door for the Major. They get out of the vehicle and begin walking towards the helicopter. The driver walks in front of them.

"We don't need an escort soldier," Robinson says.

"Yes, sir."

The driver walks back towards the SUV. Robinson and Peters walks together.

"I can tell you my logical opinion on the moon landing. The Russians were ahead of us in the late 1950's in all aspects of space and rockets. We were trying to play catch up during the entire sixties. Here is a simple concept, if the Russians didn't land a man on the moon or didn't bother trying, I don't think anyone made it to the moon," Robinson says.

"That concept always puzzled me in the back of my mind. I didn't want to think the possibilities were true. I remember reading the Russians never tried because they gave any human making it to the moon in the sixties, a 0.017% chance. One reason was the sun's strong cosmic radiation was too powerful outside of Earth's magnetosphere. Spacesuits would never be able to withstand that direct radiation on the moon. The flag waving as if there was an atmosphere present and perfect video footage behind huge spacesuits always bothered me over the years," Peters says while they walk up to the helicopter and open the door.

They climb inside and sit down.

"You are a smart man, Peters," he says with a smile on his face.

There is silence as the pilot walks towards the helicopter from a distance.

"My theory, Peters is, if you can't beat them, make up something to prove that you did beat them. It's all about having a strong hold on space and image is everything. America needed a confidence boost, since we failed to put the first man and first woman into space. We only launched two monkeys in 1959 and I'm sure the U.S. government wasn't going to just have that on record. The Russians were the first to launch a rocket into the moon in 1959. Radio telescopes from several countries backed and verified the impact on the moon. What other country verified the United States landing on the moon in 1969?" Robinson asks.

"None. That was where I read about the 0.017%. The instruments on that rocket to the moon in 1959 helped the Russian scientists determine it wasn't possible for them or anyone to land on the moon during that time. If it was possible, they would have done it already and I'm sure it would have been done in the early 60's," Peters responds excitedly.

"Exactly! Logically, if we landed on the moon in 1969, we would have landed on Mars in the 80's and today we would be landing somewhere around Jupiter's moons. The U.S. can barely go into space now without a disaster. I heard from a strong source, our next attempt to land on the moon would be around 2025. We are still developing powerful enough rockets to make it there and back safely and we are in 2000. We are developing nano-fiber materials with the Russians that can keep harmful cosmic radiation from penetrating spacesuits. Five hundred years from now humans are going to look back at the 1969 moon landing and ask how technology for the United States got worse. They had six flawless trips to the moon with primitive technology without anything going wrong. Then the next few decades, dozens of accidents and disasters just going into orbit...." Robinson stops himself to chuckle. The chuckle turns into a laugh as Peters joins in.

He coughs and clears his throat and continues with a smile, "That's like scoring A's on six advanced calculus tests then getting F's on algebra and B's in basic math. Then it takes you another fifty-six years to restudy and to attempt to get another A in advanced calculus."

"Wow. That is an amazing metaphor and concept, sir. If this were high school, any logical teacher or principal would have thought the student cheated. It boggles the mind how gullible Americans can still be twenty-seven years later. I was well convinced though for years. I do agree with you that humans in the future would look back and eventually figure it out. It is mind boggling that eighty-nine percent of Americans believe we landed on the moon while over seventy percent of people in the U.K. and Asia think the opposite."

"You gotta love the American government, with its secrets and techniques for covering up things and wanting to stay a super power in the world," Robinson says.

"You know something Major, the Russians were so smart, they knew it wasn't realistic putting a man on the moon so they put their energy into beating us again by putting the first space station into space in 1971."

"My father was heavily into the space race in the sixties. He couldn't figure out how MASA had a big fiery accident with the space program in 1968, and then the next year they had a flawless landing on the moon. He also used to talk about MASA scientists going to Antarctica to find meteors that landed from space in 1967. I miss my dad with his theories…. My dad used to say instead of two sides competing against each other, working together will take you twice as far," Robinson says.

"The Cold War was not about working together. It's interesting how the United States only landed on the moon when President Nixon was in office….."

The pilot opens the door.

"Hello sirs!" He yells while saluting. Robinson and Peters salute back.

There is silence as the pilot puts on his headphones with a microphone.

There is silence until the pilot starts to talk into the radio for clearance to take off. Peters whispers to Robinson, "I think the moon landing video should have been impeached along with Nixon."

They burst out laughing and Robinson's face turns red as he coughs very loudly.

A minute passes by and they fasten their seat belts. The helicopter blades begin to slowly rotate.

Robinson and Peters put thick headphones over their ears.

"Just keep cool and tell the truth as to what happened when in Washington!" Robinson yells over the helicopter's engine.

"OKAY SIR!"

The helicopter blades increase speed and make more noise. The helicopter takes off into the air.

"DO YOU THINK THE KID JADEN SURVIVED ALL OF THIS? DO YOU THINK HE IS STILL ALIVE SIR?"

"I DON'T THINK ANY HUMAN BEING CAN SURVIVE ALL THESE ORDEALS AND ESPECIALLY SURVIVE FLYING INTO THE SUN. THE SHIP IS DESTROYED AND SO IS HE!"

"I FEEL BAD FOR HIS PARENTS! THAT WAS THEIR SECOND SON THAT THEY LOST!" Peters continues, "I THINK THERE'S A CHANCE HE AND THE UFO08 CAN STILL BE ALIVE. THAT SHIP WAS VERY ADVANCED. IT'S PROBABLY TRAVELING THROUGH SPACE RIGHT NOW SOMEWHERE!" Peters yells.

"THAT'S IMPOSSIBLE!"

"I BET YOU $100 IN THE NEXT COUPLE OF YEARS, WE WILL GET A SIGNAL FROM THE LRSB!" Peters yells.

"YOU GOT YOURSELF A BET, YOUNG SCI-FI, STAR TREK, AND STAR WARS FAN. I'LL GIVE YOU TILL THE YEAR 2000 THAT THERE WON'T BE A SIGNAL FROM THE LRSB!" Robinson yells while grinning.

They shake hands while looking into each other's eyes while smiling.

Jaden's mind has several flashbacks

Everything is blurry, Jaden suddenly sees himself sitting in his classroom from elementary school. He is drawing something on paper, while his teacher is teaching basic math.

'I remember this and this teacher. That's Miss Hentinks! I'm in the third grade now, drawing the space shuttle Challenger. This must be around 1986.'

The teacher walked over to Jaden, "Why are you drawing, in my math class? Does this look like art class to you?" The class turned around and looked at Jaden.

"Sorry Miss Hentinks I wish I could have saved them. I did not want them to die. I don't like for people to get hurt or die. I want to be an astronaut one day."

A kid in the back of the room made a comment, "Jaden wants to be a superhero space monkey."

The entire class laughed. The bell rings and the teacher tells the class about the homework assignment, while young Jaden continued drawing.

"Space monkey, space monkey," the buck-toothed kid in the back of the room continues to shout. The bell sound fades away, so does the images he remembered.

A new image is forming, looking blurry and unclear. He hears a faint sound that he remembers that is getting louder and louder.

"Happy birthday to you, happy birthday dear Jaden happy birthday to you."

An image appeared and Jaden sees his family and friends around him. He sees his birthday cake he remembers that it said Jaden 13 on top of it. His older brother is at his side cheering for him.

"Make a wish, little brother!" Douglas yelled.

Jaden smiled and was so happy. He blew out the candles. His father, mother, aunts and his friend James are around him. He missed a candle, so Jaden blows harder.

'I remember wishing my family stayed together that year. I believe this was January 14, 1994. There was so much fighting between my parents that year. I miss my older brother so much.'

"Thirteen punches! Thirteen punches for Jaden!" Jaden's best friend James yelled. James a chubby, white boy that has cake all over his mouth, punched Jaden's arm thirteen times.

"Come on James, we are getting too old for the thirteen punches thing," Jaden said.

"Yeah, but I figured we could keep doing this until we both have girlfriends or married," James said.

James ran towards the backyard in the house with more cake in his hand. Jaden's five years older brother Douglas walked over to him. Douglas a brown-eyed, ladies man with a smooth voice, placed his arm around Jaden. Douglas wore an Aerosmith sweater, winter coat and blue jeans.

"You know little brother you're getting older and older each year. You're going to have to look after mom soon, with pop working so much. How's your karate class going?" He asked.

"They are going well I'm going to make brown belt by next year. What do you mean; I'm going to have to look over mom soon?"

"I wanted to tell you first," he paused and swallowed, "Listen younger brother, I'm going to joining the Marines when I turn 18 in June. I didn't tell mom and dad yet."

Light blue-eyed Jaden looked down at his ice cream birthday cake melting.

"The Marines? Why? Why can't you just go to college? I don't want you to go into the Marines," teary-eyed Jaden said.

"Don't worry Jaden, I'll be back twice a year and I'll have my own money for college. You know mom and dad are going through a financial situation now. I'll definitely be back to take you to your first strip club when you turn 18."

"Strip club? What's in there?"

"When you're 18, you'll know all about it."

"I don't want you go Douglas," young Jaden said.

"You'll be okay, I want the chance to explore the world and do something with my life," Douglas said.

Douglas walked to the backyard, by the apple tree while Jaden followed. Douglas pulled out a pack of cigarettes, and lights one.

"Douglas, why do you smoke cigarettes?"

"They relax me when I'm stressed and it's something I'm used to. They are not for you though. Don't smoke these, they are bad for you kid," Douglas said.

Jaden admired the white smoke floating away into the air. Jaden hugged his older brother and looked him in the eyes.

"If I had your eyes Jaden, the women would be all over me."

"What's so good about blue eyes?"

"It's something that women love and it creates a nice look for you. Us being bi-racial it's also not that common. You got pop's eyes, and I got mom's eyes."

Douglas took another pull of the cigarette and 4'8" Jaden hugged him quickly.

Douglas coughed up the smoke. "What are you doing little man?"

"Don't go Douglas; I don't want you to join the military. Please don't go, don't go, please don't go," Jaden said as the vision fades away into   *stars.*

The UFO's and Jaden's molecules are traveling faster than light through subspace. Jaden is looking through a nanoscanner as it passes through a never-ending tunnel covered in light particles. He sees thousands of stars passing by all around him in different sizes. Everything is inverted like a negative filmstrip that is not developed. Then he sees many different inverted colors. It is very quiet as Jaden is flying through sub-space. The stars have a purple bright grey color.

His mind has another flashback.

FEBRUARY 10, 1999 FRIDAY
ASTRONOMY 101 CLASS (FIRST WEEK)

"...astronomy goes way back to ancient times and became famous with the Egyptians. This was also a time where astronomy was also used in religion and used to explain the stars. It was used to help guide people from one location to another by using locations of the stars...."

'I remember this class; this is when that crazy good looking girl was hitting on me. She had long black hair, hazel eyes and a pretty smile.'

Jaden sat in the back of the lecture hall, while he listened to the professor. There is an attractive girl sitting next to him, looking at him and smiling. She passed him a note. Jaden read it: "Hey cutie, what are your parents? My mom is white and my father is black. I like your eyes. Are you single? Write back, I'm Claudine," the note read.

He turned to his left and looked at the attractive bi-racial female, smiling at him. Jaden replied and wrote on the same note.

"....We will be covering different areas of astronomy.... Procession of the equinoxes is the gradual shift in the orientation of Earth's axis of rotation..." the professor continued.

Jaden whispered, "What is this, high school, with the note passing? I'm dating someone now and my parents are the opposite of your parents. I'm Jaden."

"Hey, Jaden, nice to meet you. That is good, that you don't have a girlfriend yet. I usually don't come on to men, but I've been watching you all week and I'm attracted to bi-racial men," Claudine whispered with her hand over her mouth.

156

"Well, I'm sure you will find another mixed man, somewhere on this community college campus, but I'm spoken for already," Jaden said with his hand over his mouth.

"...Einstein's theory of relativity states mass-energy equivalence $E=mc^2$..." the professor continued to talk.

"There aren't many mixed men on campus and there aren't many good looking men that look as good as you. I think we would have good chemistry together," she said with a huge smile.

"How would you know we would have good chemistry together? You barely know me. I also told you, I'm spoken for already."

"...Einstein's theory of special relativity states that an object cannot travel faster than light in a vacuum, unless the object had special shielding around it..."

"Yes, you are right, I barely know you. But I can sense good quality and chemistry in a man when I see it. If she isn't your girlfriend then you aren't legally off the market yet. Besides, I think we can make a nice baby together, if we got together. Our baby will come out with question mark features. My eyes, your eyes or our parents' eyes. A spin on the chromosomes wheel of fortune..."

Jaden's eyebrows drifted higher, as he was amazed with her crazy talk.

"...we could connect emotionally and physically on different levels, since we both understand each other from being bi-racial. I feel we are soul mates. Our parents would accept us as being together..."

The professor walked up the stairs in the lecture hall towards the back.

"...Black holes are..."

Jaden interrupted her, "Is this what you do with your parents' money? Find the most attractive bi-racial man in college and calculate what a baby would look like with him. Then plan your future with him, before you know him?" he asked.

"My parents are loaded. I can have whatever I want. The way your eyes and face expression look now is such a turn on right now..."

"Are you on high on something? I think you need to find yourself another bi-racial experiment and you two should go on Jerry Springer."

The professor approached between them and he focused on Jaden. The entire class turned their heads to watch.

"Excuse me young man, what is your name?" Dr. Samuels asked.

"I'm Jaden Marino."

"I see you are having a private conversation in my lecture hall, I'm assuming you know everything I'm talking about," the professor said.

"I know most of it, doctor," Jaden replied.

"What is the galactic bulge and where is it?" He asked with this arms folded.

"The galactic bulge is located in the center of our Milky Way Galaxy. Our entire galaxy, including our solar system spins around this center. Every galaxy has a galactic bulge. It is made out of trillions of suns and is 80,000 light-years in diameter..."

Jaden is interrupted and the professor tried to quickly ask a question he might not know.

"What will happen to you if you fall into a black hole and what is a black hole mostly made out of?"

"If you fall into it, the event horizon, which is the area outside the black hole, will pull you in and rip you apart. The singularity is where you would be crushed down into the size of an atom. From what we know, it is made out of a collapsed star. It contains gravitational energy, dark matter and dark energy."

"Very good, Mr. Marino, I see you know something, everything was correct except the dark matter and dark energy, save the science fiction for Star Trek. There is no evidence that is what black holes are made of..."

"But how do you know or how can we know for sure it doesn't?" Jaden asked while Claudine looked forward with a smile on her face.

"Son, my lectures are about proven science, astronomy and scientific facts in space. You can watch Voyager if you want to learn science fiction. My lecture hall is not a place to rap to your neighbor for her digits. You can do that outside of my lecture classes. Now that we have spent a few minutes on Mr. Marino, can everyone please turn to page 30 in your textbooks...."

The professor walked away and Claudine passed Jaden another note. It read "I'm impressed, Bi-Einstein. We are having a party off campus next Sunday, you should come by. We are going to have a lot of liquor and bring a friend."

There is a heart at the bottom of it.

FEBRUARY 20, 1999 MONDAY
ASTRONOMY 101 CLASS

Jaden remembers this day the following week. He went to that house party with James, the day before. The psycho Claudine girl got him drunk and was trying to rape him in the bathroom. He could never remember a female so aggressive towards him.

The professor gave another lecture in class, "...22% of the galaxy has been known to be made of dark matter and 74% is thought to consist of dark energy. It is very hard to detect, but we know it is out there. It is what scientists believe holds galaxies together. There is more dark energy and matter in our galaxy than other nearby galaxies. They are smaller than an atom and they pass through solar systems and us humans as I speak...."

Jaden had his right hand on the side of his head, holding his head up with sunglasses on. It looked as if he was reading his astronomy book, but he was dozing off. He was dreaming about the party he was at the night before, where he was trashed. The memory fades away.

AUGUST 19, 1999 SATURDAY 1:45 AM

Jaden and his father Tony stand in their backyard taking turns looking through the telescope. Tony has salt and pepper hair on his head and face. His father stands at 5'8" 175 lbs with blue eyes and a full beard. Tony is full-blooded Italian, is in his mid-40's, and has glasses on. They both drank a beer and talked to each other.

"I'm proud son, that you had a good first semester in college. You graduating early from high school was a good idea," Tony said.

"Well thanks to you pops, you being the principal and all. The good grades and the few strings you pulled really helped out a lot," Jaden said.

"No Jaden, you did that all on your own son. You studied hard and graduated with the required credits."

"Well, thanks for putting the paper work through for me and getting me into this community college so fast. I kind of miss you having my back in school. I enjoyed being the principal's son throughout high school," Jaden said while he looked through the telescope.

"I enjoyed being there for you while you were in high school. So what are you going to do now with your life son? Where do you see yourself in ten years?"

"Well I hope to transfer to a four year Ivy League college. I would still like to get a physical science degree, then a master's in it. I want to try to pass the MASA's physical examination. If I can't get into MASA, then I'll settle for being a commercial pilot. I love flying things."

"Sounds like a plan son. I'm proud of you, in whatever you do. I'm glad I was able to be here for you while you were growing up. It is very tough being married and raising a family these days. My personal advice would be to get married in your late thirties and have children in your mid-forties. Be very sure before you get married or have any children. Be with the person for at least ten years before you think about having children with them. Women and men change over time, people grow into different people. They evolve into different people over time; find out what the female could grow into as early as possible. Spouses growing away from each other is the biggest problem in marriages these days. Divorce is much higher than it used to be and marriage just isn't the same anymore."

"I understand, pops. You've been telling me this for the past ten years...."

"I have to drill this into your head, because most teenagers make their life decisions around your age. Between seventeen and twenty-five are the years most men and women make their decisions for the rest of their life. Many young men and women around these ages think they know everything and ruin or change their lives forever. Men going to jail and getting criminal records for life, women getting pregnant at an early age, women being with the wrong man at an early age, getting on drugs, ruining their credit and joining the military are the biggest mistakes young people make during these years...."

His father opened another beer and guzzled it down. He started to talk with a slight slur in his speech.

"...the military stole my son from me. They used him as an infantry marine test dummy. He wasn't fully ready mentally to be on the front lines during the Gulf War. He was so eager to serve his country, to do things on his own and not listen to me. He could have joined the National Guard, non-infantry, Air Force or the navy to serve his country safely. He didn't think we would go to war the following year. I told him the United States is in some kind of war every ten years. We are always in the world's business; you never know when troops are going to be deployed..."

Jaden looked at his father with watery eyes. The moon shined brightly over them.

"You did your best pops. Douglas made his own decision for his life. It isn't your fault."

"I don't know what I'm going to do if I lose another son."

"You aren't going to lose me pop. I'll be here for you."

"Just remember, the people who run this country are very arrogant, money and power hungry. They want to eventually control us like animals. Our history proves this, cover-ups and conspiracies is the American government's way. They betrayed Douglas and covered up his

160

death. *Eventually they will betray you, son, watch your back. If all else fails, save yourself and the people you care about."*

"Pop, what are you talking about? You aren't making any sense. Pop, I think you are having too much to drink," Jaden said while he took the beer from his father's hand and placed it near the telescope.

"I'm not drinking too much, I'm fine. Give me that beer back."

"Let's talk about something else, then. You were beginning to sound like those freedom of speech protestors."

"Mark my words, we are going to be in another senseless war in the next ten years. We need another country to bully. Wasting trillions on invading another country when we can't even get our own country in good shape. Those trillions we spend on wars, that money could have been used on universal health care, giving every citizen a proper education and making our country stronger. You don't see China, Canada and Australia invading other countries..."

"Dad, dad dad! Let's talk about something else..."

"...No, I'm going to finish this last point about this country. Republicans are like religious backward thinkers fueled by money for the rich. They do the opposite of what democrats do. Democrats are like scientists and forward thinkers of change for poor and middle class. Independents are like traitors always choosing different sides. Republicans think in a collective, like the Borg in Star Trek. Special interest groups feed their pockets telling them how to think. The political system is a joke with both sides, mostly opposing each other..."

Tony's blood alcohol level passed .12. Jaden attempts to get his father out of his long politician discussions.

"Dad, what did you think of Amy last month when you met her at the BBQ?" Jaden asked.

"Your girlfriend? She's okay, for now. I don't think she is the one for you though," Tony said.

"Why not, what do you mean? You don't like her?"

"She is a good; good for now girlfriend. I don't see you being married to her. I can sense she is going to change in the future."

"How can you sense this?"

"She isn't sure of herself. She tried very hard to impress us, as if she was trying to hide something. She was putting up a front, that wasn't her true self. She is one of those people that would change ten years from now and you two would end up hating each other. Whatever you do, don't get this girl pregnant. I'm sure you will find your soul mate down the road. You would know deep down if she is the one for you."

"I know deep down now, that Amy is the one for me."

"Son, search your feelings..."

Jaden walked over to his father and placed his hand on his shoulder.

"You sound like Yoda from Star Wars now. Pop, I love Amy and I can picture myself being married to her down the road. I'm going to stay with her, no matter what happens, just like you and mom."

"You young people, with your falling in love with each other so fast. You are eighteen-years-old Jaden; you have the rest of your life ahead of you, why are you worrying about being in love so soon and thinking about marriage at such a young age?"

The question echoes in Jaden's memory. The images go black and fade away.

February 13, 2000 11:40 PM

Jaden drove home late from school after studying in the library. It was a cold, rainy, foggy night. He was on a road driving towards his home two miles away. There weren't any cars on the road. Jaden saw something glowing and floating in the air towards his right.

"What the hell is that?"

Suddenly a bright light shined from it towards Jaden's car. He pulled over quickly on a snow embankment. His tires briefly glided on the ice and the driver's door sprung open. He walked a few feet away from the car that is still running with the headlights on. Cold smoke left his mouth. The light quickly disappeared and the shiny object levitated in the air pointing towards him. Jaden felt as if the object read his mind and scanned his thoughts. The object quickly goes into the nearby field. He ran onto the private property. The images fast-forward and skip to him touching the UFO's wet outside. Static electricity came from the body of the ship to Jaden's fingers. He is hypnotized by its beauty and silver bluish color. The vision faded away.

Twenty minutes later Jaden went home and called James on the phone.

"James, James wake up," Jaden whispered on the phone.

"What? What? It's 12:05 AM."

"I found something; I think it is a UFO or something."

"Come on man, a UFO? You been eating those weed cookies again late at night? I remember the last time you ate too much of one of them. Tell Amy's friends to stop making them so potent and go by the recipe. You tripping out again and it's twelve in the morning. I'm still high from earlier and I have to wake up in six hours."

"I'm telling you man, I'm not eating any weed cookies. I saw something amazing. Then I saw government vehicles in the area when I was driving home. I'm telling you man, I saw something real. I'll tell you later, I forgot these phones could be being monitored."

"Yeah, tell me later, tell me about your new E.T. spaceship friends later. Later."

Jaden fell asleep in his room. The morning comes and he heard his parents leaving for work in the morning. He smelled the breakfast his mother left for him on the kitchen table. He woke up thirty minutes later, showered and dressed. Jaden turned on the radio and listened to the news while he ate his cold eggs, sausages, home fries and pancakes.

There was a loud knock on the door. He opened it and Major Robinson stood there with a serious look on his face. Jaden saw the military uniform and a cold chill went through his body. He stopped chewing the food in his mouth and looked the Major in the eyes.

"How can I help you today?"

"Are you Jaden Marino?" He asked.

"Yes, I am...."

The memory fades away.

FEBRUARY 14, 2000 9:30 PM

Amy pulled her Pathfinder SUV into a parking lot space outside of Saratoga Lake.

"Turn the car off and your lights," Jaden said in a loud whisper.

"Jaden, why can't you drive your car and why are you hiding in the back seat of mine?" she asked while turning around to talk to him.

"There are people watching me and following me. I saw people following me at school today."

"What people? You are paranoid baby," she said.

"I'm serious. Remember the spaceship I told you I found last night?"

"Yes. I thought you were just joking with me."

"Ever since I found it, I've been seeing government vehicles driving around town. Then I called James when I got home last night. I know the government was monitoring all phone calls in the towns. This morning, this scary looking military man knocked on my door to ask me about the UFO. James was the only person I called. I'm telling you, they are watching me and following me. They want to know what I found, so they could cover it up and make me disappear," he pleaded.

"Do you know how crazy you sound?"

"Yeah," he said while peaking out the back window.

"Baby, listen, I've been horny all day today. I'm so happy today is Valentine's..."

'Shit, I forgot today was Valentine's,' Jaden said to himself.

"...I want you to fill my hungry kitty cat up," she said while climbing into the back seat with him.

She pushed the front seats up and brought one of the rear seats down.

"Lay down on that side baby."

Jaden lies on the flipped down seat side. She took his jacket off and unbuckled his pants.

"Did your soldier miss me today?" She asked.

Jaden leaned up and looked out the side window as a car drove by.

"Baby! Your soldier friend is sleeping. He is never sleeping on me," she said.

"I guess he isn't ready for basic training today."

"I know the ancient secrets to awaken your sleeper cell soldier," she said while she climbed over him and kissed him on the mouth.

She kissed his neck, down to his chest and continued south. Jaden quickly thought about the Wheel of Fortune game show.

"Whoa! Ding, ding ding! I would like to solve the puzzle Pat: My soldier is ready for the Vietvagina jungle. You are correct! The audience applauses," he said while clapping his hands.

She giggled while Jaden laughed.

Amy pulled down his pants and climbed on top of him.

"Here's the condom right here," Jaden said as he waved it in the air as if he had a flag in his hand.

"Damn, that was quick. Did you pull that out of your ass?" She asked in a sarcastic tone.

"Yep, ass cheek pocket. I saved this special extra sensitive, almost like wearing nothing condom just for tonight."

"We can use that special condom in a second. Let me feel my soldier without his bulletproof jacket on first."

"You are a raw dog pirate matey I see," he said.

"Arrggghhhh matey, I'm taking your buried treasure and there is nothing you can do about it. Arrggghhhhh," Amy imitates a pirate while holding his arms down and slowly scratch up his arm to his chest.

A light reflected off Amy's body and the shadow of the light slowly moved behind her. Jaden entered her and she gave off a slight moan of pleasure. Jaden closed his eyes and enjoyed the instant feelings of pleasure moving up his spine up to his brain. Her eyes are closed and she had a smile on her face, while she gained momentum. She pushed up and down from his chest with her right hand. Jaden heard a car driving by from a distance and gets distracted. He held on tightly to the condom in his right hand.

"Baby, concentrate. How does that feel?" She asked as she rubbed her breast under her size 34D bra.

164

"It feels like two warm, slimy, meaty, wet fish smashed together."

"Silly! You saying my love hole smells like fish?"

Jaden opened his eyes and looks at Amy.

"Of course not, it smells like roses. But, I think we should put this on now."

"Okay."

"Hey, what car is coming up with those bright lights?"

Jaden leaned up, looked out the rear window as the slow moving vehicle pulled up closer with high beams on. Amy leaned down under the windows glass level while her ass continued to move. He gets nervous and his heartbeat increased and then the dark colored SUV parked in a parking space across from them. The images faded away.

FEBRUARY 15, 2000 5:05 PM

The doorbell rang at his parents' house. Jaden was upstairs doing his homework in the dark with a small flashlight and he heard it. Jaden's mother Stacey walked to the door. Jaden tiptoed to the staircase and listened.

"Ma'am I'm Sergeant Peters. I'm with the government special affairs unit..." he said while showing his ID.

Jaden panicked and his mind was moving 1000 miles an hour. He became very nervous and panics, but stayed focused to the conversation.

"...Your son Jaden Marino is wanted for questioning."

"How do you know I'm his mother and what are you questioning him for? Is he being charged with something?" She asked.

"No, we just want to ask him some questions about something he witnessed driving home two days ago. We also need to run some radiation tests on him."

Jaden began to pace back and forth while freaking out. He peeked out the hallway front window and saw dark colored trucks with government hazmat plates.

"Tests? What did he witness? Why aren't the local police questioning him?" She asked.

"I'm not at liberty to say."

She folded her arms and looked at him with a cold look.

"I'm not at liberty to help you then. My husband will be home in an hour, you can come back then. He was in the Air Force and he understands your language better than I do."

She closed the door and he put his foot in the doorway, right before it closed on him.

"Ma'am we need the boy to come with us now, or I will arrest you and him. Then I will charge you with interfering with a high-level government investigation. We are above local police and federal

165

jurisdiction. Let us talk to your son for a few minutes outside. You and your husband can meet us at this address," he said while handing her a card.

She looked Peters in the eyes and saw that he was serious.

"Jaden, come here for a second. Someone wants to talk to you!" She yelled.

Upstairs, Jaden's rear bedroom window was wide open.

"Jaden! Get your ass down here, when your mother is calling you. I know you hear me!"

Peters listened to his earpiece, "The jewel is on the run."

"We will be back ma'am," Peters said while he turned around and jogged to the truck.

"Jaden! Where are you?" She asked while closing the front door.

Jaden jogged through neighbors' backyards, with his head down.

'You assholes aren't getting me and making me disappear. I've seen enough conspiracy shows. I know where I'll hide, where you can't find me at,' Jaden said to himself while breathing heavy.

The images fade in and out. Another image shows him in the cornfield. Everything goes completely dark in the flashback.

ACTION BURGER WEEKLY MEETUP GROUPS.

NEW:
NFL MADDEN '15, 25TH &
NBA 2k15/2K14
tournaments. Wednesdays
6pm-12am

"ACTION AFTER DARK"
Karaoke, Just dance,
Guitar hero & Smash
bros. Fri & Sat 10pm-3am

XBOX HALO 1-4 LAN
BATTLES.
Thursdays 6pm-12am.
Bring your controller
and friends.

To join or to learn more about our meetup
groups, join our facebook page or goto:
www.actionburger.com to sign up.

Chapter 4: Virtualatrix

Jaden opens his eyes for a second and then he closes them. Jaden is on a hospital bed. His eyes open again and see a bright white light over him lighting up the room. The room is slowly spinning as if he just got off a fast ride. Sunlight is hitting the floor under the closed blinds. There are a dozen white roses on a black desk near him that his nose senses. He turns his eyes and focuses on someone entering the room he is in. A familiar looking doctor is walking towards his hospital bed with a chart in his hand. The Caucasian doctor is in his late 40's and is clean-shaven. He is wearing green scrubs.

"Jaden how are you feeling today?" The doctor asks.

"I'm feeling okay, where am I? What's going on?"

Jaden looks around and sees he is hooked up to a heart monitor machine. He looks at his hands and touches his head. Jaden feels bandages around his head.

'Something big happened to me, but I can't remember anything,' Jaden says to himself.

"Where am I? What hospital am I at? How did I get here?" He asks the doctor.

The doctor pauses for a few seconds, "You're at Stillwater Medical Center in New York. You were brought here by ambulance; you were in a car accident."

"Why do I have bandages around my head?" He asks.

"You hit the windshield pretty hard son. You had a concussion, but you're going to be okay."

Jaden looks around.

"You're my private family doctor, why are you working in the emergency room at this hospital?"

"Jaden you hurt your head pretty bad, maybe you should relax and take it easy. Your mother will be here soon," the nervous eyed doctor says while walking away.

"Oh my God, I have such a headache. What the hell is going on here? I can't remember any car accident," Jaden says to himself quietly.

Jaden relaxes in the soft, white hospital bed. A nurse wearing an all white uniform comes into Jaden's room. The nurse walks over to Jaden smiling. Jaden knows he has seen her somewhere before. She has red hair and a medium-sized figure.

168

"I'm Nurse Marge and I'm going to take your temperature young man," the nurse says in a European accent. She pulls out a thermometer. "Now if you don't mind, can you bend over so I can take your temperature?" She asks while putting lube on the thermometer.

Jaden looks at the nurse as if she is crazy.

"Bend over?" Jaden asks her in a shocked voice.

"I'm nineteen years old lady, you going to put a thermometer up my ass? You want to put your fingers up there too?" Jaden asks in a sarcastic voice.

The nurse pauses for a few seconds and says, "I apologize, can you open your mouth instead?"

She retrieves a new thermometer, Jaden opens his mouth and she places it under his tongue. He then mumbles looking directly at the nurse, "I'll put something up your ass."

The nurse gives an innocent smile and hands Jaden a small cup with a few pills. She takes the thermometer out of his mouth and says, "98.6 perfect."

"What are these pills for?"

"They will help your pain go away in your head."

"The pain only comes when I think about the past and what happened to me. Why is that nurse?" Jaden asks.

"You'll have to ask your doctor that," the nurse gets up and leaves a cup of water for Jaden.

She walks away and is interrupted by Jaden, "What day is today?"

"Today is February 16th"

"What year?"

She pauses for a second and looks Jaden in the eyes.

"Today is February 16th, 2003. Oops, I'm sorry, today is February 16th, 2000," she says as she turns back around and goes through the door.

'What is going on here? I can't remember anything short-term. Every time I do, my head hurts more and more. Let me take these pills, maybe I'll feel better.'

Jaden sees blue and red pills in his hand. Jaden takes both of them. He closes his eyes, and relaxes. He quickly falls asleep. An hour passes and the doctor returns.

"Jaden are you feeling better, how was your nap?" The doctor asks.

Jaden slowly opens his eyes. Everything is blurry; he tries to focus on what is around him. He sees the doctor sitting on the bed next to him.

"I'm a little better, my headache seems to be gone," Jaden says while he rubs his head looking around. He notices Nurse Marge is standing behind the doctor smiling. She looks as if she lost a few pounds.

"Nurse, Marge, how was your Valentine's Day yesterday?" Jaden asks.

She pauses for a few seconds, and says, "It was fine."

169

"Did Homer Simpson get you something nice for Valentine's?" Jaden asks, as the nurse rubs her red hair. The doctor turns around and looks at her.

"Yes it was fine; my boyfriend took me out somewhere."

"Where did he take you to?" He asks in an inquisitive voice.

The doctor interrupts, "Jaden, you know your mother is outside and she will be here in a few minutes. Why don't you leave Nurse Marge's personal life alone," the doctor says in a calm voice looking Jaden right in the eyes. He continues, "How was your rest? Has your head been feeling better?"

"I can't remember much about the accident, but I feel something else happened to me, but I can't remember. When I do start to think about it, that's when my head starts pounding."

"Try not to think about your past, concentrate on getting better and getting some rest. We have some more tests to run on you tomorrow."

Just then, Jaden's mother Stacey opens the hospital room door and walks straight towards Jaden with a nervous look on her face.

"Jaden are you okay?" She asks, as the doctor stands up from the bed and stands near the nurse. He whispers something into the nurse's ears. Stacey holds Jaden's hands and rubs his head as he lies in bed with scratches on his face and body.

"I'm fine mom," Jaden says as he hugs her.

The doctor and nurse walk out of the room.

"Mom, there is something going on here. A few things don't seem right. The doctor is our private doctor, but he is here working in a general hospital. I'm also in the same emergency room I was in when I sprained my ankle in karate school years ago. I'm also in a private room in the emergency room, I know this is expensive. Also, when I think back to what has happened to me, my head still hurts a lot," Jaden says quickly as he tries to catch his breath.

"Jaden, baby, everything is going to be okay," Stacey says.

"Where are dad and Amy?"

The mother pauses for a few seconds, then responds, "Your dad is at work and I left a voice mail for your girlfriend Amy."

"What happened in the car accident I was in? How did I crash?"

She pauses again and puts her right hand on his shoulder, "Jaden, baby, umm, the police said you were drinking and driving..." she is interrupted.

"Drinking and driving! How can that be?"

"I know you drink and drive sometimes Jaden," Stacey says.

"How would you know that mom?"

The mother is quiet, and then hesitates, "I'm your mom, and I know everything about you."

"Mom, are you okay? You don't sound right. You're sweating and talking with a nervous voice."

"I'm fine son; your daddy would be over to the hospital tomorrow."

"I know he is upset, especially with the car insurance being in his name."

"He isn't upset, he is just happy you're okay. He didn't say anything about the car being wrecked."

Just then, the phone rings. It rings again and Jaden answers it.

"Hey dad. We were just talking about you. I'm fine, I had a headache earlier. Now it's gone."

There is a thirty-second pause as Jaden's father speaks to him.

"Love you too dad." Jaden hangs up the phone.

"Now you get some sleep son; me, your dad, and Amy will be back tomorrow morning."

Jaden's mom kisses him on the side of the face. She walks out of the room.

'I know something is wrong here. My father isn't upset, my mom isn't talking right. Amy didn't come to the hospital first or call,' he says to himself.

"Wait a second! Amy! I don't remember what we did for Valentine's together!" Jaden yells.

He grabs his head, as it starts to hurt again. Jaden begins to feel dizzy and the room begins to spin around. The phone rings. Jaden is feeling very dizzy and his head is hurting so much that he can't answer it. The nurse and the doctor rush back into the room. The phone stops ringing. The doctor gives him a shot. The nurse and the doctor are talking to Jaden, but he can't understand what they are saying. Jaden turns his head towards the window and he sees the sun setting. Jaden closes his eyes and opens them. The sun appears as if it is rising up from the horizon and moving at a fast speed. The sun and the view look blurry like a TV with bad reception. Jaden closes his eyes and falls to sleep.

It's dark, a buzzing sound is heard, but there is no image of anything. A humming buzzing sound, that sounds familiar to him. Jaden sees quick images. He sees an image of him in the back seat of her SUV... Amy is crying next to him and he hears words.

"I don't care about what you saw, where is my Valentine's Day gift?"

The voice and images fade away. He sees an image of him flying in the air at a fast speed. That quickly fades away and it goes dark again. There is a sound of wind blowing by his ear. Jaden hears many voices at once. Everyone is talking together, while it is completely dark. A distinctive female voice is heard clearly through all the other voices, "We will come soon. We will come for you soon." The voice fades into the many other voices being heard.

"Listen you little shit... Wish you were never born. Never born, never born." Then they all fade away.

Jaden wakes up and lifts up from the bed in a cold sweat. The sun is shining bright into the room. He rips the heart monitors from his chest, turns to the right, and swings his legs off the bed. The linoleum floor is icy as he takes his first steps. Jaden looks around the quiet room. He stands up and walks over to the wall in front of the bed.

"What kind of hospital room doesn't have a TV inside of it?"

Jaden looks at the solid wall. He touches it.

'Why does it feel like I'm being watched?'

Jaden walks over to the window and feels the breeze on his body. He sees people walking around downstairs. There are many trees outside the window. Jaden is very confused as he remembers images from his dream.

'Something big happened in the last week or a few days ago. I can't remember anything that has happened. A lot of things aren't making sense.'

His headache returns and he ignores it. Jaden walks over to the door and tries to open it. However, it is locked. Jaden pulls on the door harder as he panics.

"I have to get out of here. I have to get out of this hospital."

The knob on the door is being fumbled with. Someone is trying to open it from the outside. Jaden steps back from the door. It opens and the doctor walks in with the nurse behind him.

"Jaden, what are you doing out of bed? You need to rest. I know you're not used to being in the hospital, but you need to follow the rules here."

The doctor puts his arm around Jaden and walks him back to his bed. Jaden, with a confused and angry look on his face, pushes away from the doctor. Jaden takes a few steps back.

"Something is going on here. I want some answers."

Jaden stands on the other side of the bed, looking at the doctor on the other side of it.

"Why is it I can't remember anything from the accident? Why does my headache come back when I think about what has happened to me?"

The doctor clears his throat a few times. "Jaden you had a mild concussion and you have slight amnesia. Your memory should come back soon," the doctor says while taking a step closer to him.

Jaden continues in a confused voice. "Why did that nurse agree that her boyfriend is Homer Simpson? Why did she try to put a thermometer up my ass like I was 1-year-old? Why do I feel like I was only sleeping for an hour and the sun is back up?"

The doctor and nurse just stand there and look at Jaden. The phone rings and Jaden hops over the bed. He answers the phone.

"Hello?"

"Jaden, Are you okay? I miss you," Amy says over the phone.

"Amy, what did I get you for Valentine's Day?"

"You didn't get me anything, it's okay."

'Something is wrong here, she always takes Valentine's Day serious,' Jaden thinks to himself.

"What happened in the back seat of your SUV on Valentine's Day that you were crying?"

"I don't know what you're talking about Jaden. I didn't see you Valentine's Day. I was busy studying for my test in college."

'This girl would find time for Valentine's Day. I know I saw her two days ago.'

The doctor and nurse are still standing there just looking at Jaden. Jaden holds his head while still talking to Amy on the phone. His head starts to hurt a lot. He ignores it.

"You don't remember having sex with me on Valentine's Day in the back seat of your SUV?"

"Jaden, I told you what I was doing. Now baby, I'm coming to see you in the hospital later this afternoon and....."

Jaden hangs up the phone.

"That's not my girlfriend," Jaden says while standing up.

"Doctor, I'm still waiting for the answers to my questions."

"Jaden you need to calm down, sit back down and relax in the bed," the doctor calmly replies.

"I'll relax when I get some answers that make sense!" He shouts.

Jaden picks up the phone and tries to call his best friend James.

"The number you have reached has been disconnected," the phone says.

Jaden tries to dial the number again and it's the same issue. Jaden starts to take deep breaths.

"My friend James' phone number has worked for the past fifteen years, now it's disconnected two days later?"

The nurse leaves the room.

"I have to get out of this hospital. I feel like I'm being watched. This place doesn't feel real."

"Jaden, you can't leave the hospital until you are properly checked out. You have to be checked out by a doctor. You're going to have to stay here for another two days, until I see you're fit to leave. You're getting very delusional; we might have to find you a psychologist. You might have to stay here longer than that then," the doctor orders

"You are an outpatient doctor. You work full time at a private practice. My family has been going to you for years. This is not how you normally act. You have answers for everything. Now I'm here asking you questions, that you obviously are ignoring. You do know that questions require answers right? Now stop playing stupid with me!"

173

The doctor puts his hand on Jaden's shoulder again. Jaden brushes it off. He hops behind the bed again.

"I'm remembering now. I was being chased by men in white suits…"

"Jaden, why don't you take your pills, so you can relax? You really are not well," he doctor says while handing them across the bed.

Jaden knocks them out of the doctor's hand while yelling, "I don't want any more of your pills! I'm getting out of this B.S. hospital now."

The door opens quickly as two men in security uniform walk inside with the nurse behind them. They stand by the door.

"Oh man, this is getting funnier by the minute. You two work for this hospital also? You two used be security guards in my high school. Now you work here?" Jaden asks.

"Come on, where is the *America's Funniest Home Video* cameras at?" Jaden asks.

The security guards don't say anything, but look at Jaden with a straight face.

"You see Jaden, we don't want to have to use any force against you," the doctor says.

"I can take those two guards without a problem, then I can take you out also you fake Russian KGB doctor," Jaden says in a confident voice.

"Then you would be charged with assault, Jaden. Do you want a criminal record to follow you the rest of your life?"

Jaden stands up and gets into a karate stance.

Just then, Jaden's mother opens the door. She runs between the big hospital security guards and past the doctor.

"Mom, how did you get here so fast? You said you were coming late in the morning with dad. Don't you have to work today?" Jaden asks.

"Are you okay son? Don't cause any problems in the hospital," Jaden's mother pleads.

"Mom, how are we paying for this hospital visit?"

"Son, what are you talking about?"

Jaden reaches out and grabs his mother's purse.

"Jaden what are you doing?"

Jaden is looking through his mother's bag. Everything looks blurry inside. He finds her wallet. Stacey looks shocked to what her son is doing. She tries to grab her wallet back, while Jaden pushes her away. He finds her insurance card. Jaden turns it around and it is completely blank. Jaden stands there surprised and drops the wallet on the bed, while still looking at the blank card.

"Mom, you have a blank insurance card?"

"Son, we have universal health care now. We don't need insurance cards anymore."

"Universal health care in America?" Jaden asks while starting to laugh. He continues, "Do you actually expect me to believe that? You

174

never showed me your insurance card in the past. I know this place is a fake."

Jaden walks over to the closet and says, "Where are my clothes?"

"Jaden your clothes are in a safe place," the doctor replies.

"Jaden what are you doing? You're breaking your mother's heart," Stacey says while beginning to cry.

"You're not my mother, that isn't my doctor, and this can't be a hospital."

Stacey begins to cry. The doctor pulls out a syringe and squirts it into the air. He looks at Jaden while folding his arms. Jaden walks towards the door and the big 6'3" and 6'5" guards stand in the way. The guard on the left is Caucasian and bald and the guard on the right is African American with a full head of hair.

"I have a black belt in karate and a yellow belt in jujitsu. I would suggest if you don't want to get hurt and end up being in one of these hospital beds, get out of my way."

"Sorry, we can't do," the guard on the left says while pulling out a straitjacket.

They rush to grab him and the nurse stands back towards the door. Jaden gets into a karate stance. A wind blows the blinds behind Jaden. Jaden throws two straight punches into the one guard's chest. He falls backwards and has the wind knocked out of him. He loses balance and hits his head on the wall. The black guard on the right grabs Jaden's arm. Jaden quickly grabs his arm also, gets closer to him, and elbows him in the face. Jaden then pulls him around and flips him over his back. The guard flips over and bounces on the bed and then onto the floor. Jaden is feeling energetic and stronger than he normally feels. The guard on the floor behind the bed holds his face and grunts in pain. The white guard gets up from the wall breathing heavily. He pulls out a baton and comes towards Jaden. The nurse flings the door wide and runs out. His mother is hiding under the bed crying. He jumps towards the wall and kicks off it. He forms a kick in midair, while kicking the guard directly in the face with the bottom of his bare feet. The guard falls back into the wall very hard, making the entire room shake and causing a loud thumping sound. Jaden reaches out and grabs the door before it closes. He swings the door open and walks outside. The doctor lunges from behind and tries to stab Jaden with the syringe. Jaden grabs his arm and pulls it hard forward. The doctor loses balance and hits the hallway wall headfirst.

175

"Does anyone else want some of the jujitsu/Tae Kwon Do experience? I'm giving out free universal ass whippings," he says as the doctor lies on the floor holding his head moaning.

"Hey doc, take those pills for that headache you're going to have."

Jaden walks away from the doctor lying on the floor. He turns around and walks back towards the doctor on the floor. Jaden grabs him by the shirt collar.

"What is going on here? Why are you people messing with me? Why can't you answer any of my questions?"

The doctor just laughs while blood is pouring from his head. His voice changes and it sounds much deeper.

"You don't know what you're in for. Ha ha ha. I don't know where you think you're going."

Jaden walks down the hall and says to himself, 'That dude sounds like the *Hellraiser* dude.'

"You can't leave!!" The doctor yells, while continuing to laugh.

Jaden walks quickly down the hallway. Nurses and patients look surprised as Jaden begins jogging down the hallway. Jaden is looking at their faces and they all look very familiar to him. He knows he has seen these people before. He remembers some as being in his college and two people were his neighbors that moved away. Jaden is puzzled that everyone in the hospital looks familiar to him. He looks up at a loud ear piercing voice coming from a loud speaker.

"We have a code red, on the third floor. All units please assist situation on third floor, room 305," the overhead loud speaker says.

Jaden turns around a corner. He sees an emergency staircase. He looks down the stairs and it's dark, but then it brightens up. A cold wind hits his body and face. The continuous wind brings shivers around his body. The stairs stop at the second floor. Jaden opens the door and walks slowly down the hallway. He looks all the way down the hallway on his right and sees how dark and fuzzy looking everything is in that direction. The walls look alive as if they are adjusting around his vision. There looks as if dark images are forming and then disappearing when his eyes focus. On the left, it is dark, but there is a room with light coming from it.

"This doesn't even look like a hospital now. There are no people around here."

Jaden jogs over to the bright door and opens it. He sees another door inside. He stands on his tippy toes and is amazed at what he sees. Jaden sees six doctors standing around two beds in a large room with dingy grey walls. Jaden stares as if he is seeing a ghost. His body is frozen and he can't move. Feelings of shock move around his nervous system like an S.O.S. signal.

176

Jaden sees two copies of himself lying naked, surrounded by doctors in the middle of the room. One is strapped onto a portable hospital bed. The other is on an operating table strapped in. He can't believe he sees exact images of himself. Feelings of disbelief and cold chills go up and down his spine. Jaden needs his eyes to prove he isn't seeing what he thinks he sees. He opens the door and looks around the room and his eyes open very wide. The bright fluorescent lights shine down from the ceiling. The room is moving in slow motion around him. He sees more of his lifeless bodies on the wall hung up like coats. The strong smell of being at a morgue with dead bodies attacks Jaden's nose. He covers his nose with disgust, but his mind is too determined to find out what is going on. The doctors look at Jaden surprised as if they are caught in the act. He is determined to find out what is going on and stares at their eyes behind the masks.

They have blood on their gloves and bloody tools in their hands. Jaden counts about eight clones of himself all around the room. The three on the wall are missing limbs. They are still breathing, but don't look like they are in pain. Jaden notices that the clones on the wall to the right have dark patches around where the arms and legs are cut off. There is a small room with windows towards the rear left. There are two Jaden clones walking around like zombies. There is another closed off room with a huge window to the right with another cloned Jaden with his head on the glass and hands on the side of his face watching Jaden. Jaden quickly walks over to the operating table and pushes a doctor out of the way. A feeling of shock goes from his eyes to his brain and around his body.

Jaden sees his clone in a zombie state of mind with his arms down to the bone and muscle, deteriorating. Red muscles are all around the body and the eyes are missing. Blood is coming out of its arms. The hands are just bones and veins. Jaden gets very upset at what he sees. The doctors stand there not knowing what to say or do.

"What the hell is going on in here? You people cloned me and you are doing experiments on me! You have me walking around naked with a half-sized penis!"

Jaden grabs the closest doctor near him. He rips off his mask and instantly recognizes the face. The adrenaline rushes to his muscles. He grabs the collar of the white overcoat and lifts the doctor up in the air while chocking his neck. Jaden feels puffy fur protruding from around the doctor's neck area. But he doesn't see any fur there. There is nothing but anger in Jaden's face as he tries to get to the bottom of this.

"You're no doctor; you're my fourth grade teacher! I want some answers, or I'm going to beat it out of you, Mr. Stevens. Then I'm going to beat some answers out of my clones!" Jaden yells while accidently spitting in the fake doctor's face. Mr. Stevens is speechless while gagging to breathe.

Suddenly the door swings open and something quickly enters. Jaden tries to turn around and a security guard hits Jaden over the back of the head with a baton. Jaden falls over and lands on top of the doctor. The doctor pushes Jaden off him.

They begin communicating in a high-speed alien language.

"Why is he down here?" The doctor's voice changes into a deeper voice.

"We don't need him anymore. We just need his brain, body parts and more blood. These human brains are difficult to copy while they are still in the host," the doctor that looks like Jaden's fourth grade teacher says.

Jaden lays on the floor unconscious. The five guards are standing over him. Two of them lift his lifeless body and put his arms over their shoulders. They carry him outside the room. Then they carry him down a long hallway. Jaden briefly opens his eyes and sees the hallway lighting up as he is carried down it. Looking further down past the light it is completely dark. Jaden feels like he is in a scary movie and it's moving in slow motion. He is semi-conscious and his speech is slurring.

"Where are you taking me? What is going on?"

They ignore him and Jaden continues, "Why? Why do you feel so. . . so hairy, when you have a uniform over your body?" Jaden mumbles in an incoherent voice to the guards carrying him. They ignore him.

"I don't see any hair there." Jaden smiles at the guards, while he begins to feel the pain from the blow to his head.

"Why- Why do your hands feel like . . . like claws, Mr. Security Guard? Also. . .Your breath smells like. . . like... like a dog that eats human food. Ha ha."

Something catches Jaden's attention above him; he looks up towards his right on the ceiling. Two bright eyes without a body light up near the ceiling.

Jaden still out of it and half-awake thinks he is seeing things. He hears several footsteps behind him.

Jaden turns his head to get a good look at the guards carrying him down a hallway without any doors.

"You two aren't security guards. You two are the officers that came to my house to tell my family my brother died a couple of years ago. Who are you guys trying to fool?"

They reach a poorly lit room at the end of the hallway. Jaden is coming too, but can barely move his body. He notices the room looks like an operating room. They lay him down on an operating table in the middle of the room. A doctor with a smile on his face walks up and injects Jaden's arm with a needle.

"You bastard, what did you inject me with?"

The doctor leaves from in front of Jaden.

The room looks like an all white hospital operating room, with dimmed lights.

'I can't be on Earth, where the hell am I? What is going on? I can't move my body. I can't move anything,' Jaden thinks to himself.

Four security guards stand by the door and watch. They lick their lips as if Jaden is food to them. Jaden is only able to move his eyes and mouth.

Jaden taunts the guards, "When I get out of here I'm going to break your arms and then feed you your fake badges."

More of Jaden's memory starts to come back to him. He remembers being in the UFO and flying through space.

Suddenly the doctor comes out with an object looking like a circular saw in his hand.

"So you couldn't stay in your room and go along with the program huh?" The doctor asks while ripping open Jaden's grey hospital shirt.

"Why are you doing this to me?" Jaden asks in a frightening voice, while continuing to struggle to move.

"I'm going to do a lot more to you. First, I'm going to remove your heart while it's still beating. Then I'm going to quickly remove your brain. How do you humans say it? This won't hurt a bit."

"Why did you bring me to this planet, all the way from Earth to kill me?"

"Us? Us? Ha ha ha ha," he pauses for thirty seconds and continues laughing.

The security guards at the door laugh.

"We wouldn't waste our time on a maggot human like you. We would definitely put every single one of your body parts to good use."

"I'm a maggot? You're a maggot and your mama's a big nasty horse fly that eats brown shit all day," Jaden snaps.

The doctor laughs and says, "We don't look nothing like you ugly humans. Your disgusting sweating and dirt particles constantly leaving your skin is beyond disgusting, you maggot."

"You wouldn't call me a maggot if I wasn't paralyzed in this chair," Jaden says while struggling to move.

"What kind of aliens are you people? How do you look human? You aliens look like people I know."

"Your primitive brain is so easy to manipulate into believing anything."

The doctor continues to laugh while starting up the small circular saw. Jaden tries to move, but is paralyzed like a spider's victim stuck in its web. The loud spinning blade grabs Jaden's full attention.

"Can't we all get along? There is no need for violence now," Jaden says while nervously smiling.

The doctor puts the quickly spinning circular saw towards Jaden's chest then pauses.

"That's a good one. Can't we all get along? That was from the L.A. riots a few years ago right?" The doctor asks.

Jaden thinks that they know all of his memories.

"Yeah, why can't we humans and aliens get along? Come on guys, we should have a universal friendship here. There is just too much violence in the universe," Jaden says in a persuasive voice.

Jaden begins to perspire and shake, "Didn't we learn anything from *Star Wars* and the Borg? Killing someone isn't the answer to solving intergalactic disagreements. If you want to clone me and torture my clones go ahead. If you want me to go back to the hospital room and play along, sure I can do that. But there is no need for alien on human violence."

"You humans are nothing but slightly evolved animals. You can kill animals and eat animals and you don't think anything is wrong with that..."

"I didn't kill any animals...."

"You eat meat, you are guilty, you are an animal. This is nothing more than cutting up an animal. When I'm finished removing your organs, the rest of your fat, muscles and skin will make a nice meal for the guards by the door. You humans make tasty meals. To us you taste like hamburgers," the doctor says.

"Eating me? I'm not food! I'm no Big Mac!" Jaden yells while trying to struggle.

"You won't have to worry about anything in the next few minutes. You humans are excessively violent to each other. Those memories you have, of the riots, world wars, violence upon each other and all the other things in your history are. .are. . ." he pauses, "The point is, you humans should be used to it... enough talking and stalling, okay? Time to die."

TORAGON

THE GOD OF ALL BURGERS

 # TORAGON
Ultra evil, ultra tasty.

2 beef 6oz burgers with crispy chicken in the middle. Pepper Jack, provolone, spicy mayo, grilled onions & bacon. Served on a brioche hero.

Chapter 5 The rescue

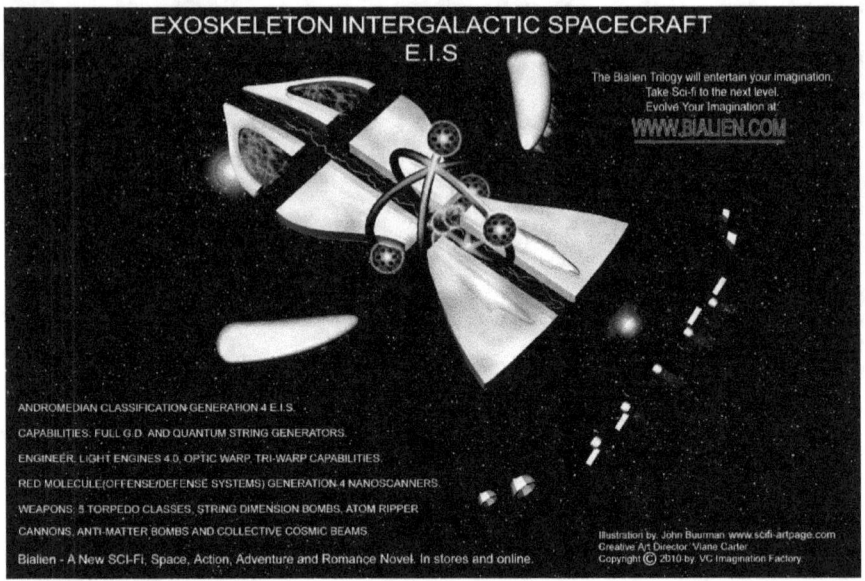

He puts the circular saw towards Jaden's chest, closer and closer. Jaden's eyes are focusing in on the high-speed blade creating a breeze towards his chest and face. The sharp circular blade pierces Jaden's chest causing him tremendous pain. Blood splatters in all directions, but floats upwards. He yells in agony and the guards begin to laugh. His blood forms half-inch round balls. Jaden blacks out and goes into shock from the pain quickly overloading his brain. As Jaden closes his eyes, he sees two bright eyes without a body on the ceiling above him. The doctor takes off his glasses and looks in confusion at the blood floating upwards. The blood bubbles disappear as they get near the ceiling. The mad doctor continues to cut downwards to his upper abdomen. The lights flicker then go out. It is completely dark in the room. The doctor stops cutting and yells to the guards still laughing.

Suddenly something falls from the ceiling and there is a lot of noise and scuffling in the dark. There is a glowing object that resembles a sword, quickly moving back and forth in the air. The glowing blue weapon has red lightning jumping around it. The yells turn into loud screeching sounds and stuff falling over. Something is sprayed over Jaden's open chest wound. Something is then injected into his neck through his jugular vein that mixes with his blood. It is completely dark in the room and it goes quiet. Jaden's large chest wound stops bleeding.

Jaden, still unconscious, is lifted from the operating table by something. His body is put over the shoulder of a warm alien being. The lights flicker in the room and Jaden regains some consciousness. He sees the doctor with blood all over his jacket and the circular saw going through his head. Jaden moans in pain as he tries to figure out what is going on. Jaden's body is being carried towards the door. Jaden hears a high pitch sound that sounds like a fax machine.

Then, a very fast speaking female voice is heard, "I'm Bellona and I'm here to rescue you. I'm trying to get you outside this virtual hospital and underground city. Your body will remain paralyzed and your lungs will stop working soon. You will be holding your breath for about ten minutes once we get out to the surface. My team and I are trying to get you off this planet. Your normal vision will be back very soon."

The fast talking voice echoing from all directions stops. He was able to make out most of what she said. Jaden sees himself being carried by a silvery alien body in the reflection of a mirror on a wall. It has two legs like a human. Jaden is able to turn his head slightly. Jaden notices this alien has six fingers that look human, with an extra thumb. The extra identical thumb is on the opposite side of the hand and is providing an extra grip on Jaden's body. He is facing down towards the ground while his legs and lower body are over the shoulder of this alien rescuing him. Jaden sees pieces of the guards lying on the floor. He looks again and the image is distorted. The pieces of the guards turn into hairy pieces of an animal with claws where the hands used to be. Bellona looks through the door in both directions. Jaden looks behind him in the room and the room changes. It changes from a bright operating room to a dark, slimy room. The skinny alien begins jogging down the long hallway. Jaden feels high up in the air, as if the alien is at least seven feet tall. His body is going up and down with the fast movement. The hallway turns into a tunnel. Jaden notices a clear force around them. Jaden hears many footsteps. They go up many stairs. He is petrified since he can't see what exactly is going on. Bellona stops running and stops against a wall. The air is turning very humid and Jaden is breathing very lightly. The footsteps go by at a fast speed down the stairs.

Jaden believes they are cloaked and invisible like the UFO spaceship. They go through a door. They continue to run down this eerie tunnel with low light. Dark colored trees and vines are appearing all over the place. Mist is in the air and reminds him of being in a sauna at the gym. The tunnel opens up into a large room with high ceilings that resembles a gymnasium. The room has vines, trees and plants all over the place, similar to a greenhouse. Bright light is shining on Jaden and Bellona from the light emitting trees. She has small light particles inside her skin as she gently puts Jaden against the wall sitting up. Jaden sees the alien figure that resembles a human body walking forward. Her body looks smooth and similar to a female human with curves. She walks like a human being.

Fourteen hairy, black animal-looking creatures approach. They are called Zetrobs. The Zetrobs are hairy creatures that look like a half gorilla with two very hairy legs with feet and an upper body like a beetle, with little antennas coming from their heads. The Zetrobs are making loud animal sounds. They also have a round arch around their backs like a beetle and four claws that extend out like hands. The Zetrobs line up and fire a green liquid from their claws at her. Bellona instantly forms a shield three feet around it. An awkward sound comes from the formation. Another smaller shield forms around Jaden as the sounds from the middle of the room go quiet. A slight humming sound is also heard in Jaden's ears. The complete bubble-shaped shield extends into the wall digging into it. His vision becomes blurry and altered by the clear shields around him. It looks similar to looking through a clear lake. He can't hear anything except the humming sound.

The two-foot long spray, that looks like flying vomit, hits her outside shield and goes around it. Smoke is coming from the ground where the alien creatures are firing their toxic poisonous acid. The shield turns completely green as all of the Zetrobs continue to rapidly fire at the same time. Jaden can see through the green material over her shield.

Jaden is hypnotized by her warrior stance as if she is ready for battle. She stands fearless as the animal creatures surround her while continuing to fire. Two red molecules suddenly appear around her wrists. The molecules look similar to the ship's molecule, but only six inches in diameter. Her body looks like a blur as she begins moving at high speed. She punches holes through her shield in the direction of the animals. Green glowing balls of energy fire like high-speed cannons towards the enemies. Their green toxin that was absorbed into the shield's energy is being used against them. They are hit and their bodies are quickly penetrated and ripped into pieces. She is moving so fast it looks as if there are two female aliens inside the shield punching holes in different spots.

Jaden witnesses this and is speechless. Bellona stands there with these red molecules spinning up and down her arms in sync. They begin to glow very bright red. She looks up towards the ceiling. She puts her arms together over her head. The two molecules slowly move upwards and leave her fingertips. They merge and get larger as they float near the top of the shield above her. Jaden sits there speechless and is unable to blink his eyes. The single molecule is about four feet in diameter. Bellona extends her right hand towards the ground. Jaden feels an invisible force quickly passing under his legs and towards the female alien. She quickly extends her arm towards the molecule above her and an invisible force leaves her arm. The force propels the molecule through the shield and towards the ceiling in a red flash of blurry light. Bellona turns around and walks towards Jaden, sitting against the wall in disbelief. Some debris falls from the newly created hole as air is quickly sucked through it like a vacuum. Branches, body parts and vines are pulled into the ceiling's new hole.

The shield disappears and the particles go into her back. Smoke comes from the lifeless body parts. Some of the creatures' bodies pull towards the ceiling. She walks back towards Jaden. Jaden is mesmerized by her walking towards him. Her beauty and brawn captivates Jaden. He knows she can't be human, but a cross between a mechanical robot and human. Bellona has something over her face that resembles some type of mask the same color as her body. He looks deep into her blank face with no hair sticking out from the mask. Her two wide eyes are glowing white, like an eyeball without pupils. Her iris reflects the light that is behind her. Her chest looks like a mannequin's breast, smooth, but no nipples. There are hundreds of white light particles slowly moving around inside her skin. Her legs are skinny and muscular. She has six fingers, but no fingernails. Jaden sees no lower female body parts. He feels she is someone here to save him, he feels safe and comfortable around her. Jaden also feels helpless since he is still unable to move. This alien female warrior stands in front of him and stares deep into his soul.

"Who are you? Why are you helping me? What's going on?" Jaden asks but doesn't get a response.

Bellona picks him up again and places him on her shoulder. She quickly walks to the middle of this large room, stepping over slimy hairy body parts. Air is sucking out of the four-foot octagon-shaped hole above them. The howling sound of wind moves around the silent room.

Suddenly the ground shakes and thirty hairy creatures begin coming from the walls in all directions. These creatures are called Blisters and they have long white and black hairs around their body. They walk upright and stand about 5 feet high. They are more organized and walk slowly in formation about thirty feet away. These Blisters have different shiny metals over their bodies. Similar to knights in the old days, but without the swords or shields in their hands. They also have a large, shiny hump like a beetle on their backs. They have two black antennas sticking from their helmets. Their eyes are at the end of the antennas. The creatures only have two arms and a metallic mask over their heads. They have an object looking like a weapon, in their right hand. The weapon looks like narrow silver Television remote controls a few inches in size. They appear to float a few inches from their hands. In their left hand, they have invisible shields over their ant-like faces.

They fire yellow energy beams at Bellona in the middle of this room that Jaden is still over the shoulders of. The yellow energy beams hit the outside of her shield and bounce back in different directions. This time it bounces back off the Blisters as each has their own clear invisible energy shields that light up over their left arms. The beams bounce onto the walls and in all directions making holes in the walls. She fires a blue six-inch round energy projectile into the air with her left arm. It passes through her shields and floats about twenty feet in the air and gets larger. It spins around clockwise very fast, drawing some kind of energy from the large room. Jaden is held tightly by her right hand.

The Blisters charge towards her from all directions still firing, weakening her shields. The shields get smaller to about two feet around Jaden and her. She begins to run towards the wall knocking creatures out of her way, with the shield following with her. The shield is getting smaller and smaller. Jaden notices her body is getting smaller. The blue projectile explodes in all directions. The Blisters dive and dig into the ground with their claws to keep from floating away. Their antenna eyes look out to see what is going on. The blue projectile makes the entire area lose its gravity. They continue to fire at Jaden and Bellona. She jumps on the wall and begins to run vertically up it. Jaden hears her loud thumping footsteps. The Blisters stop firing as they hold on tighter from the zero gravity in the room. Everything is happening so fast for Jaden; he feels as though he is in a dream. Some lose their grip and float towards the vacuum hole forty feet above, making loud screeching sounds. They are sucked in like a dust ball into a vacuum cleaner.

Jaden doesn't even feel like he is on a wall. His up and down balance makes him feel as if he is on a ground surface. They reach the ceiling and run on it. Bellona detects something coming below. Jaden looks towards the ground and he sees a different type of huge, robotic alien creature with a long neck. The Skeleborgs' are translucent down to the skeleton bodies, as if you are looking through an x-ray. They are about ten feet in diameter. Their white glowing bone structure can be seen through their synthetic skin and muscles. Their outer body suits are invisible to Jaden's eye. They have a dark helmet over their skinny faces with glowing green eyes. They have long glowing arms that resemble a weapon. Their weapons are purple and extend out where the hands would be. They walk on the ground not affected by the gravity disruption in the room. Their big size makes Jaden believe their weight is keeping it from floating away. It stands there looking up and gives Jaden the creeps. He swallows saliva as it looks up at him. Their staring at him makes Jaden's blood pressure increase.

"That thing looks very scary, it's almost eight feet tall and wide like a fat girl at an all you can eat," Jaden says while keeping his eyes on it.

The equilibrium in his ears goes out of sync and he feels very nauseous looking down. The howling octagon hole in the ceiling gets louder and louder. Jaden's lungs stop breathing on their own. He feels as if something is making him hold his breath. The robotic alien fires a fast moving orange ball with a ring around it from its left arm towards them. Bellona tosses paralyzed Jaden into the hole head first and the shield goes around his body. He feels a powerful acceleration as he falls upwards. The orange ball explodes creating a large explosion. A huge amount of debris and rocks fall all over the place. Jaden sees fire that looks like small spheres in front of him. He is surrounded by fire from the explosion. The blast greatly increases his speed as he freefalls up the dark hole. The powerful blast hits the female alien directly. Her body sustains heavy damage and is on fire. There are microscopic robotic organisms called microbots, attacking her body through the fire. Her legs amputate from the torso and suck through the hole. Her fiery left arm floats away, but quickly pulls back towards her body by a magnetic force. Her body sustains hundreds of holes through it. There are clear seals over the area where her legs were cut off. Her left arm is floating two inches from her torso, where her arm came off at.

The Skeleborg extends both of its hands upwards. Bellona's eyes glow very dim and she can't move. Her severely hurt body is caught in some kind of tractor beam, slowly pulling her downwards. The fire on the ceiling blows out into the hole. Everything is happening so fast.

Jaden is less than a mile from the surface. Jaden is falling upwards faster than an express elevator. His arms are to his side and his body is straight as he continues to fall upwards with fire all around and the clear shields protecting him. Jaden hears noises like a fax machine and dial-up modem, but much faster.

The Skeleborg's microbots are attacking the inside of her body. The defensive nanobots inside her body are trying to fight them off, but are being overpowered. Bellona is twenty feet away from the Skeleborg, when suddenly its head disappears. The upper body expands outwards. An open area that resembles a shredder with spinning teeth replaces the head and neck area. She is about to be pulled into a spinning vortex of glowing razor sharp teeth. She is fighting the tractor beam energy with pro-gravity nanobots quickly moving around her body, pulling her upwards. But it is not overpowering the Skeleborg's tractor beam around her. Most of her energy is going towards protecting Jaden and keeping the shield energy around his quickly propelling body. She needs his body to make it to the surface. Microbots are trying to enter a secure area in her brain. The force of the tractor beam slowly detaches her head from her body. There is magnetic energy pulling between her neck and head. The army of Blisters is holding onto the ground and lifts their heads simultaneously and fire at Bellona. The beams fire together and hit one targeted area on her body creating a hole through it. Her body reacts to the penetration.

An army of nanoscanners quickly enter the octagon hole from the surface of the planet. They quickly pass Jaden's lifeless falling body and reach Bellona's amputated free falling legs that are on fire. The nanoscanners quickly spin around it, dissolving them into molecules.

Her head separates from her neck by nine inches and is two feet from the spinning mouth that will destroy her. She feels tremendous pain as her body is being pulled in two different directions. Her very low energy body is not responding.

There is a dimly lit red dwarf star in the sky above. The galactic center's light is also shining brightly over the surface from the west. Jaden is moving upwards at a very fast speed and reaches the surface. His uncontrollable body continues upwards by the side of a large rocky mountain. Fire explodes around him and in different directions as he spins sixty feet into the 1% oxygen atmosphere. Jaden can see and feel bright sunlight shining over the top of the mountain. There is also some dim red sunlight shining behind Jaden. The ignited fire around him quickly goes out. His body descends as the planet's gravity takes over. Jaden is falling towards the ground, but not as fast as he would on Earth. He is about to hit the ground and closes his eyes to brace for impact. He abruptly stops a few feet from the ground, when something grabs him. The shield around Jaden's body goes off and another one quickly forms. He is being held by something invisible with feathery and hairy large arms. Jaden can't see its face, but assumes it's someone on Bellona's team. It begins to run with Jaden over a rocky surface. His body slowly bounces up and down.

There are purple and green dagger-like crystals of many sizes all around the surface of the planet. They point up as high as fifty feet from the surface. They point out into different directions and some sit on top of mountainsides.

"I'm Marco and I'm going to get you to our ships not far from here," he says in a deep robotic voice.

Jaden understands, but doesn't reply. Feelings of confusion continue to cross his mind.

The Skeleborg has its arms around Bellona's head, slowly pulling it into its mouth. The top of her head is being cut away by the hot plasma energy teeth. The nanoscanners reach down the hole where Bellona is at. They quickly spin around her body, changing her molecules into energy. Her body and separated head disappear into a flash of light into the tunnel towards the surface. The billions of microbots are left behind and float into the Skeleborg. It then jumps upwards towards the ceiling with thrust coming from its feet and elbows. The alien's huge body shrinks in size as it reaches the tunnel. It fires another large orange projectile upwards towards the flash of light moving at a fast speed.

The flash of light reaches 153 feet over the surface of the planet and stops. There is a bright beam coming from a nearby star and another source of sunlight coming from Andromeda's Galactic Bulge. Bellona's energy molecules begin to form back into her body. Hundreds of nanoscanners spin clockwise reforming her body with the help of the sunlight. Her body has trillions of yellow spinning light particles reforming her into solid matter. Nanobots are quickly moving around the inside of her body creating glowing light particles. Her silver body returns and something comes out of her back. Semi-visible wings that resemble an angel's wings come out her back and levitate six inches from her back. The wings are not touching each other and extend down to her buttocks. The trillions of spinning yellow light particles disappear from around her body. Glowing blue particles come out of her arms and disrupt the gravity around her as her wings slowly flap. She quickly flies towards the ground.

Marco is carrying Jaden, across rocks, sand and debris. He closes his eyes and he is able to see through a nanoeye. Jaden sees Bellona's body floating like alien angel in the bright sunlight. He is still not breathing and is holding his breath. It is amazing to him he is able to hold his breath for such a long time. Jaden realizes they must have done something to him when he was in the UFO.

The orange projectile comes out of the tunnel in a glowing blur of energy straight towards Bellona. She fires an invisible force from her right arm, hitting the projectile head on. It explodes into a horizontal line of spherical diamond fire, lighting up the shadow side of the mountain. She passes through the fire and continues downwards. Jaden has a front row seat to the fireworks show. She quickly reaches the ground near the tunnel and kneels from the sudden impact. The wings on her back disappear into her body. She makes two fists and puts them together. She pulls them apart and a glowing sword forms. The weapon has blue lightning jumping around a yellow light that extends 2 ½ feet. The tunnel glows and she swings her weapon downwards just as the Skeleborg exits.

Jaden witnesses a second colorful explosion splitting in two directions. The Skeleborg is split into two pieces and then explodes. The energy sword disappears into Bellona's hand as she runs towards Jaden. The nanoeye is not controllable by Jaden.

Jaden hears the low fax machine sounds around him again. The alien carrying Jaden appears and he is able to see its entire body through a nanoeye. The alien resembles a male figure and his size and shape intrigues Jaden. The blue and orange alien is about ten feet tall. His light blue semi-metallic frame is wide. He has orange fur all around the top part of his body. Around the skin of the alien is a shiny blue metallic body. There are small white light particles moving up and down inside the skin. This alien looks like a powerful fighter. He has several chrome spikes two feet long coming from his back and up to the shoulders. Red lightning particles are jumping around between the spikes on its back. There are red molecules on each wrist of the alien. His arms are long and furry and look somewhat human. His face is covered by something that looks like an exotic blue chrome helmet. His round reflective helmet glows different colors. Jaden continues to stare at the color-changing helmet.

Both aliens run together. Jaden does not feel like Marco is running. They both go invisible again. Jaden, still unable to move, turns his eyes to the right and sees a clear energy shield a few inches from his eyes.

They run across an open, rocky field. There are large, shiny metallic discs half way into the rocky ground all over the place. The galactic bulge's bright sunlight shines on them as they carefully run around the huge metallic discs that are arranged in an orderly fashion. The light is so bright that Jaden has to squint to see what is going on. His eyes cannot tolerate the bright light so he closes them. Jaden feels as if he is dreaming. Nothing feels real.

The ground starts to shake and rumble. The bright light fades away from Jaden's closed eyes. They run between a small passageway that resembles a ravine. The small mountains on each side are separated by about thirty feet and are about twenty feet high.

Six enemy spaceships approach them from the same direction. The ships are called cubfighters and look like flying brown stingrays. Each double wing is levitating a few feet from the body and they have white thrust coming from the rear of them. They stop midair simultaneously and their bodies begin to glow. They fire two sets of brown laser beams at them. Marco and Bellona's shield systems become very visible and absorb the powerful blasts. They stumble from the sudden impact of force. The ground is shot up around them creating a lot of dust. The holes in the ground go down dozens of feet. Jaden experiences the forceful movement with his new friends, but concentrates more on trying to breathe. He tries to inhale, but he feels as if he has a plastic bag over his face. His body is still paralyzed and he struggles to get some control of his body. He wants to move his arms around his throat, but he can't.

Marco tosses Jaden to Bellona. His body feels weightless as it glides ten feet through the air. The feeling instantly registers in his long-term memory as a feeling he felt when being tossed into the air by his father when he was a toddler. Jaden feels as if he is being tossed around like a Raggedy Ann doll.

Bellona holds Jaden against the wall and they are invisible. Marco runs towards the opposite wall and takes on the green laser fire. His shield takes on the powerful blasts. Suddenly, the dozens of chrome spikes on Marco's back stick up and float a few inches from his back. The red molecules on his wrist begin to spin in circles and light up red. He sticks his right arm out and a spike from his back travels through the molecule on his wrist and turns into a long metallic weapon in the shape of a spear. The weapon has light particles moving up and down it. His right hand holds the long barrel weapon that looks like a sniper rifle and a rocket launcher combined. The edge of his red spinning molecule is at the grip of the gun, somehow powering it. Marco quickly approaches the mountain and his body becomes semi-visible. His body disappears into the solid rock. Three cubfighters quickly circle around and levitate over the area scanning for them.

Suddenly Bellona becomes visible with Jaden in her arms and begins running down the ravine area. The cubfighters turn and begin firing at her. The barrel of Marco's four-foot long semi-visible weapon pokes from the top of the mountain. The weapon moves in a blur to three different positions in less than a second. In each position, a glowing silver projectile was fired towards the cubfighters at near the speed of light. Jaden hears a low popping sound from a distance behind him. The three cubfighters quickly propel backwards into the air and explode into brown fire. They are completely destroyed. There are three more cubfighters at a distance approaching. Marco pulls himself up from inside the mountain and is not on top of it. His body turns visible as he quickly begins to run. His body is moving so fast that he looks like a blur of energy. The weapon disappears through the molecule on his arm and returns with the rest of the levitating spikes on his back. The molecule on his left arm is missing. Another spike from a different area on his back floats upwards, changes direction and passes through his right molecule. A lime glowing green weapon forms in his hand. The weapon looks organic with light particles moving around inside of it.

The three cubfighters fire their green lasers simultaneously and they merge and hit the mountain behind Marco. A white energy leaves the cubfighters' bodies and quickly rides the laser down to the mountain. Marco is running on top of the mountain and his feet thump the ground shaking the entire mountain. The entire mountain explodes under his feet and he leaps into the air at the last second. Marco's left red molecule is rotating and floating about a ½ mile to the left of him in the sunlight. Rocks and fire explode around Marco's body as he falls. He fires three green projectiles from his exotic weapon without even aiming it at the red molecule. The molecule redirects the projectiles towards the three cubfighters levitating together. The molecule slightly changes directions in milliseconds. The cubfighters are hit from behind and quickly drop towards the exploding mountain. They go down and the fire explodes upwards. All three crash into the fiery mountain at high speed. Marco lands on the ground below; there is a loud thud and energy disperses in different directions. His knees bend slightly and he quickly runs towards Bellona. His weapon disappears and floats around towards his back again. Rocks and debris continue to fly in all directions. He dodges medium-sized fiery rocks as they fall. The mountain Marco was on is completely destroyed. Dozens of diamond-shaped flames form towards the sky. Marco hears debris hitting the other mountain and rolling to the ground. Fire and rocks completely cover the path behind them.

Sunlight appears again around Bellona and Marco as they run together across a rocky field. The three cubfighters that fell towards the mountain were not completely destroyed and quickly fly from the fire. Suddenly the bright sunlight fades away. Something dark is blocking most of the sunlight from the galactic bulge and local star. It looks as if a double eclipse just took place. There is a slight glow coming from where the bright light was. There is a low screeching sound coming from behind them. Jaden begins to gag and suffocate for air.

An army of one hundred beetled Blisters start coming out of different holes in the large mountain behind them. Their arms extend like legs and they run like a quadrupedal animal. The Blisters have another layer over their bodies like synthetic suits. A half dozen seven foot Skeleborgs run behind the Blisters. The Skeleborg's have transparent bodies. Their slightly white glowing bone structure can be seen through their synthetic skin and muscles. Their outer suits are invisible to the average eye. In their right hands are glowing green plasma swords. The Blisters fire their yellow lasers toward the rescuers. Jaden and his new friends helping him reach a small hill. They turn around to see the Blisters from a distance. The yellow beams strike around them, bombarding the mountainside with debris. Small light particles appear around their bodies as they jump up and float towards the top. The cubfighters coordinate their fire together into one brown laser beam. The beam creates small diamond-shaped flames around it and hits them directly. The force propels their bodies into the side of the mountain. Bellona has Jaden over her right shoulder and her left hand pushes off from going into the mountain. The powerful beam strongly disrupts their shield energy. They change direction and they begin running up the mountain. Hundreds of small rocks fall down the mountain. Marco's shields begin to get weaker as he runs faster towards the plateau area. Jaden goes into cardiac arrest and stops gagging as Bellona quickly runs up the mountain. Something sharp like a needle leaves Bellona's arm and goes into Jaden's vein. Fluid quickly enters his bloodstream.

The plateau area they are trying to reach has boulders and rocks falling over it. Suddenly the ground starts to shake all around like a magnitude 6.0 earthquake. On the far right of the large mountain is a smaller one that is about two miles from Jaden. The top half of the mountain explodes and creates a large mushroom cloud into the mostly carbon dioxide atmosphere. A UFO with a blue molecule around its hull quickly comes out of the mountain emitting the matrix plasma beams. A second ship follows with a purple molecule around its hull. This ship looks identical to the one Jaden was flying. The trotting Blisters stop running and look back at the large explosion from the mountain. It rains dirt, metallic rocks and debris into all directions.

Marco makes it to the plateau area first, which is about 120 feet from the ground. Boulders completely cover the area. Light particles come from his molecules and move through the boulders. He quickly changes his energy shield into a long horizontal rectangular shape that goes under the boulders. Marco's body goes semi-invisible and runs through the huge boulders.

The UFOs fire cannon rounds at the cubfighters. The cubfighters' shields glow pink. The UFOs fire two sets of yellow torpedoes that split into two more sets. The cubs fire dozens of red lasers towards the torpedoes. The torpedoes create their own energy shield around themselves. The red laser slows down the torpedoes causing them to break into pieces. The cubs fire mini red cubes the size of a paperback book. The glowing cubes synchronize their shield draining green lasers at the UFOs. The UFO ships quickly dodge the incoming green lasers. The torpedoes form back together hitting the cubfighters. The nanobots in the torpedoes eat away at the cubs' energy shield, creating holes in it. The cubs take cover by retreating in different directions. The two UFOs go after them.

Two of the four robotic aliens use their thrusters on the bottom of their feet and arms to go airborne.

Bellona is standing invisible and absorbing incoming fire. Her body quickly turns -200°F and Jaden's body instantly freezes. Marco begins to lift the entire boulder area with the horizontal energy shield. The area shakes and a forty square foot horizontal shield lifts with hundreds of tons of boulders on it. He lifts it over his head and Bellona runs under it with frozen Jaden in her arms. Two flying Skeleborgs fire their primary weapon from 250 feet away. Four bright orange balls propel towards the plateau at 300 feet per second.

Bellona places Jaden on the ground; he lays there as if he is inside of a coffin made of clear energy. Marco holds the boulders and horizontal shield with his left hand. His right hand disappears and the large weapon appears. It lights up aqua blue and a projectile is fired towards the orange balls. Bellona also fires an invisible energy from her right arm. They destroy three of the four projectiles. The last one explodes near them knocking them backwards. The powerful blast propels their bodies across the ground and the area is engulfed with fire and strong winds. Bellona continues to concentrate on her shield energy around Jaden. Marco lays flat on his back and the horizontal shield quickly falls within two inches of his face, but he holds it up with two hands. Bellona and Marco's bodies are on fire and take damage as they both lift the horizontal shield with boulders on top of it. The Skeleborgs charge their primary weapon system. Marco walks towards the edge of the plateau area, while holding onto the boulders above him with his left hand. He stands there, a huge flaming warrior. Bellona holds the horizontal shield area from the middle of the plateau area with two hands over her. The army of Blisters beneath him stands up on their hind legs and continue to fire towards Marco. His body takes several direct hits. Marco swings his right arm forward near the horizontal shield and downwards. A congregation of glowing huge

194

rocks propels from overhead and move in sync with Marco's arm movement. The rocks head towards the ground at 1000 feet per second. They slightly glow as they bombard the army of Blisters. Several Blisters are struck and the rest aim at the rocks. They dodge and roll to avoid being hit. The high-speed rocks create holes in the ground and debris explodes in different directions. Marco's right arm spins clockwise in 360° rotations and some rocks continue to move like cannonballs.

The fire burning in all directions shows fiery images of two other advanced looking UFOs parked behind Bellona and Marco. Microbots are in the fire attacking their bodies. Their spaceships are parked to the far right and left of the plateau area, UFO3 sits on the left side and UFO4 sits on the right. The ships have completely flat bodies and six separate floating pieces connect the ship together. There are red lightning particles in the middle and front of the UFOs. There are floating ball particles spinning under the ship and through the rings of each red molecule. A clear wave of energy from UFO3 suddenly spreads into different directions putting out the sphere-shaped fire like a fire extinguisher. The clear wave of energy contains a trillion nanobots to fight the 500 billion microbots in the fire. Bellona walks towards her exotic flat UFO4 ship and a giant red molecule appears and comes out towards her. It leaves the ship and moves over her body and creates a red light as bright as a red dwarf star. The energy balls are quickly moving around the molecule tracks. Her entire body glows red and turns as bright as the sun. The light can be seen for miles as a long flash of bright light. Marco stops firing the projectile rocks towards the Blisters. He realizes the Blisters are able to dodge each rock and he needs something that delivers a harder impact. The Skeleborgs fire their orange projectiles towards the red light from a distance. UFO4 fires a few cannon rounds, from the top of the red molecule. It passes over Jaden's frozen body and towards the orange projectiles. They collide and there is an explosion. Marco tilts and curves the horizontal shield with his right arm, into a 90° angle. Tons of rock slowly crushes together as one side is held vertically. Marco looks up into the sky as if he is doing calculations.

Everything is happening so fast. The bright red light fades back into the molecule and it goes back into the ship. Bellona's body changes into a more reflective chrome tone. There are trillions of white particles quickly moving all around and inside her metallic skin. There are alien symbols all over her body that resemble tattoos that look as if they are in 3D. The joints on her wrists, knees, upper arms, elbow, waist and neck aren't attached to her body and levitate between one-half to two inches. Magnetic energy separates and holds her joints into place. There is a small red molecule moving up and down on both of her arms. Small chrome fingernails slowly grow from her six fingers. She is still partially covering her face and looks as if she is ready for battle. She quickly runs over to pick up Jaden and puts him into her ship. In the meantime, Marco swings his right arm up the vertical side of the shield containing the rocks and boulders. Rocks the size of basketballs shoot into the sky at 900 mph. Marco continues to swing and propels hundreds into the dark sky and some the size of a car. The Skeleborgs fire towards Marco. The Blisters fire their weapons towards Marco, when they figure out what he is doing.

Suddenly, a larger shield appears around the entire plateau area in the shape of a huge contact lens. Marco's ship is creating the large shield. The other two orange balls explode outside the larger shield, creating fire and a shock wave all around the mountain. More large rocks fall from high above the plateau area and into Marco's 90° energy shield pile.

The Blisters begin climbing the side of the mountain. Marco finishes launching several thousand tons of rocks into the atmosphere of the planet. His horizontal and vertical shield disappears. His ship quickly extends the shield over the area the boulders were at. Two Skeleborgs are floating outside the shield area and pink glowing cubes come from their chest areas. The cubes quickly spin in circles around each other, emitting an infrared beam towards the shield. It slowly breaks down the atoms in the shield in a two-foot area.

The bright gigantic bulge sunlight is still blocked by something making the area dark as if it was night. Three cubfighters can be seen exploding in the far background with UFOs 1 and 2 flying behind them. Bellona sees the Skeleborgs trying to penetrate the shield with their anti-shield weapons to drop a bomb inside. Suddenly a rock comes from the sky at 9500 mph and lands where the Blisters are, just missing one. The resulting sound echoes and a three-foot crater is created in the ground. The gravity of the planet increased the force of the boulders and rocks Marco fired into the upper atmosphere. They begin to rain down over the area. Bellona runs and her body goes invisible. Her personal shield forms around her body. She leaps into the air and her shield passes through the larger shield. The shield disappears and her body slowly begins to rotate 360°. She puts her two fists together and pulls them apart. She forms two identical sword-like weapons from her fists. Everything is happening so fast and the Skeleborgs see two spinning swords coming at them. The sword has baby blue lightning jumping around a yellow light that extends two and a half feet long. The lightning jumps two inches and bounces back from a small clear shield surrounding both weapons keeping the energy intact. There are millions of anti-hydrogen glowing particles moving around the outside on the sword creating a smoky haze. Her body is spinning in circles and her arms are straight out. She quickly swings and cuts apart the cubes. The Skeleborgs see Bellona coming towards them and quickly react. The dark sky lights up like a meteor show as the rocks rain down. The Blisters on the side of the plateau area are trying to dig through the rocks under the shield area.

USE GRAVITY AS A WEAPON   BELLONA'S MILLISECONDS BATTLE

COPYRIGHT 2010 BY: VC IMAGINATION FACTORY

Location: Planet 455 Andromeda Galaxy.
Mission: Jaden's kidnapping rescue.
Take your imagination where no Sci-fi story has gone before. www.bialien.com

Bellona vs. Skelborgs/Blisters

Bellona quickly swings at the Skeleborg's head, cutting its head off before it could draw its weapon. She misses the other one. A trail of white smoke comes from the ground and up towards Bellona's spinning body. Her body looks like a glowing spinning T. The other Skeleborg she passed aims its primary weapon at her. She tosses the sword in her right hand towards the ground. Dozens of lasers are passing by Bellona; she collects some of them into the sword on her left hand. She fires a semi-invisible force from her right hand at the Skeleborg as it fires an orange projectile. The force makes the projectile explode and propels the Skeleborg's body into the shield covering the plateau area. The explosive fire and the pro-gravity force of her weapon makes the side of the mountain crumble and pulls the Blisters body down the side of the mountain. The Blisters try to hug the wall and hide in their shells, but it is too late. Screeching echoes in all directions as they all slam into the ground at three times their body weight.

Rocks and boulders rain from the sky in a blur of light, hitting dozens of Blisters. They come down in a loud whistling sound that echoes between the surrounding mountains. The high-speed projectiles smash into the iron-metallic ground creating holes. The impacts echo for miles and sound like landmines going off. Bellona's body stops spinning and she falls towards the ground, while catching her spinning second sword. She lands on a blister crushing it into the ground, like Mario steps on a turtle in *Super Mario Brothers*. She crouches from the impact and her face looks as if she is ready for battle. She is in the middle of a mob of Blisters, fleeing to get out of the way of the raining projectiles. They gallop to take cover against nearby mountains. The high-speed boulders and projectiles bombard the area. Three remaining Skeleborgs fly by overhead and two fly down towards Bellona with glowing plasma swords in their hands. All three of their chest areas glow green as if they are charging a weapon together. UFO1 lands on the plateau area.

Dozens of lasers are being shot by the Blisters towards Bellona while they seek cover. The swords absorb the energy of the yellow lasers. Bellona accelerates at high speed and moves in milliseconds. Her body also quickly rotates on its knees for faster turnaround time. The joints on her arms enable them to rotate in 360° angles and to intercept dozens of lasers a second into the two swords. Her hips and waist has magnetic energy around them helping her to rotate her flexible body. Bellona is moving so fast that everything seems to be happening in slow motion around her. From a distance, she looks like a blur of silver light. A boulder the size of a sumo wrestler comes directly over her. She turns and moves out of the way and it hits the ground where she was standing. The shock wave of sound from the impact slowly echoes in all directions. The debris and sand explode upwards in slow motion from around the impact areas. Bellona dodges lasers while striking several nearby slow moving Blisters. Her swords begin to glow bright yellow from all of the lasers that went into it. She dodges another rock impact within inches. The Skeleborgs are moving at high speed as well, and dodge the missile rocks while getting closer to Bellona. Her right arm spins around to the other side of her body collecting the yellow lasers.

The Skeleborgs on the ground are twenty-five feet in front of her. The Skeleborg flying above beams a bright green laser from its chest towards teammates on the ground. The Skeleborgs on the ground fire two bright green matter beams from their chest at near light speeds towards Bellona. She quickly somersaults foward into the air, while leaving her legs below her knees on the ground. Rocks and debris still exploding in the air, harmlessly bounce off her body. She tucks in her upper legs and narrowly misses the first and second beams by inches. The green beams create a hole through several mountains behind her for miles. Bellona also just misses being hit by another boulder projectile. The red molecules on her arms rest in the opening at her wrists. While somersaulting in thousands of millisecond revolutions, she throws her swords at the two Skeleborgs in front of her. Her hands leave her body and propel with the swords at breakneck speeds. Thrust explodes from the red molecules at the end of her hands like rockets. The swords cut through floating sand and debris. Her body stops spinning and quickly descends towards the ground and magnetic energy pulls her legs on the ground back towards her knees. The Skeleborgs quickly activate their shields and the swords explode on impact into a huge explosion of fire, yellow light and blue lightning.

The Skeleborgs fall back from the explosion and sustain damage. The explosion temporarily disrupts their defense and shield systems. Bellona's nanobots infiltrate the two Skeleborgs' bodies as she charges towards them in a blur. Her arms flip around 180° and another pair of hands form. The Skeleborgs quickly get up off the ground and the one still levitating above them aims its arms at Bellona. She puts her hands together and forms two swords full of red particles of energy. She spins around, just missing another rock projectile. Bellona's red swords strike the Skeleborgs' plasma swords and there is a spark of light flashing. They separate to two sides of Bellona. She blocks and swings at both of them as they do the same. Bellona is blocking behind her as well as in front her with her fast moving magnetic joints. Marco places Jaden's frozen cocooned body into UFO1. The inside temperature drops below -300°F.

The Skeleborg above catches Bellona in an invisible tractor beam and pulls her body upwards a few inches. The two around her try to strike her simultaneously. The alien behind Bellona strikes towards her leg and her left knee extends a few inches and the plasma weapon harmlessly passes between them. She uses pro-gravity energy in her feet to pull her to the surface as she quickly jumps and flips to the right avoiding a rock projectile the size of a fifteen-inch television. She comes down and quickly cuts off the left arm of the Skeleborg in front of her. It continues to swing its weapon with its right arm. The light particles are quickly moving around in her skin. She is done toying with the Skeleborgs as Marco signals her. Her entire back area down to her legs, glows bright white and a duplicate body comes out of her back. The identical faster moving body of Bellona comes swinging at the one-handed Skeleborg with two swords. Her stunt double quickly blocks the sword strikes and cuts the Skeleborg from the bottom up. Bellona continues to fight the second Skeleborg in front of her, while dipping and dodging the hot plasma sword. Bellona's wings form on her back. Her stunt double quickly turns around and runs towards Bellona. Bellona quickly bends down on her knees and arches her back over. The stunt double leaps off her back while taking Bellona's wings with it. The last of the rocks and boulder projectiles fall.

Bellona leans up and the Skeleborg in front of her is completely frozen. The nanobots infected its entire system. Bellona's stunt double goes after the last Skeleborg that has stopped using its tractor beam. The stunt double kicks off a high-speed boulder projectile in less than five milliseconds and propels itself towards the flying Skeleborg. The boulder projectile lands directly on the Skeleborg in front of Bellona, destroying it. Debris slowly flies around Bellona and her body shakes from the impact. The Skeleborg behind Bellona splits into two pieces and explodes. Her stunt double is about forty-five feet above her and is quickly flying and flapping its wings towards the last Skeleborg. The stunt double looks as if it is getting weak. It reaches the shield generating Skeleborg with a plasma sword in its hand. A midair battle begins. The stunt double's two swords instantly disintegrate when it touches the Skeleborg's energy shield. The Skeleborg lowers its shield and stabs the double through the chest. The hot plasma sword comes out the other side, between the flapping wings. There is no reaction from the stunt double as silver liquid pours down its lower back. The double quickly wraps its arms around the Skeleborg, stopping it from retracting the weapon or moving its arms. They look at each other face to race as the Skeleborg struggles. The light particle wings begin to flap as fast as a housefly's. It pulls them both into a backwards direction. The Skeleborg tries to fight it with its thrusters. The thrusters extend five feet down and burn the double's legs. The mask over the double's face disappears. The double puts its face close to the Skeleborg's face and kisses it. The wings continue to flap while completely confusing the Skeleborg. Suddenly they are both struck down by a high-speed boulder the size of a living room sofa. There are two explosions as the boulder hits the ground. Debris, fire and light particles explode into different directions.

Twenty seconds has passed since Bellona jumped down from the plateau area. Time speeds up around Bellona and debris and rocks land fall towards the ground around her. She walks over a surface that resembles Earth's moon. Bellona is weak from the battle and the light particles are slowly moving around her body. Her joints aren't levitating. The boulder spot where her stunt double was destroyed glows silver. The silver energy moves across the ground and back into Bellona's feet. The fifty-five remaining Blisters that sought shelter on the side of nearby mountains notice the raining rocks have stopped. They begin firing their lasers towards Bellona again. Some gallop and some run on two feet towards her, while firing. The shield around her body absorbs the yellow lasers.

The angry Blisters run up around Bellona while continuing to fire. They form a circle around her and begin to stand on top of each other like stadium seats. Her knees bend from the hundreds of lasers quickly hitting her shield. She lays down defenseless on her stomach. The shield shrinks down and turns the color of the yellow beams. Yellow and grey particles begin quickly moving around the inside shield area. The particles collide into each other. The energy shields disappear into a bright flash of light. The flash of yellow light is brighter than the sun and turns everything in the surrounding area yellow. Her body explodes into thousands of pieces straight into space. The Blisters fall to the ground and on top of each other. Eight of the closest Blisters die from the explosion. Most are on their backs. They look around and into the sky to see what happened. Hundreds of glowing silver projectiles rain down directly on the confused Blisters. They try to lie down and cover themselves with their strong armor backs, but it is too late. The silver matter burns and implodes their bodies as each one of them screeches in pain. The sound echoes into all directions. A sizzling sound can be heard from the dying bodies like eggs in a frying pan.

All the Blisters lay motionless on the ground. A clear film and silver matter comes from their dead bodies from all directions. The glowing matter forms back together in one place. It continues to form together and forms back into Bellona. Her eyes light up and red hair comes out of her head. She has her yellow energy sword in her left hand. There are dozens of bodies all around her, most inside of craters. Lightning comes from all directions. The white lightning lands in the palm of her right hand and slowly forms a sphere of bright energy. Her semi-visible wings are floating over her back. UFO2 can be seen firing at a cubfighter ship in the far background. Her magnetic joints return around her body, along with her two red molecules. There are a few marks around Bellona's body. Suddenly the sunlight from the local star and galactic bulge shines down on Bellona and around the planet. The lightning energy dissolves into her right hand. Something small and dark is quickly falling towards the planet from space.

She leaps into the air and anti-gravity particles move around her body. Her wings slowly move back and forth as she flies towards the plateau area. It looks like a black meteorite. She reaches the top and forms her own shield. She passes through the larger shield still protecting the three UFOs there. Marco walks up to Bellona to see if she is okay. The black meteorite crashes into the ground about 500 feet away. The crashing sound bounces against the mountains and causes avalanches. Rocks fall onto the top of the shield. Bellona and Marco turn around, and walk towards the edge of the plateau and look down. Debris and rocks sit midair and appear frozen in time around this black object. The all black, shiny object looks like a huge alien with four arms. It has some human features around its body. Its left leg is bending across the ground while its right leg is kneeling. Its head is bowing down and looks as if it is praying towards the plateau area. Its two lower arms and hands are touching the ground to the sides. The mysterious alien's upper arms and

202

hands have two swords in them; and point straight outwards. The swords have mysterious dark flames moving around. There are also weird alien symbols along both sides of each sword. Bellona gets angry and forms her swords. Her wings extend from her back and she is about to leap towards this unknown alien. Marco quickly reaches out and grabs her shoulder to stop her. She stops in her tracks and looks at Marco and they communicate in milliseconds. Bellona turns back towards the ships and Marco continues to stand there.

Bellona checks on Jaden and Marco's UFO3 ship hovers towards him from behind. His body turns semi-invisible and his ship passes through him. His body disappears into his ship and they both take off through the shield. Suddenly all the rocks and debris that were frozen in the air are sucked into its body and disappear. Small dark flames appear over its shoulders and upper arms. Bellona sees this through a nanoeye and can't believe what she is seeing. It reminds her of Toragon, but it reads like a small black hole. It stands up straight to about ten feet tall and looks up towards the plateau area. This alien life form has no face, just a head and red glowing eyes. It has a human-shaped body structure and pure evil is the vibe it gives off as it begins to walk forward. UFO3 quickly returns to the area and meets up with UFO4. They levitate about 400 feet away from the ground over the threat. They each fire their cannons and four torpedo weapons from the top and bottom of their molecules.

It is a direct hit and there is an explosion of fire that extends upwards. The fire, debris, and explosion force is sucked into this black alien as it continues walking at the same pace unaffected. The rescue team can't believe what they are seeing. Bellona gets into her ship and her red molecule begins to move around her ship. The ship Jaden is in also forms its purple molecule.

The rescue team coordinates an attack. UFO4 and 1 fire from the plateau area a total of four red torpedoes and two bright yellow torpedoes. The torpedoes spin around and come up behind UFOs 2 and 3. UFOs 2 and 3 fire the same amount of torpedoes and they merge together into a torpedo as bright as the sun and as huge as a Volkswagen car. There is a very loud whistling sound. There is a very huge explosion and light is everywhere. The planet shakes and rumbles like a magnitude 9.0 earthquake. Light and electricity is going into the air. A shock wave of energy expands into all directions. The mountains around the dark alien shake and rock avalanches fall down towards it. The large shield goes around the plateau area again, as it absorbs the powerful simultaneous shock waves of nuclear bomb forces. Fire and debris engulf the entire area for miles around. Everything is obliterated for miles around. A stream of fire in the shape of a diamond shoots into the sky. The sunlight from the local star is clouded by debris and fire. Avalanches of rocks and boulders fall from the mountains and topple all over the area below. Tops of mountains crumble down towards the surface and cover the impact area. The plateau area is bombarded with rocks and boulders. They land on top of the shield being created by UFO4 and 1.

Suddenly there is a low growling sound and fire begins to pull back down towards the impact area. The team uses nanoscanners to investigate what is under the rumble. They see the dark alien standing and levitating over a hundred square foot deep crater. Its four arms are in the air and its head looks up as if it is angry. It yells as if it is in a lot of pain. Dark flames about two feet high extend from its upper body. Rocks and boulders begin to rotate clockwise around it. Everything is being sucked into the dark, shiny alien along with a pair of nanoscanners that got too close. It begins to run and destroys rocks in its path. It jumps and floats up towards the plateau area.

It walks straight through the energy shield unfazed. The angry alien runs towards the parked UFOs and attacks them. It attacks UFO1 and walks right through it. It looks around confused and runs towards UFO4. Again, it walks right through the UFO as if they aren't there. It looks around confused. Suddenly the shield around the plateau area disappears, large boulders and rocks fall over the area, burying the dark alien. UFOs 1 and 4 are hovering above the mountain invisible and turn off their reimage technology. All four UFOs fire at the mountain creating another large explosion. They quickly take off and fly above the cloud of dust and debris. Some small, dark material flies down towards the explosion from different directions. The UFOs fly in formation and enter the upper atmosphere. Something is following them from the planet. The still slightly damaged UFO1 attaches and piggybacks to UFO4. They fly in the formation of a pyramid, UFO1 and 4 in the front, and UFO2 and 3 slightly lower to the sides. They reach above the planet and many distant stars can be seen against the bright sky. Two light sources shine on them. A black comet is chasing them from the planet. The UFOs change direction towards the local red star and enter light speed. At 185,900 miles a second, the UFOs move together as a long spaceship. This dark comet quickly catches up to them. It too is moving at the speed of light. UFO3 and 4 fire a red projectile at the dark comet. But it does nothing and keeps coming towards them gaining momentum. They fire a combined laser of different colors from each molecule and the powerful beam is absorbed into the dark abyss. It continues to move closer towards them.

The UFOs change paths from the nearby star and fly towards the rest of the solar system. UFOs 2 and 3 get closer and connect to 4, while UFO1 is still being piggy backed on UFO4. The ships glow while a larger vortex electromagnetic shield is created all around them. Their tails come off and morph into one larger silver tail. There is a huge explosion of colorful light from the tail. Their speed increases past light speed and the light around them begins to fade behind them. They reach 286,000 miles a second. The black comet fades far behind. The UFOs begin to rotate and go semi-invisible. Nanoscanners create a small hole in front of the UFOs. The ships break down into quadrillions and quadrillions of atoms. They enter the artificial subspace wormhole created by thousands of nanoscanners and disappear into the darkness of space.

Earth November 2005

Underground at a top-secret military base in the Nevada desert, Peters walks up to Robinson and gives him a piece of paper.

"Where is my hundred dollars? The LRSB transmitted a signal to Earth this morning. I knew that ship was still alive and not destroyed," Peters says.

"LRSB? Was that UFO09 or UFO10?" Robinson asks.

"That was UFO08, five years ago," Peters says.

"Yeah, I remember now, the exotic UFO that got away from us back in 2000, that cost us our promotions and made a mockery of the Air Force."

Robinson reads the paper with an astonished look on his face.

"Unbelievable, it transmitted a perfect signal from the Milky Way center, 28,098 light-years from here. That is unbelievable. That ship must be still flying around a thousand times the speed of light, unbelievable. One hundred dollars? The bet was before the year 2004."

"Come on sir, you still lost."

"Yeah yeah. I'll pay you later. Double or nothing for another signal in the next five years…"

…………..TO BE CONTINUED.

Written by: Vlane Carter

Creative art director: Vlane Carter

Graphic artist: John Buurman
John Moriarty
Matthew Garofalo
Kwan Wilson

VOL I Glossary of Terms

Atoms ripper – Is a molecule destroying energy similar to plasma fusion in the forward shields.

Bioparasites – Darclonians in microbial form. They wait to merge with nanomole to control a human body at high speed. Nanomoles protect bioparasites from human white blood cells. Bioparasites also control armies of microbots.

DEK – Dark Energy Knight.

DEQ – Dark Energy Queen.

DEW – Dark Energy Wraith – Mysterious dark energy that rides like a comet and fuels itself from the exhaust of a spaceship.

DHW – Darclonian Human Walkers. When nanomole and bioparasite merge. Darclonians are controlling human bodies at high speed. Making them super strong and slowly modifying the human body to turn them into super humans.

HBH – Hijacked brain Humans – See positive stage nanomole.

LRSB – Long Range Signal Beacon. It is put on UFOs just in case they get away from the US government. The top-secret technology sends transmissions through subspace.

Microbots – Darclonian robotic or organic organisms that can do a variety of things similar to the Andromedian nanobots and nanodrones. They prepare the human body to become super human.

Molevision – When the nanomoles are in a neutral stage they transmit different visions to other nanomoles when a human is suffering or experiencing pleasure from torturing someone else. It transmits and records dozens of emotions.

Nanoeyes – Invisible to the human eyes, range in size from a millionth to a billionth of an inch. Nanoeyes allow the host to hear and see things at a far distance. It can also pass through most materials. They can be controlled by host or on their own.

Nanoscanner – Invisible to the human eye and range in size between a millionth to a trillionth of an inch. Nanoscanners can do what nanoeyes can, and also analyze materials, scan through objects and determine their structure. They also have other capabilities especially in optic-warp. They can be controlled by host or fly autonomously.

Nanomoles – Are encoded particles sent to Earth over 100,000 years ago by the Darclonians. They sit hidden in the brain of humans. They reproduce in intelligent life from generation to generation, recording everything.

A Nanomole has three stages:

1. Negative - Mole is semi-hibernating and is recording and saving detailed information on the host.
2. Neutral – When the mother ship sends a high power signal to Earth to activate each nanomole in the brain. An 84 hour countdown begins. Humans go unconscious for thirty seconds before waking up, and go back into the negative stage. Some humans randomly go in and out of the neutral stage. The nanomole is expanding and preparing the neurons, axons and chemical messages in the brain to completely take over the human host.
3. Positive – HBH – Hijacked Brain Humans – The nanomole takes control of a human body and walks to upload areas. Bioparasites (Darclonians in microbes) merge with the nanomole and the humans become DHWs.
    * Humans are able to see, feel and hear everything around them, but can't control their own bodies and are prisoners.

Nanodrones – Advanced prototype organic nanobots that were specially made to work with Jaden's body. They work with his body in a collective of different groups and do many tasks.

Nanobots – Metallic, mechanical, microscopic robots that work with Andromedian biomechanical bodies and spaceships.

Optic-warp – The Andromedian species way of traveling through space at a fast rate. The ship approaches a local star at the speed of light, and then the ship breaks down into Quadrillion of molecules and slingshots through subspace at 6-90 second light-years.

Shield technologies –

Clockwise – Forward – 2 layers - First outside layer destroys objects by ripping apart its molecules and atoms. A part of plasma gasification. Second layer protects object or person inside the shield with solid energy force. Powerful projectiles can force through shield systems (gravity x force). The person, depending on the speed it traveled, can feel the force inside. The shield can change into any shape.

Counterclockwise – reverse – 3 Layers – First layer slows projectile and absorbs blast. Second layer gravity matrix analyzes material and stays in one place. It then recycles it into the shield whirlpool, which can be turned into a weapon for firing. Third layer protects objects or person inside with a solid force.

Gravity shockwave – It pulls gravity forces from ground level from all directions and leaves a smoky haze. The object caught in the pathway of the weapon instantly loses its gravity and propels forward at high speed. The object suddenly changes directions towards the ground at 3-4 times its body weight.

TC-100 – An instrument that scans through foreign material. It's like a high powered x-ray scanner that can see inside of aliens and foreign materials.

UF1-retrac team – The UFO police team that specializes in analyzing a UFO and preparing it for transport to Area 51 for research. They analyze the ship, check for radiation. They work for the government in a special sector and are mostly civilians.

Wraithstalkers – Lightly armed Darclonian ships used for recon missions.

BEST & CRAZY ACTION BURGER YELP REVIEWS

TOP 20 "BEST"

Carol B.
Ridgewood, Queens, NY
278 friends
687 reviews
Elite '15

→ Share review
♀ Compliment
✉ Send message
↓↑ Follow Carol B.

 12/29/2013

✓ 3 check-ins

Listed in The Yelp 100 Challenge NYC Twenty13!

Ahem, un ode à l'Action Burger:

On Graham Avenue, who could imagine you'd find,
a wonderful land still a secret to mankind.

Step into this wonderful land,
collages of comics and video games on hand.

What's your fancy?
Order it here.
A boozy milkshake? A burger stacked a mile high?
Chicken fingers, tots, mozz sticks, oh my!
Every concoction of which you've ever dreamed,
all on their menu...what heaven it seems!

Take a seat, your food's cooked fresh to order.
It might take a few minutes, so be patient, alright?!

And in the meantime, there's plenty to keep you busy.
A blockbuster hit on the big screen TV,
a round of Streetfighter or Mortal Kombat on the house!
Or maybe rock out to some Guitar Hero tunes.
Whatever you like, it's all here waiting for you!

When you've stepped into Action Burger,
you've stepped into a game.
You've stepped into more than a burger establishment,
you're the star of this domain!

The owner is nice and he'll chat about it all.
Attend a meet-up and make new friends.
At Action Burger, there's good ol' fun at every end!

Was this review ...?

 Useful 3   **Funny** 3   **Cool**

TOP 20 "CRAZY" YELP REVIEWS

J P.
Brooklyn, NY
👥 0 friends
📷 25 reviews

↗ Share review
🎖 Compliment
✉ Send message
👣 Follow J P.

 8/29/2014

Horrible food, burger was bland (reminded me of high school cafeteria food), fries were too oily, delivery takes too long, and its overpriced. I like the concept of the place but the execution is terrible. As a comic book/gaming fan and foodie, its upsetting they half assed this place. So much lost potential. Much fail.

Was this review ...?

💡 Useful 2   😊 Funny 1   ❄ Cool

 **Comment from Erica V. of Action Burger**
Business Owner

9/3/2014 · I'm sorry to hear about your experience. Little confused by your response. Since when does something bland = horrible? Okay something is missing some flavor or not up to your standards in seasoning (according to you), so it's automatically horrible? Like the worst food you ever had in your life. I happened to like high school cafeteria food.

Since when are fries not oily? Our fries are fresh cut fries (meaning we make them ourselves), they are made in a deep frier, drained of oil, placed in a wax bag, then paper-bag, then plastic bag for delivery. The wax bag can only soak up so much oil.

Honestly i'd prefer freshly made oily fries over chemically salty, like mc donalds does. In fact mcdonalds have chemically processed fries that barely soak up any oil. Maybe these fries might be more your preference:
youtube.com/watch?v=VO3D...

Overpriced? Well in comparison our meals are slightly more expensive than Mc donalds and we make things fresh. We make our own burgers, own fries and many other things. Big mac meal super sized (burger, fries, soda) comes out to $9-$11. Our cheese burgers, fries, and soda comes out to $11.

What is considered delivery taking too long? Did the food take 2-3 hours like dominoes pizza on news years eve? or did it take 30-60 minutes like most businesses delivering food in the area?

All yelp reviews responses are by Vlane Carter.

212

www.ingramcontent.com/pod-product-compliance
Lightning Source LLC
Chambersburg PA
CBHW070831120626
46556CB00002B/716

9 780983 469032